YOU ARE MINE

MIRANDA RIJKS

PROLOGUE

She grabs her throat. Her legs give way and she sinks onto the antique Persian carpet; the bloody, foaming spittle on the edges of her lips matches the fine reddish brown and cream threads on the floor.

He stands there and stares at her.

She gasps, trying but failing to speak.

He crosses his arms and blinks. Her eyes roll back into her head, and her body convulses.

'Perfect,' he murmurs, watching her with a detached curiosity as if she were an insect captured in a jar.

'No one is going to help you now,' he murmurs.

Everything is panning out perfectly. A prolonged and painful death, but one where she is conscious. Many minutes during which he can enjoy her anguish. A time when he is in control.

Her body stills. A damp lock of hair falls across her forehead. He is about to bend down to touch the silken strand when her eyelids flicker open.

Her pupils are wide and dark. A trickle of blood slips from

her left nostril. She opens her mouth, but only a gurgling sound comes out.

He bends down now, squatting at her side. 'You promised me so much, but you betrayed me.' His voice is deeper than normal. 'You're just a filthy whore!'

Her fingers clutch at thin air, the translucent moons on her nails so very perfect. He swipes her hand away and it falls heavily onto the carpet. Her body convulses again.

'There's no one here to save you. We're alone in the house. I am going to watch you die.'

And then there's a stench and he turns away in disgust as he realises what has happened.

He strides across the room. For a moment he hesitates, but then he decides, no, he must not look at her again. He must remember her as she was. Vibrant, capricious, exotic. He won't look, but he will listen.

'I did my research, you know,' he says as he settles into a chair that faces away from her, positioned on the far side of the room. 'The mixture you've drunk will burn through every cell in your body, nice and slowly, so you writhe in pain in exactly the same way as you've made me suffer.' He smiles as he cracks his knuckles, slowly bending back one finger at a time. 'It's the strychnine in the rat poison that causes the pain. It switches off the nerve signals to muscles, which is why you're having these severe spasms. They hurt, don't they?'

There is a strange scratching noise. He is tempted to turn around to check if the poison is doing its job, but he doesn't. He is a master of self-restraint. And patience; patience is a virtue that he has learned. If his research is correct, it will take three hours. But that's alright. He has time. He leans his head back against the hard-backed armchair and sighs. He will wait for however long it takes for the final rasping breath to leave her body.

'I chose this poison especially for you, because your

consciousness and brain won't be affected at first, and it'll give you time to think about how you've betrayed me. You'll have three long hours to think things through and to suffer unimaginable pain. And then you won't be able to breathe and it'll be all over. Finito. Gone forever.'

1

CHARLOTTE

'Charlie, this looks great!' Jodi claps her hands and twirls around.

I nod. I know I should be happy, but I'm not feeling it. Mum walks over and plants a kiss on my cheek.

'Dad would be so proud of you,' she says, squeezing my forearm. 'And I'm proud of you too.' Her voice catches.

'And so am I, big sis!' Jodi throws her arms around me.

I stride to the back wall and straighten the painting I've called, rather unoriginally, *The Shaggy Dog Story*. It doesn't need adjusting. They have hung my pictures well, perfectly grouped and lit. Everyone has told me it's a coup having The Titanium Gallery host my first solo show. It's located on the high street in Alderley Edge, no less. Home to the WAGS and the nouveaux riche of Cheshire, the place to be seen in the North West of England. And as Bernadette Titus – the middle-aged, surgically enhanced, peroxide-blonde gallery owner – declared, my paintings have a certain naive charm and will look equally good in a Macclesfield semi or a Prestbury mansion. Apparently. She has high hopes for a sell-out show, and with her art pedigree including the Saatchi Gallery and Sotheby's, she has told me on several occasions that her eye for spotting talent is second to none. Modesty isn't one of her virtues.

'Why didn't you persuade Charlie to wear something a bit more colourful?' Mum may think she's whispering, but as we're the only people in the gallery, I hear every word. I turn around and catch Jodi's eye. She grimaces.

I think my black jumpsuit and simple court shoes are à propos. I'm not one of those extrovert artists who calls everyone darling. In fact, I don't describe myself as an artist. Surely that title should only be bestowed on someone who earns their living through their art? I'm a long way away from that.

'Charlotte, have some bubbly.' Bernadette's assistant hands me a glass of Prosecco. I can't remember her name.

'Thanks.' I take a large glug. 'When do you expect people to arrive?' I bite the edge of my nail. It's gone 7.45 p.m. and the invitation was from 7.15 p.m. to 9.30 p.m.

'People are always late,' she says, flicking her auburn hair over her shoulder. 'Bloody rude, if you ask me.'

I nod. As if on cue, the front door opens. Two women and a man walk in, dressed to the nines in designer gear. Bernadette rushes over to greet them. They accept glasses of fizz and help themselves to the canapés on the front desk.

It's a small gallery with whitewashed walls and discreet lighting. There are artfully placed angular flower arrangements on tall glass tables, with white arum lilies and sharply pointed green foliage. The floral art, as Bernadette calls the arrangements, are in whites and greens and designed to enhance rather than detract from the paintings on the walls.

'It's so refreshing seeing paintings of animals, don't you think, Boo? I can't bear those abstracts that could be splodges of anything.' The tall woman wearing glitter-encrusted skinny trousers speaks with a broad Mancunian accent. She comes to a halt in front of my pig painting. It's large, life-sized. I don't hear what she says to her friends because the door opens again and a cluster of Jodi's friends enter, chattering loudly, waving at me, hugging my sister.

I make small talk with the few people I know, but it's awkward. Most of them haven't seen me recently and they are tongue-tied. Why aren't we taught how to deal with grief? Shouldn't we have lessons at school practicing conversing with the broken-hearted? After all, death and disappointment come to us all.

There must be twenty or so people in the gallery now. I'm not sure if that's a good or a bad number. I glance around, desperate to see a little red sold sticker on the paintings, but so far there are none. If they don't sell, I wonder if Bernadette will chuck my paintings out of the gallery before the agreed ten days are up.

I am pinning everything on this show. If I don't earn some money quickly, I won't be able to stay on in the flat. I am three months overdue on my rent. The landlord took pity on me back in May, but his patience has worn thin. I have already received a solicitor's letter threatening eviction within thirty days. I have another five unopened brown envelopes shoved in a kitchen drawer. Two of them are stamped with the words *final demand*. Jodi knows my finances are tight, but she doesn't know the full extent of it. She offered for me to move in with her, but I don't want to live in the centre of Manchester, and the last thing I want is to be a further encumbrance. She's done quite enough already. And I know Mum would like to help out, but Mum is living off her pension and she's also suffered enough.

I'm lost in my maudlin thoughts, standing at the back of the room, drinking too much Prosecco. I try to look at my paintings objectively. Most of them are of animals; there are two landscapes and a portrait of the Bedouin man who guided us on our last holiday in Morocco's Atlas Mountains. I paint mainly in acrylics but oils too, and this time last year I was heavily into mixed media. I say I paint, but the reality is I haven't picked up a paintbrush in six months. Heartache and creativity are incompatible bedmates. It's just as well Bernadette booked this exhibition nearly a year ago and I had a sufficiently large number of completed artworks in stock.

'Charlie!' Jodi appears in front of me and makes me jump. 'See that man over there?' She has her hand over her mouth and speaks in a whisper. 'He's just bought three of your paintings. The Bedouin, the horse and the field of sheep. He wants to talk to you.'

'That's great!' I try to do some quick mental arithmetic, but alas, the sale of three paintings isn't going to have a substantial impact on my financial mess.

'It's bloody brilliant!' Jodi says. 'This is the first evening, Charlie, and you've just sold three paintings!'

A man is striding towards us. 'That's him,' Jodi murmurs. He has a warm, wide smile with straight bright-white teeth. He is smartly dressed in a well-cut navy suit and a red bow tie that befits a much older man. I guess he must be late thirties or early forties. His face is smooth and unlined, and he has wavy mid-brown hair that bounces on his forehead in a foppish manner. I would use Vandyke brown if I were painting those locks. He stands very close to Jodi and me.

'I understand that you are Charlotte Aldridge. I am in total awe of your extraordinary talent.' He extends his hand. Manners force me to return the gesture. He squeezes my hand and then holds it for a little too long while his eyes scour my face. They are green with amber flecks and slightly too close together. He has a deep cleft in his chin and the squarest jaw I've ever seen. His palm is clammy, and when he releases my hand, I have to stop myself from wiping my palm on my trousers to get rid of the residue.

'Thank you very much for buying my paintings.' I smile. Jodi winks at me as she slips away.

'That is my greatest pleasure. I know exactly where I will be hanging them. I have just had a charming conversation with your sister, Jodi. How long have you been painting, Charlotte – if I may be so bold as to call you that?'

'Yes, of course,' I say. 'I've been painting all of my life on and off. I went to art college but then took a series of real jobs because painting doesn't pay unless you're one of the greats.'

'Which I believe you are.' He speaks with a plummy voice, with lengthened vowels, and he has a tendency to either swallow the final syllable of each word or finish sentences with a croak. 'What are you working on at the moment?'

He steps a little closer to me. I step backwards. I hate it when people invade my personal space.

'I'm not,' I say, glancing away. 'Life has somewhat got in the way.'

'Yes, I know what you mean. If I am experiencing emotional stress, I find I can't write poetry.'

I look at him in surprise. 'You're a poet?'

'Goodness, I wouldn't call myself that!' He flushes slightly. 'It's just a little hobby. I think we all need a creative outlet of sorts, don't you?'

I nod.

We fall silent for a moment. The gallery seems quite full now, and people are jostling us as they move around the room. The noise levels are high.

'I have a proposition for you, Charlotte.' He places his hand on my arm and then removes it again. I notice small beads of perspiration on his upper lip. It's warm in here but not that warm. 'I would like to commission you to paint my portrait.'

I hadn't seen that one coming. 'Gosh, that's very flattering, but I don't paint people. My specialty is animals.'

'Which, of course, isn't strictly true, is it, Charlotte? I've just bought your exquisite painting of the Bedouin man. I simply adore your style.'

'I've never had a commission to paint a portrait,' I say feebly.

'So it will be a great honour and privilege that I will be your first.'

I am screaming inside. *I can't. What if I screw it up? What if I can't even remember how to paint? Should I tell this stranger that I haven't picked up a paintbrush in six months?*

'It is somewhat of a family tradition to have one's portrait painted. All of my forefathers are displayed on the walls at the Hall, and up until now, it's something I've been putting off. I'm not keen on the formal oil style, whereas you seem to have the ability to capture personality with your looser brushstrokes and fabulous palette of colours. Forgive me, I am not an art critic, so please excuse my inability to articulate properly, but I simply adore the saturated, harmonious tones that you achieve, and the thought that goes into your compositions, and the way you are influenced by such diverse artists yet still achieve a style and technique that is so very uniquely your own. I was thinking that my portrait should be perhaps a half-length in size, which I believe is fifty by forty inches.'

'That's very flattering, but–'

'I believe fifteen thousand pounds might be an appropriate figure. If that's insufficient, of course, there is room to manoeuvre.' He puts his hand in his jacket pocket and produces a business card, which he hands to me.

'Thank you, but–'

He cuts me off again. 'I have been monopolising you for too long. Please mingle with your other guests, and I will catch up with you later. I would like to have another look around the gallery.' He bows his head to me and walks away.

'Fifteen thousand pounds,' I mutter under my breath. 'Shit.'

I run my finger over the embossed black lettering on the thick cream business card. *Sir Rupert St John Baskerville Bt., JP, Sesame Hall, West Sussex.*

2

RUPERT

I know I should be looking at the paintings. They're lovely, of course they are. But my eyes are drawn to Charlotte. I feel her presence so acutely, as if I were being bathed in an aura of golden light simply by being in the same room as her. She is exactly as I had imagined, but oh so much more beautiful in the flesh. The photograph in the art magazine did not do her justice. It captured her delicate heart-shaped face and those pure blue eyes; it showed her cascading platinum tresses, but it failed to portray the true essence of her. Perhaps I am being unfair to the photographer. Perhaps it is simply impossible to reproduce such unique loveliness in print.

I clasp an orange juice and walk around the gallery again. It is fascinating listening to what other people are saying. But their comments are so trite. They are looking at the surface of the paintings, not trying to understand the state of mind of the artist or the symbolic values and emotional responses she intends her work to evoke. It is a relief when people start to leave. I feel I can breathe again. I hang back, in the corner of the gallery, behind a pillar. Not obviously hidden but not in full view. It affords me time.

It is almost 9.50 p.m. and now there are just five people left.

'Congratulations, darling.' The older woman gives Charlotte a kiss on the cheek.

'Have a wonderful time, Mum,' Charlotte says. 'Remember to call us on Skype.'

'I'm not sure how to, love.'

'Don't worry. Uncle Richard is a techie pro. He'll help you. Have a safe flight and let us know when you've arrived.'

'I will do, darlings.' She gives both Charlotte and Jodi a kiss. They help her put on her raincoat and she leaves.

Now is my time to emerge from the shadows.

'I can't tell you how much I've enjoyed your show,' I say, beaming at both Charlotte and her sister.

'Gosh, I didn't realise you were still here.' Charlotte looks a little startled.

'I was wondering if I could buy you ladies a drink to celebrate the success of your exhibition. I believe there are some fine wine bars here in Alderley Edge.'

'Just a few!' Jodi laughs.

'I think champagne is the order of the day, don't you?' I suggest.

'Actually, I don't–' Charlotte speaks at the same time as Jodi.

'That would be lovely!'

Charlotte lays her hand on Jodi's arm and turns to one side as if to whisper in her ear. Fortunately, Jodi is having none of it.

'It will do you good to go out and have a drink. And we do need to celebrate. You've sold nine paintings this evening. That's bloody fantastic!'

Charlotte's shoulders sink a little. I don't understand why she isn't reacting in a more ebullient fashion, but I am sure I will find out in due course. Fortuitously, we are interrupted by the grande dame of the gallery, who flounces over to us.

'A good solid start, Charlotte. I told you your style will

appeal to the masses. We're shutting the gallery now, but I will keep you posted on sales over the coming days.'

'Thanks, Bernadette.' Charlotte smiles at her.

'Come on, sis,' Jodi says, dragging Charlotte towards the door. I follow closely behind.

It's bitter outside and threatening to rain. I always forget how much worse the weather is up here in the north-west of England. Luckily for me, I don't feel the cold, but I worry that Charlotte and Jodi don't have thick enough coats. I stride quickly towards The Fascinator Bar, and the ladies clip-clop behind me. I spent the afternoon doing a recce of the drinking establishments in the village. The Fascinator is by far the most upmarket. Not to my taste, it has to be said. I can't abide purple velvet chairs and artificial gold bauble lights, but it has a fine wine list.

I hold the door open and we are met by a blast of hot air and the sound of a saxophone. The maître d' hurries forwards and, in an overtly camp manner, takes our coats and leads us to an alcove. Charlotte and Jodi sit next to each other and I face them. A second later, a waiter arrives, wearing a black shirt and a black apron tied around his midriff.

'What can I get you to drink?' he asks, handing me the wine list.

'A bottle of your finest Krug champagne,' I say, handing back the wine list without glancing at it.

'Of course, sir.'

'Gosh, I'm not sure I've ever drunk Krug before,' Jodi says. 'It's very generous of you.'

'Have you sampled it, Charlotte?' I ask.

She shakes her head. 'I don't drink much alcohol.'

'Very wise.' I am glad to learn that.

'So tell me about yourselves,' I say, leaning back on the velvet banquette, laying my arm along the top edge. I thought I might feel nervous, but I am pleased to feel very comfortable in their presence.

'She's my older sister.' Jodi has an annoying laugh. One of those silly, high-pitched giggles.

'Are you also an artist, Jodi?'

Charlotte sniggers. Jodi elbows her in the ribs.

'No. I can't paint. I'm a midwife,' Jodi says.

'A very worthy profession. And, Charlotte, have you always been an artist?'

She shifts and looks away coyly. 'No. I don't paint full time. Until recently I worked in a bookshop.'

'You mean you ran it,' Jodi interrupts. 'She's always too modest.'

I smile. That doesn't surprise me. 'And do you ladies live together?'

'No. Charlie lives in Macclesfield, where we're from, and I live in Manchester now, near the hospital.'

I turn my body, so I am facing more towards Charlotte. 'Does everyone call you Charlie, Charlotte?'

She shakes her head. 'Only Jodi and a couple of close friends.'

'So would it be alright with you if I call you Charlotte?'

'Yes, of course!' She lets out a little laugh, which fortunately is nothing like her sister's.

'Where are you from, Rupert?' Jodi asks.

I am not aware that I told Jodi my name, so I wonder if Charlotte has explained my proposition. I am slightly irked that she hasn't called me Sir Rupert, but perhaps she isn't au fait with formalities.

'I live in West Sussex, in a large house nestled at the foot of the South Downs,' I explain.

We are interrupted by the waiter returning with the bottle

of Krug and pouring it into champagne glasses. He places the bottle into a silver bucket filled with ice, drapes a white napkin over the side and leaves us.

I raise my glass. 'To you, Charlotte, and your success as an artist!'

She blushes. Jodi blows her a kiss.

'Thank you,' she says, her eyes lowered unassumingly.

'Has Charlotte mentioned my proposal to you?' I ask Jodi.

'Very briefly,' Jodi says. Charlotte keeps her eyes downwards. She has long, dark, silken eyelashes.

I place my champagne glass on the table and lean forwards. My legs are so close to theirs I can almost feel their body heat. It is intoxicating and I try not to let it distract me.

'I will explain more. I live in a big house called Sesame Hall that has been in my family for nine generations. The head of each generation has commissioned a portrait of himself, and the pictures hang in the hallway and up the main staircase. Sadly my father passed away many years ago, and it is one of those things I know I should have done already but haven't gotten around to. Perhaps it's because I have never found the right artist. We have a Joshua Reynolds, a Francis Bacon and a Lucian Freud, so it's a rather special collection of paintings.'

'Why on earth do you want me to paint you?' Charlotte exclaims.

I knew she would be humble, and thank goodness she is. 'Every great artist was unknown at some point. I think you are on the cusp of phenomenal success, and I would like to be one of your early patrons. If, of course, you will accept my offer.'

'It's a bloody amazing opportunity,' Jodi says. Her glass of champagne is nearly empty.

'I suggest you come and stay for a couple of weeks – more if you need more time. The house is large, so you would have your own space. I would sit for you as required, but I am rather busy, so often not at home. You would have free run of the place. It's in a very scenic location and we have a swimming pool and gym, which you are welcome to use. All food and drinks would be provided, of course. In many ways it would be like a holiday for you, Charlotte. Your only obligation would be to paint my portrait, and for that I will pay you. I did a little research into the going rates, and if you feel twenty thousand would be a more suitable figure than fifteen thousand, then I would happily pay that.'

'Bloody hell!' Jodi whispers. I notice her nudging her knee against Charlotte's.

'Wow, that's amazing and really generous!' Charlotte says, but then she lowers her eyes again and fiddles with the small watch on her left wrist. There is a long pause before she reaches for her purse and says, 'Could you excuse me a moment. I need to go to the ladies'.'

She edges off the bench seat and stands up, smoothing down her all-in-one trousers, or jumpsuit as I think they call them. I watch her walk away. She is very slender, almost too thin, although her curves are all in the right places. As she disappears around the corner, I turn my attention back to Jodi.

'Your sister seems rather subdued, considering her success.'

'Some crap stuff has happened to Charlie recently.'

'I'm sorry to hear that. May I ask what?'

She shakes her head. 'It's in her personal life. This is the break she needs. It would be amazing for her to get away, especially now. Mum has been her rock, but she's flying off to New Zealand for five weeks to stay with her brother.'

'I'm sorry to hear that Charlotte has had a difficult time.' I pause. 'I hope you might be able to persuade Charlotte to take me up on this offer. I am very happy to provide her with references, and she could even come for an initial visit, all expenses paid of course, should that be more comfortable for her.'

'It's an awesome offer. Leave it with me. I'll talk to Charlie.'

Charlotte returns to the table.

'Do you often come to Alderley Edge, Charlotte?' I ask.

'No. It's too expensive here for me, with all of these fancy boutiques and stuff.'

'Yes, I can see that it may be a little nouveau and pretentious,' I concur.

We are silent whilst we all sip our champagne.

'What brings you to this part of the world?' Jodi asks.

I hesitate formulating my answer. Should I pretend I was in the area and stumbled across the exhibition by chance, or should I be up front with my answer? I decide that Charlotte deserves truthfulness; after all, honesty really is the best policy.

'I have to admit I came to Cheshire especially for the opening of your exhibition. As a collector, I get invited to many gallery exhibitions and probably attend one in ten. Your work piqued my interest and I'm very glad I made the effort to attend.' I don't mention the hundreds of times I have watched the video I found of her on YouTube talking about her work.

'Gosh, it's a long way to come from Sussex,' Jodi comments.

We make small talk for a while, but I can tell Charlotte is tired. She tries to stifle her yawns and there are dark rings underneath her eyes. When she suggests it's time for her to go home, I don't try to dissuade her. Sleep is exactly what she needs. Jodi insists on accompanying Charlotte. I am glad of that. I wouldn't want her making her way home alone.

I walk them to the door, where the maître d' hands them their coats.

'It was a great pleasure getting to know you both,' I say, kissing Jodi on the cheek first. I inhale deeply as I lean in to kiss Charlotte. Her aroma is of peaches, strawberries and something else I can't define. It is sublime. I feel a jolt through my body as my lips briefly touch her silken, soft cheek.

Our eyes meet and I know she feels it too. There is a long pause as we both digest the exquisite moment.

'I look forward to hearing from you, Charlotte,' I say, bowing my head very slightly.

'I'll be in touch,' she replies. Those captivating eyes still appear sad and I am surprised. It's been six months. Six long months where I have waited, oh so patiently. Surely that is long enough?

3

CHARLOTTE

I have a pounding headache when I awake. Too much Prosecco, I suppose, followed by that obscenely expensive champagne.

Groaning, I sit up in bed and run my fingers over Matthew's photograph. I take stock of last night. The sale of nine paintings isn't bad, but I don't know how long it will be before I actually receive the money. Two weeks, a month? Weeks I don't have. I need the money now.

'I wish you were here,' I whisper to Matthew's photograph. 'I really don't want to paint the portrait of that posh man in Sussex, but perhaps I'll have to.'

Sometimes I hear Matthew's answers. His beautiful baritone voice resonates inside my head, pointing me in the right direction, giving me the very best advice.

'Do it, Charlie,' his voice says. 'It's quick money, good money, and perhaps the commission is the push you need to get back to painting. Commissioned portraits of pets are good, but if you branch out to do portraits of people, you'll be able to charge way more money. Twenty grand for a couple of weeks' work is amazing.'

I sigh. Matthew is right. This is a golden opportunity. I bring his photo to my lips and kiss it gently. Then I swallow a couple of paracetamols and make my way into the bathroom. Peering in the mirror, I realise I look a mess. My complexion is almost grey; dark mauve circles encase my eyes; it's as if the pain in my heart is reflected in my face. At least my hair is looking ok. I went to the hairdresser's yesterday morning. Lovely Hank put some highlights in and dried it all smooth and glossy. It was worth every penny I can't afford. As I'm brushing my teeth, my mobile phone pings. I grip the toothbrush between my teeth and march back into the bedroom, grabbing my phone. It's Jodi.

Brilliant show last night. Congrats!

Thanx

What are you going to do about Sir R?

Dunno

You should do it. Easy money

Not sure. Find him a bit creepy

I don't mention Matthew's words from the grave. If I told her I hear my dead fiancé speak and that I listen to his advice, she'd march me straight to a shrink. The last thing I need is to regurgitate the horrors of the past few months. Immediately after his death, my lovely GP suggested I see a psychologist. I declined. I am grieving. I'm not insane.

I know what you mean. He's quite good looking though. Do some research

Yup. Good idea. Probably will do it

R u home later?

Yes

I'll call tonight. Have a good day. Luv u xxx

Luv u 2 xxx

JODI and I were two peas in a pod when we were growing up.

We did everything together. Most people thought we were best friends, and when we explained we were sisters as well as best friends, they stared at us in disbelief. We used to giggle about it. I'm petite and blonde; Jodi is three inches taller than me and naturally mousey. She dyes her hair dark and keeps it short in a pixie cut. It suits her. We went our different ways when I got into art school and she went off to train as a midwife. Any mum who has her at their birth should count their blessings. Jodi is the most caring, calm and resourceful person I know. These days she's a city chick, riding around Manchester on her bike and frequenting cool clubs on her rare evenings off.

I, on the other hand, have no desire to live in the city. Matthew and I planned to move to a little cottage somewhere between Buxton and Bakewell in the Peak District, near enough to Manchester airport so that Matthew could commute to his well-paid pilot's job. We even talked about having our own smallholding and a menagerie of animals. Particularly a dog; I've always wanted a dog. Instead, I'm still in the flat that we rented as a stopgap between moving in together and getting married. And I want to stay. It brings me comfort that I am sleeping in the bed he slept in. That I sit in his chair and stand in the shower where we washed together.

I finish in the bathroom and shuffle into the tiny kitchen to make myself a bowl of cereal. It's not even a particularly nice flat, with no views or outside space. But it's where I feel most comfortable and where I can grieve in solitude. My neighbour, who owns the whole of the adjacent house, is a professor of piano at the Royal Northern Academy of Music in Manchester, and she also has a regular flow of students whom she teaches at home. Mainly adults in the daytime and teenagers after 3 p.m. I like listening to the repetitive phrases. It used to drive Matthew mad.

This morning Mrs Leadbetter is teaching her best students. I've seen the bald-headed man in his sixties a couple of times.

He carries a battered leather satchel and arrives on a bicycle, which he chains to the lamppost. He is playing Chopin Polonaise in A-flat major, Op. 53. It sounds impossibly difficult and it always makes me cry. One day I met Mrs Leadbetter coming out of her front door and I asked her what her Thursday 9 a.m. student has been learning for the past four months. She smiled, her grey-haired head tilted to one side, and said it was the most beautiful piece of music in the world. She wrote the name down on a scrap of paper and recommended I listen to Vladimir Horowitz's version on YouTube. I did as she suggested, and that was the first time I felt Matthew's arms around my body and his lips on my neck since the day he died.

This morning Mrs Leadbetter's student is playing the Polonaise from beginning to end. I have a horrible feeling that he may shortly be moving on to another piece of music, and I will be deprived of my weekly fix of Chopin. Perhaps it's time I move on too. Perhaps the posh man's offer is manna from heaven. It crosses my mind that perhaps Matthew has organised it for me.

I grab my laptop, place it on the kitchen table and fire it up. Whilst I'm waiting, I make myself a coffee and eat half a bowl of cornflakes. Then I sit down and search for Sir Rupert St John Baskerville. What a ridiculous name. I bet he got ribbed something rotten at school.

I peer at the screen. Plenty of information comes up about him. He is a magistrate and a local councilor – quite the pillar of society. I want to be sure that he's got the dosh to pay me; it's looking promising. LinkedIn shows that he studied land management and is now the chief executive of The Sesame Estates. Sesame Hall, where he lives, has been in his father's family for many generations. The family is listed in Debrett's and on ThePeerage.com. After ten minutes or so, I shut my laptop down. I've seen enough. Sir Rupert is who he says he is, and the commission is obviously genuine.

Eight months ago, after Matthew proposed to me, I quit my job managing an independent bookshop in Congleton. Matthew knew how badly I wanted to be a full-time artist and, with his good salary being sufficient to support us both in the short term, said that I should concentrate on fulfilling my dreams before we started a family. It was a typically generous offer from the man I was ecstatic to be spending the rest of my life with. Between the day I quit work and the day that Matthew died, I was my most prolific. I painted ninety percent of what is on display at The Titanium Gallery during those couple of months. I think it was the first time in my life that I was genuinely happy, doing what I adore, living with the person I loved more than anyone else in the world.

But now I wonder whether true joy is sustainable. The past six months have been the worst of my life. All my dreams were ripped away when the police knocked on my door. I haven't worked; I haven't painted; I've barely survived. Many a day I wished I were dead. But I'm not. Jodi and Mum wouldn't let that happen.

I sigh. My choices are stark. I accept the commission and get my finances back on track. Or I don't, and will most likely have to declare myself bankrupt, even if all the paintings sell. There really is no choice.

After a second cup of coffee, I drag my easel from the corner of the living room, pull out my box of paints and find a small canvas, which I prop against the easel. I stare at it. In the past I used to be buzzing with inspiration. Everything was a potential subject. Now I am uninspired. But if I'm going to accept this commission, I need to be sure I can still paint people. I'm so out of practice. I could try to paint Matthew, but that might break my heart even further. Instead my eyes settle on a photograph I took of Jodi and her then boyfriend on our birthday, just under a year ago. I will paint my sister.

I place the photograph on the table in front of me and

lightly draw her outline on the canvas. Four hours later, when my stomach is rumbling and my head feels fluffy, I realise I haven't forgotten how to paint, but I have forgotten to eat or drink. I make myself a quick omelette, switch on the news and send Jodi a text.

Decided to accept Sir R's offer. Cx

I put his business card on the mantelpiece when I got home last night. I find it and grab my phone. Hesitantly, I dial his number. I almost hang up before it connects, but instead I breathe deeply and listen to it ring.

'Sir Rupert Baskerville.'

'Um, Sir Rupert, this is Charlotte Aldridge. We met last night at my art exhibition. Thank you very much for treating Jodi and me to a drink.'

'Ah, Charlotte, I'm delighted to hear from you. How are you?'

'I'm very well. I am calling about your offer.'

'I am all ears. I hope you will be making me happy.'

'I'd love to paint your portrait if the offer still stands.'

'It certainly does.'

'In which case I should be able to complete it within a couple of weeks, three at most. I normally ask for one-third of the payment up front with the remainder due on completion. Is that ok?'

'Indeed it is, Charlotte. Needless to say, I am delighted. How soon would you be able to start?'

I hesitate. 'It would suit me to start as soon as possible.' I don't need him to know that I am desperate for the money, that if he wires me £6667 today, I will have plenty of money to pay my landlord what I owe and more.

'That's convenient for me too. Would you be able to arrive on Saturday? It will give me time to show you around over the weekend. Perhaps you could email me your bank details and I will make an immediate payment. I'll send you directions, oh, and remember to bring some wellington boots. Goodbye, Charlotte. I am looking forward to spending more time with you.' He hangs up.

I screw up my eyes. Goodness, that is the day after tomorrow! I have just committed myself to go and stay with a complete stranger on the opposite end of the country.

A FEW HOURS LATER, Jodi calls me again.

'I've taken the commission,' I say.

'That's fantastic. It will do you so much good to get out of the flat and away from all of those memories.'

I don't attempt to disagree with her. My memories are what sustain me, but Jodi doesn't get it.

'And it's a stack load of money! I'm so happy for you, sis!'

'Will you come and visit me?' I ask.

'Of course, if I can get some time off work.'

When I end the call, I wonder again. I could paint him from photographs. Do I really need to go all the way to Sussex?

But then my phone pings and my banking app tells me that £6667 has just been deposited into my account. An email arrives from Sir Rupert.

Dear Charlotte, Just to confirm that I will be paying you £20,000 in return for painting my portrait, the sittings to take place at my residence, Sesame Hall. I have wired you the first third, and the remaining two-thirds will be paid when the painting has been completed. I look forward to welcoming you on Saturday, and in the meantime, please find attached directions. Yours, Rupert.

'I'm going, Matthew,' I whisper under my breath.

He doesn't reply, or perhaps he does, but I can't hear him.

Sussex. Bring it on.

4

SIMONE, JULY 1994

Mon dieu! This place is amazing. The woman at the agency said I was lucky to get this posting, but she didn't tell me it would be like *this*. I got off the train at Pulborough station, exactly as instructed, and there was a man standing there dressed in a dark grey chauffeur uniform, holding a piece of card with my name written on it.

He insisted on carrying my rucksack and my suitcase, and I followed him out to the car park. And there was an *énorme* fancy Rolls Royce all shiny in navy blue. It looked brand new. He held open the back passenger door and I climbed in. The seats were made from camel-coloured leather and smelled amazing. I have never, ever been driven in such a fancy car.

I tried to make small talk, but perhaps my English isn't as good as I think it is, because he answered in curt monosyllables. But I didn't have to wait long. Just ten minutes later we were pulling through some large iron gates and crunching along a long, long gravel private boulevard. At the far end was a big house and a semicircular driveway. He stopped the car in front of the imposing front door, and I hopped out before he had the chance to open the car door for me. He threw me a disapproving stare.

And now I am standing on the steps of this mansion, looking at parkland all around and gentle, rolling hills in the background.

'Simone Durand?'

I jump. I didn't hear the door open behind me. There is a man standing in front of me, actually the most handsome man I have ever seen. Which is weird because my friends all told me Englishmen are ugly and boring, not like our Frenchmen. He extends his hand.

'Welcome to Sesame Hall, Simone. I am Sir Oswald Baskerville, father to Rupert. Please come in. Arthur will bring your luggage.'

I feel my knees weaken as he releases my hand from his firm, cool grip. I try not to blush as I walk past him into the grand hall. There is a massive dark wooden staircase rising upwards on the left-hand side and one of those medieval suits of armour (although hopefully without the skeletal remains inside it) standing next to a huge grandfather clock. Paintings line the staircase wall and the hallway. Most of them are portraits and some look positively evil. I shiver. I wasn't expecting to stay in a museum.

'I know this all looks very formal,' he says, 'but we're not. Our family has lived here for many generations, so the house is chock-full of antiques.'

'I've never seen anything like it,' I say in a quiet voice.

'Most people are overwhelmed when they walk in for the first time,' he says. 'Come through to the drawing room and let's have a little chat.' I follow him along a dark corridor. He opens a door to a bright room that looks over the parkland.

'Have a seat. I'll ask Mrs Cherry to bring you a drink. What would you like? Lemonade, coffee?'

'Water is great. Thank you.' I sit on the edge of a sagging floral chintzy armchair. It looks like a hotel in here with a large stone fireplace, low tables, various groupings of sofas and chairs and more paintings, mainly in ornate gold frames, on the pale blue walls.

Sir Oswald sinks onto one of the sofas and stretches his long legs out in front of him. He has movie-star good looks, somewhere between Jeremy Irons and Kevin Costner. His dark hair is greying around the temples, and he stares at me with magnificent dark eyes. His lips are thin and his jaw chiseled, but his face is pale. Very pale. His button-down shirt is open at the top, and dark, curling hairs escape. I love a hairy chest in a man. I imagine myself running my hands down his washboard stomach, then placing my hand over his heart and kissing him better. He would thank me for healing his emotional wounds and I would–

I am jolted by my name. 'Simone?'

'I am sorry,' I say. My hands rush to my cheeks. 'I was, how do you say in English, miles away?'

'Your English is fluent. I'm impressed. Don't worry, you must be tired after your journey. I just wanted to tell you a bit about my son, Rupert.'

'Yes, of course.' I lean forwards. A woman with tightly permed white hair walks in carrying a tray and places a glass of iced water next to me and a silver coffee pot and small cup and saucer next to Sir Oswald.

'Thank you, Mrs Cherry,' he says. She nods and turns away without saying a word.

'Rupert is a bright boy, but he doesn't fulfil his academic potential at school. He has suffered deeply from the death of his mother.' He sighs and his eyes glance at a photograph of a beautiful woman wearing a silver evening dress. 'My wife passed away three years ago, and Rupert has found it extremely hard to adjust to life without her. He mopes around doing nothing during the school holidays. The boy doesn't appear to have any friends, or if he does, he never invites them home. He sobs like a baby when it's time to return to boarding school after the holidays. He needs some structure in his life, and I would like him to become fluent in French. Language skills are so important in today's day and age. So that is where you come in.'

He pours himself a cup of coffee and drinks from a cream and gold porcelain china cup. I take a sip of water from a cut-glass tumbler. For some reason my hand is shaking, so I put it down again quickly. I hope he doesn't notice.

Sir Oswald carries on talking. 'It's time that we stop namby-pandering to the boy. He needs to be taught discipline. That's the objective for this summer. Self-restraint and getting into shape. I suggest that his days are structured so that he spends the mornings with you, learning French. In the afternoons you will be free while Rupert takes exercise, and then you will join us for dinner at 7 p.m. I would like you to converse with him in French only. How does that sound to you?'

'Very good. Thank you. I wasn't expecting to have every afternoon free.'

'You won't have weekends off. You will be expected to be with Rupert every day of the week.'

'That's fine,' I say, although it isn't really. I had hoped to meet up with friends in London during the weekends.

'We have two full-time members of staff. Arthur Stone, who is our chauffeur and oversees the exterior of the house, and Mrs Cherry, who is our cook and housekeeper. We used to have a full complement of staff, but as it's just me living here alone most of the time, I felt it necessary to downsize. I am sure they will both make you feel at home.'

He picks up a little brass bell and rings it. A few moments later Mrs Cherry scuttles back into the room.

'Would you mind showing Miss Durand to her room,

please, and then introduce her to Rupert. I need to get back to the office.'

'Yes, of course, Sir Oswald.' Mrs Cherry nods deferentially.

MY BEDROOM IS A DREAM. The carpet is so thick, my toes sink into it. The bed is a small four-poster with oak bedposts. On top of the claret-coloured bedspread, there is a pile of flowery tapestry cushions in maroons and dark greens that match the curtains. The room smells musty and it's not to my taste, but it's still plush. There is a kidney-shaped dressing table and a wall full of built-in cupboards. The large bay window looks onto the same breathtaking view as the drawing room. I dance around. I got so lucky coming here!

I even have my own bathroom. It's only got a bath in it and no shower, but I think that is typically English. I wonder if Sir Oswald likes to share a bath. Oh goodness, he is so hot! I don't know how I'm going to last a full summer without combusting around him.

My bags have been placed on a luggage rack, just like in a hotel, so I start unpacking, placing my belongings in drawers lined with lavender-scented paper. And then there is a knock at the door.

'Come in!'

Mrs Cherry appears and holds the door open. 'Would you like to come with me and I'll introduce you to Rupert.'

'Yes, of course,' I say. I'm eager to meet my charge for the next two months.

I follow her along the corridor, past the staircase and into another narrower corridor where the ceiling is lower; it feels slightly claustrophobic. She knocks on a door and opens it.

'Simone Durand is here to meet you, Rupert.'

There is no answer. She opens it anyway and holds the door back, gesturing for me to go inside.

For a moment I think the room is empty. It is so dark; the curtains are closed and the walls are painted black. There is a musty, unpleasant smell. And then I notice the television in the corner, and a mound is shifting slowly on the red sofa.

'Rupert, can you switch that thing off?' Mrs Cherry says.

There is a grunt and the mound becomes a boy. A very large boy. Not tall, just fat. Obesely fat.

'I'll leave you to it,' Mrs Cherry says. She lets the door swing closed behind her.

I walk forwards so that I am standing next to the sofa. I extend my hand.

'Hello, Rupert. I am Simone and I am your au pair for the summer.'

He ignores my hand and rolls his eyes.

'I know exactly who you are.' His voice is croaky. Not fully broken, but almost. 'I can already speak French, so I don't know why Father insisted on employing you. *Quelle perte de temps.*'

'It may be a waste of time, it may not be. We will see.'

He sits up and stares at me. His face is red and raw with virulent acne, and the T-shirt he's wearing is too tight, showing the rolls of fat around his stomach. This boy looks and sounds nothing like his father. I wonder if they are really related.

'Your father suggested we spend the mornings together learning French, and then I understand there are other activities for you in the afternoons. I suggest we start at 9 a.m. and finish at lunchtime. Perhaps tomorrow morning you could show me around and we can find out more about each other. How does that sound?'

He grunts.

I am not sure what to say. This isn't the first time I have been an au pair, but my previous charges were younger children, and they lived in normal houses, not a mansion like this. I've never had to deal with a fifteen-year-old boy.

'You can piss off now.' He turns away from me and switches the television back on.

Charming. Absolutely charming.

5

CHARLOTTE

The drive to Sussex takes me nearly six hours. The traffic is lousy, and by the time I am weaving my way through Petworth towards Pulborough, I can barely keep my eyes open. Thank goodness for my satnav, but even so, I almost miss the turning to Sesame Hall. There is a discreet wooden sign on the right side of the road, and I turn a little too quickly without indicating. Iron gates are set further back, but they look rusted, as if they haven't been used in decades. The car behind me hoots loudly as my tyres screech and then crunch along the drive. I have to take several deep breaths to calm my nerves.

Despite the fading light, the scenery is beautiful. Ancient yew trees with vast scaly reddish-brown trunks and branches bowing low, laden with dark-green needles, line the edge of the drive. Behind them are iron railings fading into the distance, separating the fields from the road. The grandeur suggests this is the estate of a stately home; it's only the weeds growing along the centre of the drive and the long, unkempt grass on either side that suggests this may be a property that is down on its luck. I'm going slowly, but nevertheless this must be the longest private driveway I have ever been on. And it makes me nervous. My heart is pounding a little too hard and my breathing is fast.

And then the house appears straight in front of me. It's red brick, and although it appears to have Georgian proportions, it is disappointingly ugly and lacking symmetry. It's big, but not as large as the impressive drive and grounds might suggest, and I wonder if it's a modern, lesser version of what stood here originally. There are six rectangular windows with white frames along the ground floor and eight on the first floor. I'm not sure what I was expecting, but it wasn't this. As I pull up in front of the house, lights come on and reveal single-storey red brick buildings off to the side of the house.

I climb out of the car and stretch, walk around to the boot and take out my suitcase and my box of painting equipment. Then I walk up the stone steps to the front door and press the gold buzzer. The door swings open immediately and there is Sir Rupert. He must have been watching me through the spyhole in the door.

'Welcome to Sesame Hall,' he says. I put out my hand to shake his, but he leans forwards as if to give me a kiss on the cheek, and my hand jabs his stomach. Awkward. We step away from each other as if we have been stung. He lunges for my suitcase, saying, 'Please, let me.'

As he steps backwards, I follow him into the big hall. This looks more like the stately home that I was expecting, all dark wood panels and austere oil portraits and armour from distant years. A large staircase built from matching dark wood rises to the left. There is a musty scent along with the faint odour of wood polish. The hallway is lit by a wrought-iron chandelier, perhaps three feet in diameter, with far too many candle-shaped bulbs to count.

'This is amazing,' I say.

'Thank you.' He stands to one side and his eyes flit all over the place. As I glance at him, I get the impression that all of the bonhomie and confidence of the evening of my exhibition has dissipated. I'm not sure why. I would have expected him to be more secure in his own surroundings, rather than less. What it does do is extinguish my nerves.

'How was your journey? And would you like a drink?'

'It's kind of you to offer, but I stopped for a cuppa only half an hour ago. I hadn't realised quite how long it would take me to get here.' I stifle a yawn.

'In which case, let me show you to your room and you can have a rest.' He leans down to pick up my box of paints and brushes.

'Where will I be painting?'

'In the study. I can show you that first if you like, and then we'll go to your room.'

I follow Sir Rupert along a corridor to the left of the hall-way, past a couple of closed doors and into a dark wood-paneled room with built-in bookshelves housing hundreds of leather-bound books. There are large French windows that I assume lead out onto a terrace. It's dark now, so I can't assess the light. As if he is reading my mind, Sir Rupert says, 'I have chosen this room because it has northern light and is a room where I feel particularly comfortable.'

I nod. I can envisage him reclining in the high-backed leather armchair, selecting one of the antique tomes to read, perhaps playing a recording of Bach on an old-fashioned gramophone. I know exactly the colour palettes I will use to depict him.

'Of course you will have brought your own supplies, but nevertheless I took the liberty of purchasing you an easel. I visited a splendid art supplies shop in Brighton this morning.' He crosses his arms and puffs out his chest.

It's a fabulous, large easel that would have cost him at least three times the price of my battered old thing that I've left in the boot of my car. I'm impressed.

'Thank you. That is very kind. This is a lovely room.'

He nods. 'My father enjoyed spending time in this study, and I write my poetry in here.'

We walk back out into the corridor. He picks up my suitcase and I follow him upstairs, past the wall crammed full of portraits and along the upper landing, the walls of which are also packed with paintings. I wonder where he intends to put his own portrait, and for a moment, my nerves resurface. My style is nothing like the traditional artworks displayed here. I hope he won't be disappointed.

'This is your room,' he says, holding the door open and letting me walk through. The curtains are pulled. They are dark wine red and green in a floral print and remind me of a faded, country house hotel. The room has a musty smell, but it is clean, albeit tired looking, and the bed is made and piled high with cushions.

'I hope you will be comfortable here. There is an en suite through there.' He points to a closed door on the opposite side of the room. 'Why don't you have a little nap now and then please join me for drinks at 6.30 p.m. in the drawing room followed by dinner at 7 p.m. You're not vegetarian or, heaven help us, vegan, are you?'

I chuckle. 'No, I'm a full-on carnivore.'

'I'm relieved to hear that. We're having lamb shanks for dinner.'

'Lovely,' I say.

He hesitates in the doorway for a moment and then turns around. 'See you at 6.30 p.m.'

The door closes with a creak and I hear his footsteps fade down the corridor.

This really is like a country house hotel. Drinks at 6.30 p.m. followed by dinner at 7 p.m. How very formal.

I unpack my suitcase and hang my clothes up in a large oak armoire that smells of mothballs. Then I sink onto the bed. After texting Jodi to tell her I've arrived, my eyelids close and I drift off to sleep.

I awake with a start, my throat dry and my heart thumping in my chest. I turn to the right side of the bed, looking for Matthew, and then as I do every time I wake, I swallow a little sob when I realise he isn't with me. He will never be with me. It takes a few moments to orientate myself. I glance at my watch and shake off the horrible fogginess of an afternoon slumber. It's 6.34 p.m. Shit. I was meant to be downstairs.

I jump up and race to the bathroom, only halting when I hear the sounding of a gong. Is that what woke me up? I splash my face with water, put some mascara on, and pat down my crumpled blouse. I'm wearing jeans and they'll have to do. I grab a pale pink V-necked jumper from the cupboard and hurry out of my bedroom. Fortunately I turn the correct way and find the large staircase. I am on the bottom step when Sir Rupert appears as if from nowhere. I jump.

'I was just coming to look for you. I wondered if you had got lost.' Sir Rupert has changed out of his casual chinos and plaid shirt and is wearing a blazer and bow tie. He looks me up and down and I see a flash of disappointment on his face. I suppose I was meant to have changed for dinner.

'Sorry, no. I fell asleep.'

THE DRAWING ROOM is a large room, with several clusters of armchairs and sofas; some look as old and tired as the house itself. There is a metal trolley on the far side of the room. Sir Rupert strides over to it.

'What is your tipple?'

I bite my lip to stop myself from grinning. He is so formal and speaks in such an antiquated manner.

'I'll have a G&T if you have it.'

'Most certainly.'

He pours me some gin from a brand I have never come across, tips in a can of tonic and drops in a couple of cubes of ice and a slice of lemon. He motions for me to sit in an armchair near the fireplace. A log fire is lit and the wood sizzles and spits as it burns. He makes himself a whiskey and sits down next to me.

'Do you live here alone?' I ask.

'Yes, alas, I do.' He puts his glass down with a clunk. 'I haven't been fortunate enough to be married. It would be wonderful to share my life with someone. This is a big place to be rattling around in all by myself.'

I had hoped he might have a wife, which would make my stay here slightly less awkward. No such luck.

'Do you have help with the house?'

'I had a couple who used to keep things shipshape. He looked after the gardens and she cleaned the house and cooked. Alas, she passed away and he retired, so now I use a local agency to clean. It's far from ideal having different people snooping around, but needs must. How about you, Charlotte? Do you have anyone to look after you?'

'Um, no. I'm alone. I live in a small flat.'

There is an awkward silence for a while, until Sir Rupert stands up and says, 'Please join me in the dining room. Dinner will be ready now.'

'Do you cook?' I ask.

'Um, just a little. I have some help.'

He ushers me out and into the adjacent room, which houses a very long, gleaming mahogany dining table, probably large enough to seat twenty-four people. Two place settings are laid. One at the end and the other next to it on the right.

He pulls out a chair for me and I sit down. I don't object to his gentlemanly manners, even if I am betraying my feminist tendencies. After disappearing for several long minutes, he returns pushing a metal trolley piled high with steaming dishes.

'I would have liked to have had a waitress here this evening, but unfortunately the woman from the village who normally helps me out is otherwise engaged. So please forgive me, but I will have to serve you.'

I stifle a giggle.

He pours me a glass of red wine and then passes me the dishes of food.

How I wish Jodi were here. She would find all of this formality absolutely hilarious. On second thoughts, it's just as well she's not, as we'd probably be rolling around on the Oriental carpet in fits of very rude laughter.

The food is surprisingly delicious, and whilst we're eating, it takes the pressure off making small talk. We start with pea and mint soup, followed by lamb shanks, mashed potatoes and an array of steamed vegetables. Every so often I glance at Sir Rupert and he quickly averts his eyes. It's like he's staring at me, and it is making me feel extremely uncomfortable.

'I was wondering whether you might like to make a start on the portrait tomorrow? I realise it's Sunday, but I don't have to work, and afterwards I could show you around the local area.'

'That sounds lovely.'

I help him clear the plates and we pile the dirties back onto the trolley, which he pushes back out of the room. It is very strange and I wonder why we don't just eat in the kitchen like normal people.

He returns with a platter of cheeses and a silver box.

'Do you eat puddings?' he asks. His close-set eyes are wide, almost fearful in expression.

'Rarely,' I say, which isn't strictly true, but I get the feeling that that was the correct answer.

He lets out a puff of air. 'I'm glad to hear it. I don't have much of a sweet tooth and try to avoid too much fattening food.' He pats his flat stomach. 'I was worried you might be disappointed that I don't have an array of desserts on offer.'

'Not at all,' I say, helping myself to a small piece of goat's cheese.

When we have finished, he asks me if I would like a nightcap.

'No, thank you, Sir Rupert, but a cup of coffee would be lovely.'

'Please call me Rupert. Coffee coming right up.'

The coffee is bland and I am nearly sure it is decaffeinated. I am used to strong coffee and drink far too much of it at home.

'Can I help you clear up?' I ask as we both stand up.

'Absolutely out of the question. Please have a seat back in the drawing room and I will join you shortly.'

'Would you mind if I got an early night? I'm really exhausted after all that driving.'

He hesitates for a moment and then says, 'Yes, of course. Absolutely. How thoughtless of me. Please sleep well and stay in bed for as long as you like in the morning. Would you like me to bring you a cup of tea or coffee in bed?'

I am startled and taken aback by the suggestion. 'No, thank you. I'll be fine. I rarely sleep in. Is it ok if I help myself to breakfast?'

'Of course. It's in the kitchen, which is the next door along from here.'

I say goodnight, making an awkward little wave with my hand, and hurry upstairs to my bedroom.

Grabbing my phone, I send Jodi a text message.

Weirdest place. Super formal. Strange bloke, but I'm sure all will be ok. Need to remember the £20k! Sleep tight & let's speak tomorrow. Cxx

She doesn't reply. I suppose she is out on the town having fun. I take the photograph of Matthew out of my wallet and kiss it goodnight. I wipe my face as the tears fall.

How I miss him.

6

RUPERT

When you have dreamed of something or someone for as long as I have, it is nigh on impossible to dampen down the feelings of excitement when that individual arrives in your personal orbit.

Charlotte is utterly beautiful. I can't deny that I was a little disappointed she didn't make the effort to dress up for dinner, but she seemed quite relaxed, and we had a delightful meal. After I had cleaned away the plates and dishes and scrubbed the kitchen until it was sparkling clean, I indulged in a nightcap before creeping upstairs to my bedroom. I stood for a long time outside her bedroom door, listening. But all was silent. I cursed the solidity of our doors. I would have liked to have heard her breathing.

I slipped into my bedroom, stripped off and stood in front of the mirror. I am in very good shape, my abs well-defined, my chest hairless in line with what millennial women apparently prefer. Waxing is ridiculous and bloody painful, but as the old cliché goes, there is no gain without pain. I am sure Father would approve. Just the thought of such loveliness lying in the bed next door awakens Percy. I try to subdue my thoroughly inappropriate thoughts, but even after a lengthy shower, sleep evades me. I toss and turn for many hours, and when I eventually awake, I am dismayed that it is already gone 8 a.m. I jump out of bed, pull on a pair of corduroys and a thick jumper and hurry downstairs.

Charlotte is seated at the kitchen table, her slender fingers clasping a mug of tea, a vision of loveliness in my ordinary surroundings.

'Good morning!' I say breezily. 'I hope you slept well. Have you found everything you need for breakfast?'

'Thank you. I just have a cup of tea in the mornings.'

'Gosh, that won't sustain you. You're such a slight little thing. Can I make you a cooked breakfast?'

'No, thank you, but I appreciate the offer.'

'In which case, I suggest we convene in the study at 9 a.m. and you can make a start on the portrait.'

She gets up from the table. I hadn't meant to suggest she leave, but unsure what to say, I simply smile at her. She rinses her mug in the sink. I wish she hadn't chosen the earthenware. I use that for tradespeople; she should be drinking from our finest china.

'May I suggest that you paint in the mornings. I work from home on estate business most mornings, with the exception of Wednesdays when I am in court, sometimes for a half a day, sometimes for the whole day. I am a magistrate.' I pause for her reaction, but disappointingly she just nods. 'Perhaps you could have Wednesdays off.'

'Thank you,' she says demurely, drying her mug with a tea towel.

'What do you enjoy doing when you're not painting?' I ask.

'Anything to do with the outdoors – walking, swimming, being around nature.'

'Please feel free to use the swimming pool. It is heated. I also have a gym, which you are welcome to use too.'

She nods and leaves the room.

AN HOUR LATER, she has unpacked her paints, set up the easel with the large canvas and has turned the leather chair so that it is facing her. I settle down into it and smile.

'What would you like to wear in the portrait?' she asks.

Goodness, I haven't even thought about that. Stupid me. I think of the portrait of my father in his Lord Lieutenant uniform and my grandfather in his hunting pinks. I feel a kernel of panic. I am not a member of any official body; I don't have a uniform; I don't hunt. What will I be remembered for?

'You don't need to decide now,' Charlotte says in her typically kind manner, immediately quelling my panic. 'I'm going to be concentrating on your face first anyway.'

'Where should I look? Straight at you or to one side?'

'Just look straight ahead and don't worry about keeping still. We'll be having plenty of sittings. I just want to get a general feel for your features.'

I love those words; they melt into the cool autumnal air. *Feel for your features.* I wish she really were feeling my features. I cross my legs.

She is sketching me now, seated on a stool, her knees demurely together, her eyes roaming my face. What is so fabulous is the chance this gives me to study her: the way the tip of her tongue comes to rest just under her straight top teeth. How her long eyelashes flutter up and down as she glances at me and then back to the canvas again. Lines appear on her forehead as she concentrates. I would like to stroke them away. How tendrils of her hair escape from the clip she has used to pile her beautiful locks on top of her head. I had thought I would struggle to sit still for any length of time, but in fact two hours pass as if it were ten minutes, so lost I am in studying every movement she makes, imbuing her expressions with meaning, wondering whether she likes what she sees. I pray that she does.

Just before 11 a.m. she stands up, rolls her head on her neck and then stretches her arms up into the air. Her jumper rides up, revealing a quick flash of her smooth, pale stomach and her perfect, neat belly button. It reminds me of Simone's, although Simone's stomach was slightly rounded, not as washboard flat as Charlotte's.

'I think I've done enough for now,' she says.

I jump up from the chair. 'Can I get you a drink or something?'

'You're very kind, but I am quite happy to help myself to something from the kitchen if I may?'

'Of course. Please make yourself at home.'

SHORTLY AFTER NOON, I pull the Aston Martin up to the front of the house. I note how she raises her eyebrows. It is a beautiful car and I am glad she appreciates it. My father chose it and had it built to order, the bodywork sprayed in a subtle pale blue to match the colour used in our family crest.

I go slowly along our uneven drive, but when we turn out onto the lane, I put my foot down, and full throttle, the car roars and races forwards. I glance at her and can tell that she's impressed with the motor and my control of it.

'All the land that you see around here is part of our estate. It is mostly laid to arable and managed by tenant farmers. It provides me with a healthy income and keeps me out of mischief.' I laugh, but she simply smiles.

'So what are your hobbies, Charlotte?'

'Painting,' she says.

'Of course.'

I wait for her to ask me what my hobbies are, but she stays silent, admiring the view. I assume she is still a little coy around me, so I volunteer the information. 'My hobbies are poetry and various modalities of exercise. I practice Krav Maga.'

'What's that?'

'It's a form of self-defense and fighting developed by the Israeli army. I am quite proficient in it. Combined with daily workouts in my gym at home, I manage to stay reasonably fit.'

'I hope you don't need to defend yourself too often!'

'Fortunately not.' I laugh. I am glad Charlotte has a sense of levity.

'We also have a shoot on the estate. Do you shoot?'

She shakes her head and gives a little shiver.

'It's nothing to be scared of,' I say. 'We breed pheasants. It's very sociable and we have a syndicate that meets up throughout the season.'

She is staring out of the window and clearly not interested in shooting. I must try a different tack.

We are entering the village now, so I slow down to keep within the speed limits. As a magistrate, I have to be very careful to obey the law. The humiliation of being caught for speeding would be too much to bear.

'The Baskervilles used to own the whole village, but my grandfather gave many of the cottages to his workers on the estate, and other buildings were sold off shortly after the war. Now we are just ordinary members of the local community. I suggest we have Sunday lunch at The Chicken and Hen public house. Would that suit you?'

'Thank you,' she says as I turn the Aston into the parking lot. I have reserved a table in anticipation.

'GOOD AFTERNOON, MRS CARTER,' I say brightly as I approach the bar. A few of the locals turn to look at me and greet me with a nod. Fortunately I'm well liked around here.

'Good afternoon, Sir Rupert. I've reserved your normal

table for you.' The landlady grabs a couple of menus and walks around the bar, leading us to our table in the corner of the dining room.

'May I introduce you to my friend Charlotte Aldridge. She is a renowned artist and has come to visit from the north.'

'How do you do,' Mrs Carter says, plonking the menus on the table. 'The specials are roast lamb and roast pork with all the trimmings. What can I get you to drink?'

Charlotte asks for a sparkling water and I order half a pint of lager. She seems a little uncomfortable, shifting around in her chair, not meeting my eyes as often as she did when she was painting me. I hope I haven't done anything to offend her. I assume she is simply tired after the long day of driving yesterday and painting me this morning. I excuse myself and go to the gentlemen's. A quick look in the mirror confirms that all is ok.

After our meal, I suggest a further drive around.

'Would you mind if I walk back to Sesame Hall?' Charlotte asks.

I am, of course, a little disappointed. I would have liked to have joined her, but as I have the car, I will have to drive home.

'Of course,' I say graciously. 'Please make yourself at home.' I hand her a duplicate key for the front door and watch her stride away. On second thoughts, perhaps it's not such a bad thing that I will have an hour or so alone in the house. It will give me an opportunity to have a little peek through her things.

7

SIMONE, JULY 1994

Teenage boys are a mystery to me. I know at nineteen I am still a teenager myself, but I am so much more mature than any adolescent boy I have ever met. I have absolutely no interest in them. Rupert was quite the little brat the first day we met, but in the week since then he has morphed into an eager learner. In fact, he is too eager.

Our mornings follow the same routine. An hour practising writing, followed by an hour of conversation, normally outside, as the weather has been lovely. We then have an hour of reading and comprehension, followed by conversation over lunch.

In the afternoons, I tend to lie by the pool or take a stroll through the park or read my book, with my legs tucked underneath me in my bedroom. Invariably, wherever I am, Rupert is too. It is beginning to get on my nerves.

Today it is particularly hot, the weather more reminiscent of the Côte d'Azur than southern England. It is too hot to do anything except lounge by the swimming pool. After lunch I go up to my room and change into my yellow bikini, slipping an oversized shirt stolen from Gerard, my ex-boyfriend, over the top. The house is cool and silent. I have not seen Sir Oswald in the past three days, much to my disappointment. I assume he has been away on business.

I put my towel on my sunbed, take off my shirt and lie down. My body is a pale bronze, and the vibrant, sunshine yellow of the bikini sets off my tan beautifully. It isn't long before my eyes close and the heat of the sun makes my body feel as if it were melting. When I eventually open them again, a shadow has fallen across my torso. I look up with a start and Rupert is standing there staring at me.

'What are you doing?'

'Looking at you.'

'Well, don't.'

He is wearing a tropical print shirt, which makes him look even grosser than normal. The sun has made his pimples worse, oozing and pus-filled. He wobbles over to another sun lounger and heaves himself onto it. I shut my eyes, but after a minute or so open them again. Rupert is staring at me. I open my mouth to say something, but then I take pity on him. This is a boy who has lost his mother. He attends an all-boys' boarding school. I don't suppose he's ever seen a woman's body as exposed as mine is in this skimpy bikini. Although it creeps me out, I will forgive him.

I let my eyelids close again and sometime later am awoken by male voices. I don't have the energy to open my eyes, so I just listen to Sir Oswald's deep, molten voice.

'You really are disgusting, Rupert. What are you doing to lose some of that weight?'

I open my eyes just a fraction so I can look through my lashes. Rupert is sitting on his sun lounger, his shirt off, his head hanging low over his man-boy boobs and rolls of stomach fat.

'Speak up, son!'

Rupert tugs on his shirt to cover himself but doesn't say

anything. His eyes are bloodshot and cast downwards, and his lower lip is trembling. His face is looking particularly red, and I can't tell whether it's from the sun or because he's blushing.

'You'll never be a Baskerville with a weak chin like that. Heaven knows where it's come from.'

Sir Oswald sighs and turns away from his son. He peels off his clothes and drops them onto the ground. He walks around the pool to the deep end, his swimming trunks tight, showing off his beautiful physique and rippled muscles. Although he must be in his forties and old enough to be my father, he is a staggeringly beautiful man. He pushes himself up onto tiptoes and dives into the pool, barely making a splash, completing length after length, firstly doing the crawl and then butterfly strokes.

Whilst he is in the pool, I rearrange myself, pulling my bikini top a little tighter, increasing my cleavage. I turn around to lie on my stomach, with my face towards the pool. When Sir Oswald climbs out of the swimming pool and pads towards me, dripping water from his chest hair and firm body, I look up, leaning on my forearms, my cleavage on display, my bottom in the air. I smile at him and he smiles back.

'How are you, Simone?' he asks.

Oh my goodness, I am so horny, him standing this close to me. I would like to grab him, but instead I look up and flutter my eyelids. 'I am very well, thank you, Sir Oswald.'

'Jolly good,' he says. 'How is Rupert progressing with his French?'

'He's making good improvements. He's a diligent pupil with a quick grasp for the language.'

'I am glad to hear that.' Neither of us glance at Rupert, who can definitely hear every word. Sir Oswald strides towards one of the sun loungers and pulls it over so that it is next to mine. As he lays a white towel on the lounger, I turn onto my side so that I am facing him.

He lies down and stretches his arms above his head. 'It's such a relief to be home.' He sighs.

'Where have you been, if you don't mind me asking?'

'To London. I have complicated business affairs that need settling. The lawyers make such a meal out of everything, creating problems just so they can charge more. Anyway, no need to bore you with that. Has Rupert told you about the history of Sesame Hall?'

'Not much,' I say. 'I'd be interested to learn more.' I'm not really, but I want to engage him in conversation.

He looks at me long and hard, and my stomach melts. His dark eyes appear to get larger, and I can tell he likes what he sees.

He tells me some history of the house and the estate, but I don't absorb his words, I just listen to the timbre of his voice and watch his face.

But then suddenly his tone changes.

'What the hell are you staring at, Rupert?' he shouts.

I turn to look at his son. Rupert gets up. I think he has tears in his eyes, and his shoulders are hunched up under his ears. He hurries, or rather waddles, away, towards the house.

'Please excuse me,' Sir Oswald says. He gets up and strides after Rupert.

I wait a long time, but neither of them return. Eventually, when I am too hot and in need of a cold drink and a cool bath, I return to the house. It is totally quiet; perhaps everyone has gone out.

When I am washed and have slipped into a floral summery dress, I wonder what is up with Rupert. I decide to go and look for him, but I can't find him anywhere. He's not in his bedroom or his study; he's not downstairs. Perhaps I was right and he has gone out. I am just about to return to my room when I walk straight into Sir Oswald.

'I was looking for Rupert.'

'He is being punished.'

'But he's not in his room,' I say.

'No. We have a special room for punishments. It's something of a family tradition. I was appalled by his lascivious behaviour. He was staring at you as you lay by the pool. I'm just glad you didn't notice.'

'He's only a boy,' I say, my imagination running riot as I think of this special punishment room.

'An adolescent who should know better. Please don't worry yourself about Rupert. Would you like to join me for an aperitif in the drawing room before dinner?'

'Yes, please,' I say a little too quickly.

The thing is, I am worried about Rupert. As much as I think he's a revolting teenager, he is sensitive, and he is still grieving the loss of his mother. No one should be made to suffer more than is absolutely necessary. Sir Oswald disappears into his study, and I try to find Rupert. He certainly isn't in any of the main rooms of the house, so I wander around outside, peeking in the outbuildings, admiring a collection of fancy cars kept in garages. Eventually, I return to the house through the back door, where there is a large utility and laundry room. Mrs Cherry is bustling around, preparing dinner in the kitchen.

'Can I help you?' I ask. I haven't offered before, mainly because the woman seems very dismissive of me. She looks up with surprise.

'I ain't had anyone offer to help since her ladyship died,' she says, chortling. Perhaps she's not as grim as I assumed. 'If you'd like to peel and chop those carrots, I wouldn't say no.'

I walk over to the wooden butcher's block. She hands me a vegetable peeler and a knife and I start chopping. We work for a while in silence.

'You've settled in well here, unlike the au pair from last year.' It's not clear whether she's talking to me or articulating her thoughts aloud. 'Young Rupert likes you, as does Sir

Oswald. Not surprising, I suppose. The last au pair looked like the back end of a bus.'

'Where is Rupert?' I ask.

'Dunno. Haven't seen him in a few hours.'

'Sir Oswald said he was being punished.'

Mrs Cherry immediately stops stirring the pot she is cooking on the large Aga. Her lips tighten.

'What does it mean, he's being punished?'

'It's not for you to worry your pretty head about. Sir Oswald has his ways, and it isn't for me or you to question them. This family has been following its traditions for centuries, and they've all grown up into fine men.'

'I feel sorry for Rupert,' I say.

'You, young lassie, need to stop asking questions.' She turns her back to me and stirs harder and harder, and I wonder whether the wooden spoon will snap in her grasp.

8

CHARLOTTE

Rupert is intense. It was kind of him to treat me to a pub lunch, but I need my own space. I am tired, and whenever I'm tired, I miss Matthew more than ever. Walking back to Sesame Hall gives me a boost of much-needed energy and time to myself.

I take advantage of the walk to call Jodi.

'He's quite weird,' I say.

'He's entitled to be weird if he's paying you twenty grand to paint his portrait!' She laughs. 'What's the house like?'

I explain how it is big but tired, and that he lives there alone.

'He's probably not used to having company,' Jodi surmises. 'What's he like to paint?'

'Fine. I think the painting will be ok, but it's early days. I miss you.'

'I miss you too. Uncle Richard sent an email to say Mum has settled in, and they're going away for a few days to the coast, so we won't hear from them for a week or so.'

'I'm glad she's having a lovely time. She's been so supportive of me since Matthew died, and she needs the break,' I say.

'I've got back-to-back shifts this week, but send me a text message if you want to talk and I'll call you on my break.'

'Ok. Love you.'

'Love you back,' Jodi says and hangs up.

I feel so alone as I stride along the drive up towards Sesame Hall. Mum is on the other side of the world, and Jodi is consumed with her own life. My friends are there in the background, but there is a wide, gaping hole that Matthew left, and it's so raw and painful. I assumed that coming somewhere new, to a place Matthew never visited, might have eased my loss, but all I can think of is how Matthew never got the chance to see this place or experience the things I'm experiencing. And when I think that, I can't help but go over the horrific events surrounding his death, searching in vain for new clues, new thoughts and conclusions as to why it happened.

It was the first May bank holiday weekend and the weather was surprisingly fine. We got up early and prepared sandwiches and stuffed them in Matthew's rucksack, along with bottles of water. We left his car on the side of the road up by The Cat and Fiddle Pub, the highest pub in Britain. The air was fresh and the views awe-inspiring. We walked all the way up to Shining Tor, then did the full circular route, along Goyt's Clough, passing all the rocky outcrops and skirting the moors, catching our breath leaning against tumbledown dry-stone walls. We stopped for our picnic and admired the stunning vistas. And over five hours later we stumbled back to the car, exhausted but happy. I had two large blisters on my feet, but I didn't care.

That evening we were due to go into Manchester to meet with some university friends of Matthew's, but I was exhausted, lying prone on the sofa. 'Do you mind if I don't go?'

'Yes,' he said, and then he blew kisses onto my neck. 'But I'll forgive you this once, you lightweight! I expect you to paint a picture inspired by the Peak District and those views we saw today.'

I didn't answer as he kissed me on the lips.

An hour later, showered and looking ridiculously handsome in a pair of jeans and a pale blue button-down shirt, his leather jacket flung over his arm, he blew me a kiss goodbye and said he'd be back before midnight.

He wasn't.

I never saw Matthew again.

His father identified his body, and my life was destroyed.

THERE WERE no security cameras in the place where Matthew died, and no doubt I was thinking about that, as I do over and over again, as I approached Sesame Hall. Blinking above the front door is a security camera. I hadn't noticed it last night. I suppose Rupert must be a bit vulnerable living here in the middle of nowhere all alone. I take my boots and anorak off and carry them upstairs. My eyes are drawn upwards and into the corners of the rooms as I move inside the house. And there are more cameras discreetly tucked into the cornicing of the hall and upstairs on the landing.

I shut my bedroom door, take off my clothes and slip into bed. This time, I set my alarm for 5.30 p.m. so I have time for a bath before dinner.

THIS EVENING, I have made a bit more of an effort and have put on a full skirt in a black and white floral pattern teamed with a cropped black cashmere cardigan. I have only brought one skirt and one dress with me, so I hope Rupert will forgive my informal dress code. Dinner is coq au vin, delicious again. I assume he has a deep freeze full of pre-prepared food, but I decide not to ask him.

He tops up my glass of wine.

'You have quite a lot of security cameras around the place,' I say.

'Yes. Unfortunately, as I am a magistrate and live in a big house, I am somewhat of a target for the local riffraff.'

'Have you been burgled?'

'Just the once, but once is too many. They broke into the garage and took the quad bike. Fortunately, they didn't break into the garages where I keep the Rolls and the Aston Martin. That really would have been a disaster.'

'Quite,' I murmur.

'But you don't need to be scared.' Rupert leans towards me. I shift backwards slightly. I'm about to tell him that I'm not in the slightest bit scared, when he says, 'I'll look after you.'

I try not to flinch as I smile at him.

I drink too much. I know I shouldn't, but conversation is so stilted that I fill the gaps with wine. Besides, the wine is delicious and far superior to anything I would drink at home. By the end of dinner, I feel a little tipsy, but in a nice way.

'Do you fancy a stroll outside?' Rupert suggests. 'It's a clear evening, and with so little light pollution, the stars are out in all their glory.'

'Sure,' I say, holding onto the edge of the table as I stand up.

'I'll get your coat for you,' Rupert says.

'Don't worry, it's in my room–'

'No, it isn't,' he interrupts. 'We keep coats and boots in the cloakroom downstairs. I took the liberty of putting yours in there.'

I raise my eyebrows, but he doesn't notice because he is already striding away towards the back of the house, where I assume the said cloakroom is located. When did he go into my bedroom to remove my coat and boots? For a horrible moment, I wonder if it was when I was asleep. I consider asking him but chicken out as he helps me into my old, navy anorak.

He leads me to the back of the house, along the wide terrace and down some steps onto a path I hadn't noticed before. It's chilly and I give a little shiver.

'Are you cold?' Rupert asks. He puts his arm around me. He is tall, so my head is far below his. Surprisingly I don't mind too much. At least he is transferring some warmth.

'Look up,' he says. 'You might catch a shooting star.'

I do as he suggests, but a strand of hair flicks across my face. He leans across and gently removes it. He is standing too close, gazing at my eyes. The discomfort kicks in and I take a step backwards. I am creeped out. I clutch my arms around my body.

He inhales as if he is about to say something but then appears to change his mind.

'Shall we walk?' I suggest.

'Good idea. We can stroll down to the lake. It's a stone path the whole way, so you won't ruin your shoes.'

A bird or an animal scurries across the path in front of us. I jump. Rupert laughs.

'Are you scared of mice?' he asks.

'A little,' I admit. 'Actually quite a lot. I don't like rodents or spiders. How about you?'

'You get used to them, living in the countryside.'

We are silent for a few more steps, and then he asks, 'So tell me, Charlotte, what do you want from your future?'

'Um-m-m,' I stutter.

'A husband, children perhaps?' he asks.

I can't help the tears smarting my eyes. Yes, I should have had a husband. Maybe I would even be pregnant with our first child by now. Oh, Matthew. I miss you so much.

'What is it, dear? I'm sorry. Have I upset you?' Rupert puts his arm around me again.

'I'm sorry. It's all a bit raw.' I swallow a sob.

'What is?'

'I was engaged to be married. In fact, I should be married by now, but my fiancé died six months ago.'

'I'm so terribly sorry to hear that,' he says, coming to a halt. 'What happened?'

'Matthew died...suddenly.'

'My dear, please don't upset yourself. No need to tell me any details. You are such a beautiful woman. I am sure you will find happiness again soon.'

'Thank you,' I murmur, sniffing. But I don't feel like taking a walk now. I just want to go to bed and lie with my memories.

'Do you mind if we go back and do this walk another day?' I suggest.

'By all means. A good night's sleep will do wonders.'

I DON'T KNOW if it's the wine or just sheer exhaustion, but I fall asleep quickly, weighed down by the heavy duvet and multiple blankets. But I awake with a start. The room is pitch black. I fumble for my alarm clock. It's 2.09 a.m. My heart is beating rapidly as if I have had an adrenaline rush. And then I hear it. A creak. Is that what awoke me?

I lie with my eyes open, my fingers clutching the top of the duvet, my ears straining. But there is silence. I reassure myself that this is an old house. It is bound to creak and move as the air temperature falls. Perhaps there is even a friendly ghost. Did all that talk about cameras and security send my brain into overdrive?

My breathing settles, and I am just falling back to sleep when I hear it again. Footsteps. Creaks. They sound as if they are outside my bedroom door. Should I go and look? Or is it Rupert walking around in the middle of the night? I hold my breath. Waiting. But all I hear is the blood pounding in my ears.

When I next wake up, pale silvery light is shining through

the curtains. It is 7 a.m. and time to get up. I sit up in bed, run my index finger over Matthew's photo and yawn.

And then I notice it.

The curtains are open about an inch in the middle. I am positive I pulled them fully last night. I am always careful about closing curtains properly because I need the darkness in order to sleep. Did I forget? I drank more than usual, but no. I am sure I pulled them. I remember that my fingers were still wet from the bathroom, and I was worried I might have left a stain. They were most definitely fully shut when I switched out the light.

What the hell?

9

RUPERT

Charlotte isn't like other women. I assumed that before I met her, but now I know her, I can say so with certainty. She has a sensitivity to her that needs to be cherished and nourished. It is evident that she is still hurting from the unexpected death of her fiancé. I am fortunate not to have experienced profound anguish, but I suppose an exceptionally sensitive person such as Charlotte will feel the effects of grief for longer than most. It is clear that six months isn't long enough. My strategy must be to take her mind off her dead fiancé and show her that life is full of exciting possibilities.

Yesterday I had a lot of work, including meetings with my accountant and one of the farm managers. I sat for Charlotte for a couple of hours in the morning and then had to leave her to get on with the mundanity of my day. We had a brief supper, this time at the kitchen table, and then she excused herself immediately and went up to her room.

This morning I am up bright and early. I go into the study to have a sneaky look at her painting. She has moved the easel so that the picture is facing the wall. Carefully, I lift it up and turn it around. The outline of my face, neck and shoulders is there, and I can see that she has started with the differing tones – the lights and the darks. I like the squareness of my jaw and the hint of a piercing gaze. Even though she is at these early stages, she has definitely captured a good likeness of me. I am pleased. Very pleased.

I turn the easel back to the wall and stride down the corridor towards the kitchen. As I pass through the great hall, I stop to look at the portrait of my father. Yes, he was a fine-looking man. But me, I am more handsome. Women stare at me. They are aware of my masculine magnetism. Of course, such a view may be perceived as delusional, vain even, but really I am not. I could easily step out of the pictures of any magazine. My lack of success in the relationship arena is simple. Up until now, I have not found the correct woman.

Although I normally work out in the gym, this morning there is a clear blue sky, and I feel like going for a run. In the cloakroom, I find my running shoes and search through the pile for a lightweight jacket. My fingers run over Charlotte's anorak. My eyes alight on her boots. They are both cheap and frayed. I must do something about that.

By the time I have returned from my run, had a shower and eaten breakfast, I am late for my portrait sitting.

'Please excuse my tardiness,' I say, slipping into the chair.

'It's no problem. I have plenty to do.' Charlotte smiles. There is a levity to her words and she has a gentle pink bloom in her cheeks. My vision of loveliness.

'I have decided what I should like to wear in the portrait,' I announce.

'Oh yes.'

'Simple black tie, perhaps with a pale blue bow tie and waistcoat, to represent our family colours.'

'Sounds good,' she says, but her mind is clearly on her painting, and she descends into silence, her face a picture of concentration. Once again, I lose myself in her gaze, imagining her lying in my arms, her perfectly formed ear pressed up against my chest. I am tugged from my daydream by her voice.

'I was wondering if you would like me to cook supper tonight?' she asks.

'But we agreed that I would provide the food. You must tell me if it is not up to your standards.' I feel a kernel of concern.

'The food is absolutely delicious. It's just that I enjoy cooking and thought it might save you.'

What a kind woman she is. Perhaps I should have told her that I am not slaving away in the kitchen, that I have asked a local caterer to supply me with dishes that I place in the deep freeze and take out to defrost after breakfast. But I don't want to disappoint Charlotte. If she thinks I am a good cook, that can only be a positive.

'I would be delighted to accept your offer. Would you like me to do a shop for you?'

'No, that's quite alright. I'll take my car and nip into Tesco in Pulborough.'

WHEN I ARRIVE BACK at home shortly before 7 p.m., there is a heavenly scent coming from the kitchen. Charlotte is standing at the Aga, an apron around her midriff, humming gently under her breath. How marvelous that she feels at home here.

'Did you have a good day?' I ask. I get a thrill in asking her that. We make such a good couple.

'Yes, thank you. And you?'

'I did and I had just enough time to nip into Chichester to make a couple of purchases.' I place a large paper carrier bag on the table. 'I have a little gift for you.'

She wipes her hands on the apron and turns to look at me. 'Thank you.'

I move the bag towards her. She steps forwards and takes out the Barbour coat and Dubarry boots.

'Oh my goodness,' she exclaims, charming little pink spots appearing on her cheeks.

'I hope it's not presumptuous of me, but I felt your coat and boots needed upgrading.'

'It's very kind of you, but I can't possibly accept these,' she says.

'Why on earth not?'

'They are much too generous, and you're paying me quite enough already.'

How modest she is.

'I'm afraid, my dear, that I win this argument. They are yours, and I hope you will enjoy wearing them.'

'Thank you very much,' she says quietly.

Charlotte has made a very fine shepherd's pie. How did she know that it is my favourite? That it reminds me of happier times when Mrs Cherry made me special meals at the behest of Mother. And as if that wasn't enough, Charlotte has created an apple tarte Tatin, which she serves with ready-made vanilla ice cream. I had assumed with her slender physique, she wouldn't have a sweet tooth, but perhaps I presumed wrongly. I will have to offer her desserts in future.

Despite having eaten in some of London's finest restaurants, I am not sure I have ever had such a delicious and satisfying meal. I cannot praise her enough. They say that food is the language of love, and Charlotte has just given me a very large dollop.

She insists on washing up the dishes, so I stand next to her and dry them. I wonder if now is the moment to gently place my lips on hers. I try to recall what some of the dating books say. Go with your intuition, I believe, and my intuition is screaming, *take her in your arms*. I lay the tea towel on the draining board. She is focused on scrubbing a saucepan, her hands and forearms encased in yellow rubber gloves.

'May I?' I ask huskily, stepping towards her, my lips puckered, ready to kiss hers.

'Oh, thanks,' she replies, handing me the saucepan. It drips soap suds onto my shoes, and I stand there wondering how I just missed the moment.

When she finishes washing up and wiping down the kitchen surfaces, she undoes her apron and hangs it up on the hook behind the door.

'I need to make a couple of phone calls, so I'll say goodnight now.'

'Oh,' I say, remembering that tomorrow is Wednesday, and as I'm due in court, I may not see her all day.

'Goodnight.' She smiles as she leaves the room.

I RETREAT TO MY BEDROOM, laden with disappointment, but then I remind myself that it is early days. We have found each other at long last and will have a whole lifetime together. There is no need to hurry and risk scaring her off. When I first laid eyes on Charlotte, a thunderbolt hit me. Naturally it wasn't what I intended to happen, but my feelings were, and still are, so overwhelming that denial is hopeless. In many ways, it is a relief. Love at first sight. That in itself is perfectly normal, isn't it?

I have a pile of self-help books on modern dating that arrived courtesy of Amazon in anonymous brown boxes. I keep the bulk of the books hidden at the base of my wardrobe, as God forbid, I wouldn't want anyone knowing I have to turn to them for advice. My favourite is titled *You've Got The Looks, You've Got The Body, So Why Aren't You Pulling? Dating Tips for Handsome Men*, and that I keep next to my bed.

The thing is, I *have* had dating success. In fact, when I'm at social engagements, women frequently throw themselves at me.

I'm probably one of Sussex's most eligible bachelors. Eighteen months ago, shortly after my final operation, I had a liaison with a lady in her mid-thirties. She had come out of what she described as a long-term toxic relationship. She arrived in my life thanks to my short stint using a dating app. Roxana swiped me and I swiped her back. We met for drinks and then for dinner. After our second dinner at the very splendid Amberley Castle, she asked if she could see where I live. I brought her here, and as soon as we walked into the hallway, she pulled my face towards hers and began to devour me with kisses. It was so unexpected and quite glorious, so I had high hopes that all would work out just fine. I led her up here, to my bedroom. We undressed each other. She admired my physique and I ran my hands over hers. But then Percy realised I was making love to a woman who had black hair, a vast bosom and looked nothing like my ideal type. And Percy decided to go to sleep. Roxana took Percy in her long-nailed hands and tried to coax him back to life, but it wasn't happening. I apologised profusely. She was surprisingly kind about it and said it often occurred on initial sexual encounters. That may be so, but I knew it wasn't Percy who was the problem, it was Roxana. I asked her to leave. She then turned into a slut, calling me all sorts of vile names. I threw her out.

My next encounter was at the end of last year, and that time I was more careful. Carol was blonde and petite, a shy schoolteacher. We had many dates and I became increasingly confident that although she wasn't the one, she may potentially be sufficient. I had been working out regularly, and my body was almost as honed as it is now. She was a regular churchgoer and claimed not to believe in sex before marriage. For the first couple of months, that suited me. But then I thought, what if I did marry Carol and Percy decided she wasn't good enough, what then? It would be too late. I told her we needed to make love. And thank heavens we tried, because Percy was having none of it. Carol sobbed like a baby when I told her to leave. I realised then that she wanted me for my money and my status. Carol was not deserving.

I flick through my well-thumbed guidebooks, but for the first time, they don't throw up any answers. Perhaps it isn't surprising. My love for Charlotte will not be explained in any book. It transcends the written word. It is complex and mysterious and so very unexpected. I shove all of the books, except my favourite, back in the box and kick it under my bed. I strip off my clothes, and now, as I'm standing naked in front of the mirror, Percy and I are thinking of Charlotte. My beautiful Charlotte, who is just a wall away.

10

SIMONE, JULY 1994

I scream.

Was it a nightmare, or is there someone here? I am soaking wet with sweat and shivering. Perhaps I'm ill? No. My heart is racing. Something has scared me. I lie very still, trying to control my breathing.

I hear it again. A creak, right next to my bed.

There is someone in my bedroom, and it's the middle of the night.

A torchlight flickers on.

'*Qui est là?*' I whisper, my voice croaking. And then I remember I'm in England. 'Who's there?'

I clutch my sheet and pull it up over my bare breasts. I am shaking.

The torchlight goes off and my heart feels as if it has jumped into my throat.

'I'm sorry I woke you. I didn't mean to.'

'Bloody hell, Rupert. What the fuck are you doing in my bedroom?' I screech as I switch on my bedside lamp, after ensuring that I am fully covered by the sheets.

Rupert is standing next to my bed, dressed in navy and

maroon striped pyjamas, his hair bedraggled and up on end.

'Please be quiet!' he says. 'You'll wake everyone up.'

'I don't bloody care. You're freaking me out.' I glance at my clock. 'What are you doing in here at 3 a.m.? You scared the living daylights out of me.'

'Please be quiet. I beg of you, Simone.'

He looks like an oversized forlorn schoolboy, his lower lip trembling.

'Please don't tell anyone,' he mutters. He turns his face away from me.

'Why are you here?'

He just shakes his head.

I sigh. 'Pass me the T-shirt on the chair.'

He does as instructed.

'Now turn around and don't look.' I wait for him to turn his back to me, and then I slip the T-shirt over my head. 'You can turn around again now.'

He faces me but continues to stand at the side of the bed with his head hanging low.

'For God's sake, Rupert. Just bloody sit down.' I pat the end of my bed.

He sits and turns to look at me. 'I didn't mean to scare you. I just wanted to see you. That's all.'

'You can't go creeping around the house at night and looking at naked women in their sleep.'

'I'm sorry,' he whispers. 'It's just that you're very beautiful.'

I sigh. The trouble is Rupert creeps me out at the same time as making me feel sorry for him. He's a harmless teenage boy who probably doesn't have access to porn magazines and certainly doesn't have any women in his life to put him on the straight and narrow. Thinking of which, I remember what Sir Oswald told me earlier.

'What was the punishment your dad gave you?'

Rupert blushes. 'It's nothing.'

'You can tell me.'

'Don't want to talk about it.'

I sigh and yawn. 'I want to go to sleep now. Go back to your own bed.'

But Rupert doesn't move. 'You're very pretty,' he says, and then he blushes again. Bright red patches flourish on his cheeks and creep up his neck.

I flop back onto my pillow. 'Thank you, Rupert, but you need to go now.'

'Please can I stay? Just a little bit?'

'No,' I say wearily. For a horrible moment, I wonder if he's going to force himself on me, but fortunately he carries on talking and I sigh.

'If I just lie down next to you and don't touch you, please can I stay?'

'No. I'm here to teach you French not sex. Go back to your own bed.'

But still he doesn't move. I haven't got the energy to sit up or get out of bed, so I decide to change tack. I could tell him that I'll be asking Sir Oswald for a lock on my door in the morning because I don't like to be disturbed in the night by his lecherous son, but that would be too cruel. I wonder what punishment Sir Oswald would mete out if I said that. Instead I try the light-hearted approach.

'Are you a virgin, Rupert?'

He nods and then says in a barely audible voice, 'But I'd like to lose my virginity with you.'

'You what?' I exclaim and then start laughing, so much so, I'm shaking the bed. This boy is hilarious. But when I look up and see his face and the pained expression, I take pity again. I don't want to scar him for life. If he ends up looking anything like his father, he certainly won't have trouble picking up any woman he wants. But right now, that seems most unlikely. Sir Oswald is right, Rupert does have a weak chin, and all of that fat is positively gross. I assume he will grow out of the acne, but if he stays an overweight, unattractive slob, then he's going to find dating very hard. Although I suppose some girls will forgive his looks and love him for his wealth and status.

'Are you a virgin?' he asks.

'Of course I'm not. I'm nineteen!'

'That's not very old,' he says. 'Do you have a boyfriend?'

'Not at the moment, but there's someone I like.' I think of Sir Oswald and his chiseled face. If I get together with him, I could end up becoming Rupert's stepmother. That's a horrifying and rather disgusting thought. I wonder if Sir Oswald wants more children. I've always wanted kids. Preferably four: two girls and two boys. Twins would be good. And this is such a big house, there would be plenty of space for a large family.

'What are you thinking about?' he asks.

'Nothing.'

'Can I make love to you?'

'No,' I splutter. I bite the inside of my cheek to stop myself from giggling.

'Why not? Don't you like me?'

'Yes, I like you, Rupert. But it's totally inappropriate.'

'Mother was four years older than Father,' he says.

'Yes, but I'm sure they didn't hook up when your dad was fifteen and your mum was nineteen.'

'Please, Simone. Most of the boys in my class at school have done it.'

We are silent for a moment, and then Rupert says, 'You like Father, don't you?'

Now it's my turn to blush.

And before I know it, I utter a promise I know I will never keep. 'Look, if you lose a lot of weight and are a good boy for the next five weeks, I'll seriously consider it. It might be my going-home present to you.'

'Making love to you? Oh goodness!' He stands up and gapes

at me. 'Oh my goodness, thank you so much, Simone!' He throws himself on top of me then, his heavy, malodorous bulk squashing me into the mattress.

'Get off me!' I shout.

'Ssh!' he whispers. But he does get off me. He stands up, grabs the torch from where he placed it on the carpet, and scurries out of my bedroom.

I cannot stop laughing. I bury my face in my pillow to stop myself from squealing out loud. It is the most ridiculous thing that has ever happened to me. Poor Rupert. Oh *mon dieu*, it's hilarious! Eventually I am laughing so much, tears pouring down my cheeks, that I have to get up and pee in the bathroom to stop myself from wetting the bed.

Poor, overweight Rupert, with a sex god for a dad. As if I'd ever think about sleeping with him. Nevertheless, before getting back into bed, I lift up the chair in front of the dressing table and wedge it under the door handle of my bedroom. The last thing I want is Rupert trying it on again.

11

CHARLOTTE

I am mighty relieved it's Wednesday. I waited until I heard Rupert leave at 8.30 a.m. and then made my way to the kitchen. He has left me a note propped up against a bottle of marmalade.

Dear Charlotte, I hope you have a relaxing day. I will be home around 4.30pm. Rupert

There is something very intense about Rupert that makes me nervous around him. Perhaps it's because he's not used to living with anyone else, but I get the feeling he's watching me. And it's not just when I pass under the security cameras. It's that sixth sense that someone is there, standing still in the shadows, observing my every move. But would he really have come into my bedroom in the night and opened the curtains? Surely he's too proper for that?

I make myself some toast and boil the kettle. It's an old-fashioned one that heats up on the Aga, and when it whistles, it makes me jump. I keep my hands around the hot mug. It's turned really cold in the house and I need to put on another sweater.

Back in my bedroom, it seems even more bitter. I check that

the windows are closed and then tug on another two sweaters. I am now wearing all the clothes I have brought with me. It's ridiculous. I thought it was meant to be warmer in the south of England.

I message Jodi, and a couple of seconds later my phone rings.

'I'm at home. I swapped shifts,' she says. 'How are you?'

'Ok. Actually, I'm bloody freezing. The house is so cold and my bedroom is like an icebox.'

'And the painting, how's it going?'

'It's going fine, but I really want to go home. I'm thinking of taking a load of photos of Rupert and saying I'll finish it at my place.'

'Do you think he'll mind?'

'Probably,' I say, biting the side of my lip. 'I think he likes having me here.'

'He's single, good-looking, loaded. What's not to like?'

'Ergh, please!' I groan and shiver melodramatically.

'What are you going to do today?'

'I'll take a walk, have a look around, maybe watch some Netflix on my iPad. He bought me a Barbour jacket and some Dubarry boots.'

'Blimey. That's kind of him.'

'Odd, if you ask me. Anyway, what are you up to?'

'I'm about to go to sleep. I was on the night shift.'

'Let's talk tomorrow. Sleep well, sis.'

I AM restless and decide to have a snoop around the house. Hopefully the internal security cameras aren't working, but even if they are, Rupert wouldn't have left me alone in the house if he minded me peeking into all the rooms. I turn right out of my bedroom, towards the main staircase. There are four doors on the left-hand corridor and another four on the right.

Most of the rooms are bedrooms, unused, stale smelling and frigid, decorated in a variety of muted colours, mainly with old-fashioned, chintzy fabrics. The bathrooms are tired. One has an avocado suite; another one has a pale rose bath and sink embossed with a floral design. There are no personal effects in the bedrooms, and I doubt they have been used for years and years. Nevertheless, they are dust-free and kept clean.

I walk back past my room and open the door adjacent to it. For some reason I assumed Rupert slept further along the corridor, but no, this must be his room, because the window is slightly open and there are some clothes neatly folded on a chair. I fully open the door gingerly, guiltily. There is a double bed covered with a wrinkle-free navy-blue duvet and, unlike the other rooms, no bedspread. Opposite the bed is a chevalier mirror framed in dark wood, a large mahogany chest of drawers and a high-backed wooden chair. Two extra-wide dark mahogany wardrobes are positioned on the wall adjacent to the door. They make the room look smaller, even though it is probably the largest bedroom in the house. The navy and cream curtains frame a bow window with views to the South Downs in the distance.

On the bedside table next to a simple lamp that looks as if it was bought at IKEA, there are a couple of books. I pick them up. William Boyd's *Love Is Blind*. I approve of that. But it's the book underneath that makes me giggle. *You've Got The Looks, You've Got The Body, So Why Aren't You Pulling? Dating Tips for Handsome Men.* Bloody hell. Can you imagine going into a bookshop and purchasing that title? What if you think you're good looking, but everyone else thinks you look like the back end of a bus? I control my snort and put it back where I found it.

After checking out the remaining old-fashioned damp and stale-smelling bedrooms, I make my way downstairs. I've been in most of the rooms down here, but I haven't ventured to the far end of the house. I open the door and gasp. It is a big room, probably a ballroom, with a beautiful chevron parquet floor, a grand stone fireplace and several large portraits hanging on the wall, including one of a man who looks very similar to Rupert. His father, I suppose. An impressive crystal chandelier hangs from a plaster ceiling rose. Other than a dark brown baby grand piano placed in front of the double doors leading on to the terrace, the room is empty. I assume this was where they held parties in days gone by. I can imagine the women in beautiful long dresses and the men in white tie, dancing waltzes around and around. How sad that this house is empty and barely lived in. I turn and gently close the door behind me.

I try the door adjacent to the ballroom, but it is locked. It makes me wonder what is inside.

I return to the study and pick up my paintbrush. Even though there are numerous portraits hanging in the hall and up the stairs, there are no photos anywhere, not even in Rupert's bedroom. I wonder why. For a few minutes, I try to paint, but I really am not in the mood. Besides, I'm still cold. Perhaps if I go for a brisk walk, I might warm up.

I stride to the cloakroom and find the jacket and boots Rupert gave me. They feel odd; it's as if I am wearing someone else's clothes, although I'm certainly not, as they still have their labels on them. I realise that it is the first time someone has given me a present since Matthew died, and it brings tears to my eyes. Biting my inside cheek, I lock the house and stride down the road, determined not to give in to the tears. But I can't help thinking about Matthew, wondering what he would think of my country attire.

The police gave me back Matthew's trainers and leather jacket last month. They were no longer needed for evidence, apparently, or perhaps forensics had done everything they could. The edge of his leather jacket was stained with blood, and I couldn't bear to look at it. But I held Matthew's trainers against my chest and cried for hours. They were all I had. The killers took his expensive watch, a Zenith El Primero Chronograph with a chocolate-coloured leather strap, given to Matthew by his parents for his thirtieth birthday. It was worth stealing. And his wallet was gone too, not that it would have been much use to the muggers because he never carried more than ten quid in cash. A man walking his dog found Matthew dying from stab wounds behind the dumpster bins on the pedestrianised cul-de-sac just a couple of streets back from Manchester's Deansgate. By the time the emergency services arrived, he was dead.

They never gave me back the rest of his clothes, and I didn't ask for them. I suppose they were torn and bloodstained, analysed by forensics, and either burned or stored away. I don't know. I try not to think about it. I fail.

I walk for about two hours, trudging across waterlogged fields, following a public footpath along the side of hawthorn hedges until the rain turns from a drizzle to a heavy downpour. Then I stumble back.

After hanging my wet outerwear in the cloakroom, I go to the kitchen and force myself to make and eat a tuna sandwich, but I can't finish it. Guiltily, I tip most of it into the rubbish bin. Then I trudge up the stairs to my bedroom, with a glass of water and an apple.

When I open the door, I am met by a wall of heat. It is stifling hot. How is that possible? It was freezing when I left. I walk over to the radiator, and it is so hot, I almost burn my hand. Perhaps something has gone wrong with the time settings of the boiler.

I peel off all of my clothes until I'm just wearing my underwear, and it's still baking. Flinging open the window, I lean out and welcome the cold air.

A few moments later, I collapse on the bed.

.   .   .

'Hello! Anyone home?'

Rupert's voice pulls me out of a deep sleep. I hate sleeping in the afternoons. It makes me feel woozy and disorientated, but here I am having done it again. My mouth is dry and my head pounding. It feels as if I'm going down with something. I rub my eyes and sit up in bed.

There is a knock on my bedroom door.

'Just a moment,' I say, frantically grabbing my clothes and pulling on my T-shirt.

'Are you alright, Charlotte?'

'Yes, you can come in now.' I'm still sitting in bed, but at least my upper body is decent.

Rupert pokes his head around the door. 'I was worried about you. I saw your car was here, but there was no answer in the house.'

'Sorry, I fell asleep. I went for a walk, and when I returned, it was so hot in here.'

'Ah yes. The engineer came earlier on and got the old boiler working again. Is it more comfortable for you?'

'It's rather hot, and I can't find a way of turning down the radiator.'

Rupert strides to the radiator, which is under the window. He bends down and tries to turn the knob. 'It's well and truly stuck. I'll get my tools and have another go a bit later. I was about to make a start on dinner.'

'Do you mind if I take a rain check this evening? I'm not feeling great and would rather stay in bed.'

Rupert tilts his head to one side and frowns at me. 'Goodness. Do you need me to call a doctor? Are you alright?'

'I'm fine. It's kind of you. I think a good night's sleep is likely to do the trick.'

'Well, it is rather important that you are recovered for tomorrow. I have a surprise planned for tomorrow night. I'll open a can of soup and bring it up on a tray for you.'

'Thank you, that is very kind.'

When the door shuts behind him, I peel off the T-shirt again and walk to the window. I make sure they are open as wide as possible and welcome the cold air. It's not surprising my head is pounding, with the insane heat coming from the radiator. My phone pings. I return to the bed.

How are you today? Jodi writes.

Stonking headache. Rupert so weird. Wanna come home.

Then do it.

Grr. What's new with you?

And then the door opens, and I'm sitting cross-legged on the bed, wearing my old, nude-coloured bra and knickers from M&S, and Rupert is staring at me, his mouth agog. I drop the phone and grab the duvet.

'Goodness, I'm so sorry. I should have knocked.' Rupert looks away from me, his face flushing bright red. The items on the tray are shuddering. He turns and lets the door swing closed behind him. I feel like chuckling. The look on his face was classic.

Hurriedly, I put my T-shirt back on and pull on my jeans.

'I'm decent now,' I shout. But there is silence. I open the door and see he has left the tray on the floor. A bowl of tomato soup has splashed orange over the sides and is puddling on the tray. There are two pieces of brown bread on a plate, along with a little silver and glass dish holding a slice of butter. I glance up and down the corridor, but there is no sign of Rupert.

When I return to my room and pick up the phone, ready to tell Jodi why I was interrupted, I see her message.

Gotta go. Will catch up with you tomorrow. But come home if he's creeping you out too much xx

12

RUPERT

As much as I loathe clichés, I am a great believer in grabbing the bull by the horns. Procrastinators never achieve anything in life. I have decided that tonight is the night. The night when my dreams will become my reality.

I was both delighted and embarrassed when I walked in on Charlotte wearing just her underwear. It was not a gentlemanly thing to do, and I of all people should know better. I know it is wrong of me to lust like this, but I really can't help myself. Of course, it did give me a preview of her body, which is absolutely as beautiful as Percy and I have imagined. Even so, I didn't sleep well last night. Most probably it was the excitement about what is to come.

I was nervous about seeing her this morning, but she sauntered downstairs to the kitchen shortly after 7.30 a.m. and asked me breezily if I had slept well. When I discerned that she was feeling better after a decent night's sleep, my worries abated. I apologised for not reducing the temperature of her radiator, which was a little white lie, as all the heating is managed by remote control ever since I upgraded the systems within the house. I have to say that I am slightly confused about Charlotte's reactions this morning. I thought she might have been embarrassed for me to see her semi-naked, but it appears not. Does that suggest perhaps she is a little louche? Surely not? Perhaps she is simply confident in her own skin, just as I am in mine.

Besides, now that I have seen her almost-naked body, it is time for her to see mine. She has moved on to painting my body within the portrait, so yesterday I posed in my black tie, and this morning I am doing the same. It is enthralling how her eyes scour my torso and her hand moves quickly across the canvas. All the while I am plotting how the day must unfold. This afternoon, I will give Charlotte a little taster of what is to come.

After the painting session, I disappear into my office, but I watch her set out on her daily after-lunch walk. When she has disappeared out of view, I rush upstairs and push a note under her bedroom door.

Please join me in the gym. R

Most days she is out for approximately an hour; consequently I time my workout so that I am glowing rather than red in the face and sweating buckets. That would be very unpleasant. When eventually she knocks on the door of the gym, I am on my cross trainer.

'Come in!' I am unable to keep the smile off my face. 'Apologies, I have just finished my workout.' I slip off the machine and grab a bottle of water and take a sip. I am wearing a pair of black Lycra shorts and nothing else. I place the water bottle on the floor and reach over for my towel and slowly wipe myself down, my muscles rippling. Poor Charlotte. She doesn't know where to look. I would like to grab her and tell her that it is quite acceptable for her to watch me, that her reactions are perfectly normal, and that she shouldn't be embarrassed. I have worked hard for this body and want her to enjoy it as much as I do.

'How was your walk?'

'Good,' she says, without meeting my gaze.

'I have something for you,' I say as I walk towards the garment bag hanging from the hook on the back of the door.

'I can't–'

I interrupt her. 'Please open it, and I'm not accepting no for an answer.' I hand her the long canvas bag. My eyes are fixed on her face as she unzips it and peels it back to reveal what is inside. The dress is long, in silver satin with little spaghetti straps, and I know without a shadow of doubt that Charlotte will look absolutely stunning in it.

'This is a designer dress, but why...' Her words peter out as she touches the delicate fabric.

'There is a pair of satin silver shoes in the pocket of the bag,' I say. 'I hope they will be comfortable. They are your size, but you have such delicate, slender feet, I wasn't sure if they would fit.' I bring my hand up to my mouth. 'Goodness, and I almost forgot. This is to go with the outfit.' I reach for the small black box on the console table behind me. 'It was my mother's and I would like you to wear it.'

I can't make out Charlotte's expression as she gingerly accepts the box. Her hair is loose and covering much of her face. I would like to lean forwards and hold her silken locks to one side, but I restrain myself.

'Please open it.'

She does as instructed, and when her eyes settle on the sparkling diamonds, she lets out a little gasp.

'It will go perfectly with the dress.'

'I couldn't possibly–'

I don't like interrupting her, but needs must. 'We are having a special dinner tonight. Please wear the dress and the neck-lace; otherwise you will feel underdressed.'

'Have we got people coming for dinner?' she asks. I am delighted that she can't keep her eyes off the Cartier diamond necklace. It has forty stones in graded sizes. I remember my mother wearing it to the annual summer ball. How she shimmered; how beautiful she was, and gracious.

'Tonight is a surprise. Dinner is at 7 p.m.'

She opens her mouth as if she is going to say something, but then closes it again. Carefully, she picks up the jewellery box and carries the garment bag out of the gym. Her reticence, her graciousness, her modesty bounce off her in waves. How wonderful that Charlotte is not only beautiful but also has such fine manners.

I am pumped with excitement and don't have a moment to lose. Everyone is arriving at 6 p.m., and I need to be ready to direct them. I hurry to my bedroom and take a hot shower, followed by a quick shave. I put some gel in my hair and then I douse myself with Vetiver by Creed aftershave. My father used Creed's Royal English Leather, and when it was discontinued, I felt as if a little part of my father was wrenched from me forever. With a heavy heart, I chose another fragrance from the same brand, as similar as possible to the scent Father wore.

I put on Father's white evening shirt, fastening it with the diamond studs that match my mother's diamond necklace, do up the black bow tie and finally slip into his suit. For years, my father's clothes were too small for me, but now I am lithe and in good shape, they fit as if they were made to measure for me rather than him. The quality of the garments is unsurpassed. The finest wool suits with silk linings. I doubt one can buy such suits today. I take my black evening shoes out of the cupboard. The result of fifteen minutes of rigorous shining last night was worth it. The shoes are like mirrors. I look at myself and smile. Father would be very proud.

I hear the crunch of tyres on gravel and rush downstairs just in time to open the front door to the caterers. The main woman, called Susannah something or other, stands on the steps with two waitresses dressed in black with white aprons.

'Could you go to the back door, please? It's nearer to the kitchen. Turn left around the house.' I point to where they should go. Since when do staff think it's acceptable to come in through the front door? I try ever so hard to be modern, and on the whole, I succeed – particularly when it comes to technology – but there are some standards that must never be allowed to slip.

I have given a great deal of thought to the menu for tonight and have had to pay well over the odds to acquire a good caterer at such short notice. Fortunately it is a Thursday and not their busiest day of the week. Nevertheless, this woman and her crew have come from Guildford. According to their online reviews, they are the leading catering outfit in the south-east of England. Let's hope that isn't hyperbole.

I let them in through the back door.

'Please, can you show Zofia where you would like the table to be laid,' Susannah says to me. She has one of those Sloaney-type voices and wears a thick Alice band that sweeps her straight blonde hair off her face.

Zofia, who has wide Slavic features, mousey brown hair pulled back harshly from her broad forehead, and a thickset body, trots behind me as we walk to the ballroom. I hold open the door and watch as she gasps. Everyone adores this room. I picked up a beautiful floral table arrangement of white roses from the florist in Petworth and have placed our canteen of silver cutlery on the sideboard.

'As I explained to your manager, please lay the table with a white linen cloth and use my cutlery. It has been in my family for generations, as has the china and glass. If you break anything, I will hold you liable. Place the flowers in the centre of the table.'

She nods. I leave her to it, and as I'm walking back towards the kitchen, the front doorbell rings again.

This time it is the musicians. I have booked a strings trio

from London, trained at The Royal Academy of Music and offering themselves for hire for special occasions. I sent them a list of the music I want playing, ranging from Beethoven to the Beatles. Once again, I direct them to the back door and lead them into the ballroom so they can set up. It has been so long since we had live music playing in the house. It sends shivers of anticipation down my spine.

I return to the kitchen, where Susannah is busying around, finishing off her pre-cooked food. The aroma is wonderful and I sincerely hope it tastes as good as it smells.

I open the fridge and show them the white wine, Château Pape Clément 2008, the dessert wine and the vintage champagne. It's Dom Perignon Rosé 1996. I thought a rosé would be more appropriate for the occasion, and at £815 per bottle, I know it's ridiculously expensive, but tonight, money is no object. I have already decanted the Château Margaux into the antique cut-glass crystal decanter, allowing it time to breathe, and I carry it through to the ballroom. What's the point in having beautiful things if you don't use them?

It is seven minutes before seven p.m. Auspicious. I run up the stairs to have a final glance in the mirror and to collect the most important item of the evening. Excitement and anticipation flow through my veins.

Today is the last day of my old life.

Tomorrow, all my dreams will start to come true.

13

SIMONE, END OF JULY 1994

Rupert is in a sulky mood. It is very unattractive, the way he sits at the breakfast table like a big lump, smearing a thick layer of chocolate spread over his toast. When he hears his father's voice in the corridor, he stuffs the toast into his mouth, his cheeks bulging out like a hamster. He hides the pot of chocolate spread under the table.

Sir Oswald has given Mrs Cherry strict instructions to manage Rupert's diet. No sugary foods, limited carbohydrates and lots of salads. The problem is, Mrs Cherry feels sorry for Rupert, so rather than blatantly flouting her employer's instructions, she leaves out the chocolate spread and the Mars bars and the baguettes so that Rupert can help himself.

Last week I made a sarcastic comment about his overeating, and he went apoplectic, telling me I was shallow and judged people on their looks, and his body was his own to do with as he wishes. I've kept my thoughts to myself since then.

We are interrupted by the beep-beeping of a lorry and lots of male voices.

'What's going on?' I ask Rupert, but he ignores me. After a while Sir Oswald strides into the dining room, helps himself to a cup of coffee and a hard-boiled egg, and sits at his place at the head of the table.

'The men are here to put up the marquee,' he says.

'Why do you have a marquee?' I ask.

'Hasn't the stupid boy told you?' He rolls his eyes as he looks at Rupert, who studiously ignores his gaze. 'It's our annual summer ball on Saturday night. We haven't held one since my wife died, but I thought it was time we rekindled the old traditions. What have you got to wear?'

'You are inviting me to the party?' I ask.

'Of course!' He laughs. 'You're a member of our family this summer.'

'Thank you.' His words fill me with hope. Love and hope. And then I think of my clothes. 'I don't have anything suitable to wear.'

He laughs as his eyes roam over my body and back to my face. I feel myself flush. 'You can choose something from my wife's wardrobe. We have kept her formal clothes just because—' He doesn't finish the sentence. Rupert scrapes back his dining room chair and thumps out of the room like a hippopotamus. 'Surely he should have outgrown his moodiness by now?' Sir Oswald sighs. 'Anyway, I have a busy day, so make your way to my wife's dressing room and choose whatever you like. I'm sure some of her evening dresses will fit you. You're slender like she was.'

After I help clear away the breakfast things, I have a word with Mrs Cherry.

'Sir Oswald has said I can borrow one of Lady Oswald's dresses. Where is her dressing room?'

Mrs Cherry raises her eyebrows so high they almost hit her widow's peak. She mutters something indistinguishable under her breath. 'It's in their bedroom suite. You can go in this afternoon after you've finished your classes with Rupert. Make sure your hands are clean and your face make-up free. We can't risk dirtying any of her dresses.'

I wonder why. Lady Baskerville has been dead for three years.

RUPERT's foul mood extends throughout the morning. Eventually I snap.

'You either want me to teach you or you don't. If you don't, I'm going to talk to your father and I will go home. I don't want to waste my time here.'

Rupert's lower lip trembles. 'He shouldn't have suggested that you wear one of Mother's dresses.'

'Why not?'

'I miss my mother every minute of every day. Father is cruel and thoughtless. I don't want you wearing one of Mother's dresses.'

'I'm sorry, Rupert, but I have no choice. I don't have anything else to wear.'

'Buy something, then.'

'And where am I going to do that in the next two days? I don't have enough money to buy a train ticket to London let alone a party dress.'

Rupert storms out and I don't have the energy to go after him.

I FEEL AWKWARD GOING into Sir Rupert's bedroom. I have fantasised about lying in his bed for the past few weeks, but as this is the first time I have actually seen his room, it is only now that I can flesh out the detail. The pale mint-coloured walls; the cream brocade curtains and bedspread; the wall of built-in wardrobes and a trouser press. The room smells of Sir Oswald, a musky, cedar, intoxicating scent that makes me tingle all over.

A large photo of Lady Baskerville in a silver photo frame takes pride of place on top of the chest of drawers. I don't want her in my fantasy.

My feet sink into the silvery plush carpet as I walk through the bedroom and into the dressing room. It is lined with wardrobes and drawers, much like you see in a dress shop. Lady Baskerville's side is largely empty. It must be very hard for Sir Rupert when he walks through here every day. But there is one tall wardrobe full of clothes. I open it and a floral scent wafts out. The dresses are all full-length in an array of colours. Most of them are sleeveless, either with a halter-neck, spaghetti straps or strapless.

My eyes are drawn to a pale blue dress, almost silvery, like the pale moonlight sky after the sun has set on a hot summer's day. I lift it out and hold it in front of myself, looking in the mirror. It is a beautiful colour. I take off my clothes and step into the dress, but my bra shows, so I whip that off too. I stand in front of the mirror and let my hair down, fanning it out over my shoulders. The dress fits as if it was made to measure, which it quite probably was, just not for me. I twirl around and admire myself from every angle. It fits like a dream and I love it. I find a pair of silvery shoes at the bottom of the wardrobe. They are too small and my toes are squashed together. The pain will be worth it.

I walk back into the bedroom and run my fingers across the bedspread. I can't help myself. I kick the shoes off and lie down on the bed, lifting up the bedspread and pushing my face into the pillows. I inhale the scent of Sir Oswald, and then I lie back with my arms above my head and let my eyelids close.

'It suits you.'

I open my eyes, and to my dismay, Sir Oswald is standing there, his head tilted to one side, an amused smirk on his lips.

'I'm so sorry, I didn't mean to. I just fell asleep.' I jump off the bed, pulling the bedspread so it is smooth, picking up the discarded shoes and rushing towards the dressing room.

'Wait.' He holds out a hand, and his warm, firm fingers rest on my shoulder.

'You look very beautiful in that dress.' His eyes narrow and his glance moves across my face, down to my breasts and onwards to my feet. 'Very beautiful.'

I shiver.

'Perhaps you will do me the honour of a dance on Saturday night?'

'Yes, of course,' I say, hoping that the deep blush I sense blooming in my cheeks isn't too visible. And then I move away, reaching behind my back to undo the zip. I can feel his eyes on me, but then I hear his footsteps, and the bedroom door closes with a gentle thud.

I HONESTLY DON'T KNOW how I get through the next two days. I am beyond excited for the summer ball, imagining Sir Oswald's fingers stroking my neck and holding my waist. I put music on in my bedroom and practice dancing, and by the time the first guests arrive on Saturday evening, I have never been so ready.

I walk down the main staircase, clutching the smooth wooden bannister because the tight shoes make walking precarious. Sir Oswald is standing near the front door, welcoming his guests, but he glances around and sees me. He nods to the couple he is talking to and walks to the bottom of the stairs, holding out his hand.

'You are breathtakingly beautiful,' he whispers huskily into my ear. My legs want to give way.

The first part of the evening is purgatory. I am sitting at a table with Rupert on the other side of the marquee from Sir Oswald. I have to make polite small talk with some dull distant cousins of the Baskervilles'. After the interminable dinner, the guests file back through the house and into the ballroom. The patio doors are wide open. A jazz band is playing and the lights are low. I stand on one side watching all of the beautiful people.

When warm fingers brush my bare back, I jump.

'You promised me a dance,' Sir Oswald says, his breath tingling my ear. Taking my hand, he leads me to the centre of the dance floor, and we dance the quick step, the salsa, the waltz. I lose count of how many dances we do together, and then when slow music starts up, I wait for him to pull me close to him, but a woman with black hair piled high in a chignon, wearing a low-cut scarlet dress, places her long crimson-painted nails on Sir Oswald's arm.

'May I take you away from this charming young lady, Oswald?'

'Of course, Alicia. Please excuse me, Simone.'

I walk quickly towards the side of the room but am accosted by Rupert.

'Wanna dance,' he says as a statement rather than a question. He grabs my hand and places a hot, sweaty palm on my back.

'Not now,' I say, trying to shrug him off. 'I need a drink.' But we are surrounded by dancing couples and I do not want to make a scene.

I try to hold Rupert as far away from me as possible. He hasn't got a clue how to dance and almost stumbles several times.

'I'll teach you,' I say. 'Slow, slow, quick, quick, left foot forward.'

He almost pulls me over.

'No!' I laugh. 'It's like this.'

And then they start playing *'Can You Feel The Love Tonight'* by Elton John, and Rupert grabs me and tugs me towards him.

'Let me go!' I whisper urgently.

'I can't wait until your last night in England.' He blows the words into my ear.

'Rupert, it's not–' but we are interrupted.

'I think it's my turn again,' Sir Oswald says, nudging his son to one side. What a relief. 'Was the boy hassling you?'

'No, it's fine. I was just teaching him a few steps.' Rupert's face darkens as he slinks away to the side of the room, and then I am swept up in the dance and the joy of being in such a beautiful man's arms.

After a couple more dances, Sir Oswald leans towards me, his breath tickling my cheek. 'I think it's time we have another drink. My back is killing me.' He takes my hand and we walk across the room towards the bar.

'A glass of champagne?' he asks.

'Excuse me, Sir Oswald.' Arthur Stone, the chauffeur-cum-butler, appears, dressed in his uniform. 'I am sorry to disturb you, but Mr Rupert has passed out in the living room. I was wondering if you wanted me to call for a doctor?'

'Oh, for heaven's sake! The idiot boy will have drunk too much. Why the hell does he have to behave so badly? Take him downstairs to the basement and leave him there to sober up.'

'Are you sure, sir?'

'Kindly don't question my orders, Stone.'

Arthur turns on his heel.

'Why do you want him to take Rupert to the basement?' I ask, remembering how Rupert was sent somewhere for punishment on previous occasions.

'I think we should dance again, don't you?' Sir Oswald ignores my question.

Various women throw me daggers, but I don't care. I am with the most handsome man in the room. Around midnight, people start departing. Sir Oswald leaves me for a while to say his goodbyes. I sit on a chair at the side of the room watching, my sore toes recovering from being shoved into tight shoes. I am tipsy, but not drunk. Just very happy.

Eventually Sir Oswald returns.

'I need to take a little stroll outside to wind down. Would you care to join me?'

I don't hesitate.

He takes my hand and leads me out onto the terrace. The air is cold and the stars are sparkling in the sky. He takes off his jacket and places it over my bare shoulders. I inhale deeply, breathing in the jasmine and the lingering scent of cigar smoke. And then when we are standing in the shadow of a large cypress tree, he places his hands on either side of my face and brings his lips down to meet mine. We kiss. The most passionate, breathtaking kiss of my entire life.

14

CHARLOTTE

As soon as I am back in my room, I hang the dress over the back of the bathroom door and call Jodi. Frustratingly, there is no answer. I assume she is on a shift at work. Instead I send her a text.

R just gave me an evening dress and his mum's diamond necklace to wear to some dinner tonight. Totally freaked out. Call me. Cx

I have no idea what Rupert's plans are, but I'm not comfortable. It is not normal behaviour to buy a dress and give it to someone you barely know. Matthew bought me some lingerie once. It was much too large, and even if it had fitted, I would have looked like a tart from a porn magazine, in red with black lace. We laughed until we cried. He took the set back to the shop and swore he'd never buy me clothes again – unless, of course, I had tried them on first.

But Matthew was my lover and soon to become my fiancé. Rupert is a stranger. And a strange stranger at that. I start chucking some of my things into my suitcase, but then I stop and let out a groan. If I leave now and tell him I'll finish his portrait at home, I'll be in breach of our agreement. The deal was for me to paint him here in situ. If I go home, he might decide not to pay me, and I am desperate for cash. Despite sending a couple of emails to Bernadette Titus to ask if any more of my paintings have sold, she hasn't got back to me. I sit with my head in my hands for a while. *Oh, Matthew, why did you die?* If he were alive, I wouldn't be here, and for a moment I am furious. How dare he leave me! How dare he not take better care of himself!

I want to go home. I reckon I am three-quarters of the way through the painting. If I work on it all day every day, I can be home in time for my birthday on Saturday. And if for some reason it's not finished by then, I will take the painting home with me and finish it there. Surely Rupert will understand that I want to be home for my birthday? But in the meantime, I suppose I should comply with Rupert's weird wishes, whatever they may be. After all, he has been unfailingly polite towards me, quite the gentlemanly host. It's not his fault that I find him unattractive and odd. And it's not like I'm scared of him. If anything, he's rather pathetic.

Sighing, I take the dress out of its bag, get undressed and slip it on. How the hell did he know that it would fit me? It's as if this dress were made for me. I look in the mirror, turning around, looking over my shoulder. It seems to hug my curves in all the right places, giving me an hourglass figure, even though I am too thin. I tie my hair into a ponytail and affix it on top of my head, line my eyes with eyeliner and put mascara on my lashes. My lipstick is a pale peach colour.

I can hear the clatter of crockery from downstairs, and it sounds as if a band is warming up. Perhaps Rupert has organised a party and will be introducing me to some of the locals. That wouldn't be such a bad thing. At least I won't be stuck with him alone all night. And maybe some of his friends would like their portraits painted, and then my financial woes will end forever.

Finally, I take the necklace out of its box and fasten it

around my neck. It's surprisingly light. I assumed a real diamond necklace would be weighty. Or perhaps it isn't real after all? I snigger. That would make me feel better.

Just before the grandfather clock in the hall strikes 7 p.m., I slip on the satin shoes and walk down the stairs. Rupert is there at the bottom and he holds out his hand to take mine.

'You look stunning,' he says, his eyes welling up. He bows his head and sniffs gently.

He is wearing black tie and looks quite smart himself, but I don't intend to give him any compliments. We walk towards the ballroom and then he opens the door.

My heart sinks.

In the centre of the room is a table laid for two people. The room is lit by a couple of large silver four-foot candelabras with the central glass chandelier turned down low. A waitress stands to one side, holding a tray with two champagne glasses. Rupert nods at her and she walks towards us, proffering us each a drink. And then the music starts, some classical piece I don't recognise. I turn to see a string trio.

'I thought you were holding a party,' I say, trying to keep the disappointment from my voice.

'And indeed I am.' Rupert walks over to the table, places his glass down and pulls back a chair for me.

'But it's only us,' I say. It's no good. The dismay is heavy in my voice.

'Yes.' He smiles but doesn't expand. I feel sickened.

'But what is all of this?' I wave my hand towards the string players.

'This is my thank you to you.'

I sit down, although there is nothing I would prefer than to run out of the room, out of this house and never return. But I am not rude and I don't want to humiliate Rupert in front of other people. He walks to the other side of the table and sits down, smiling at me.

The waitress brings us smoked salmon parcels, with a salmon paté inside. I am not hungry and I toy with the food. Rupert talks for both of us, and mostly I zone out, not paying attention to a word of what he is saying. His chatter has a hurried, nervous edge to it, and it makes me feel even more uncomfortable. So I drink. A lot. Champagne. Red wine and then white wine. After the waitress has cleared away our plates of beef Wellington, cooked to perfection, the chandelier is switched off and the room is lit just by the flickering candles. The trio is playing some cheesy love song. Suddenly, Rupert stands up and walks around to my side of the table. I wonder if I should stand up too. But then he bends down onto one knee and grabs my hand with his right hand.

'Charlotte Aldridge, I love you. Will you make me the happiest man in the world and accept my hand in marriage? This is my mother's ring and I would like you to have it.' He proffers a large ring – the biggest sapphire I have ever seen, surrounded by diamonds.

I tug my hand from his grasp, push my chair backwards, its legs scratching the parquet floor, and I jump to my feet.

'What the hell! I don't know you! I'm not in love with you! And you don't know me. This is crazy. A joke. A total joke! You must be out of your mind!'

The string players stop mid piece. They are gawking at us, but I don't care, because all I need to do is get the hell out of here and away from this delusional madman.

Rupert stares at me and then frowns, uncomprehending. He opens his mouth and shuts it again. It's as if he is frozen with shock, one knee on the ground, his green hooded eyes looking up at me. Surely he couldn't have expected any other reaction?

And then he jumps up. The ring clatters onto the floor and rolls under the table. I move as if to run away.

'Wait!' Rupert grabs my hand again. 'But I'm in love with you. We are meant for each other!'

I try to tug my hand from his grasp, but Rupert's fingers are gripped tightly around my wrist. 'No, Rupert. This is madness. Leave me alone! You're hurting me!'

The viola player stands up and places his instrument on his chair. I think he is about to walk over towards us. But then Rupert releases his grip on my wrist and I run, skidding in the high heels. I race along the corridor and then pause for a moment at the bottom of the stairs. I remove the shoes before running up the stairs, tripping over the dress; the ripping of fabric sounds unnaturally loud. I grab on to the stair rail and look behind me. I'm alone.

There is a deathly silence in the house.

I carry on running, into my bedroom, and throw myself onto the bed.

Why the hell didn't I listen to my intuition earlier? I knew he was weird, but asking me to marry him, that is off the scale of delusional.

To hell with his money, I can't stay here any longer. I pull my suitcase out of the wardrobe. And then I realise I have drunk way too much alcohol. There is no way I'm under the legal limit. I let out a sob and collapse onto the bed. The room spins. It's 10 p.m. and I've drunk a lot. I try to count how many glasses. At least two glasses of champagne, three of red, two of white. And how long does it take for alcohol to leave your system? I'm not sure, but it must be at least several hours. And I'm small, so I'm probably more drunk than larger people. I could call for a taxi, but where would it take me at this time of night? Besides, I'll have to return in the morning to collect my car. I've got no choice but to wait until tomorrow. As sure as hell I will be leaving first thing in the morning.

I grab my phone out of my handbag and call Jodi. There's no answer. Of course, she's on a night shift. I don't want to worry her, so I send a short text. *He's a f-ing maniac. Asked me to marry him!!! Coming home for my bday. So much to tell you. Cxx*

I undo the zip of the dress, but it gets stuck halfway down my back. I don't care, I rip it off my body and dive into the bathroom. I feel dirty, sullied by Rupert, even though he didn't touch me. I want to wash away this evening and purify myself for Matthew, despite Matthew only reaching me in my dreams.

15

RUPERT

One woman and two men. The musicians stare at me, and then the woman violinist catches the cellist's eye, and her shoulders quiver with laughter. The bitch.

'Get out! Just get the fuck out of my house!' I gesticulate and scream at the trio.

Hurriedly they grab their cases and zip away their instruments, rushing to get out of the ballroom and back to wherever they have come from.

And then I realise that stupid waitress woman is standing there like a statue, staring at me. 'And you too. Bugger off, all of you. Go!' I yell.

What the hell just happened? Charlotte's face was meant to light up with joy. I was meant to slip my mother's engagement ring onto her finger, and then we would have embraced, my lips tenderly pressed against hers. How can she destroy everything that we have? The fury rips through me. I hurl the wine glasses at the wall, one after the other, splashes of wine marking the silk wallpaper, glass splintering onto the parquet floor. I hear Father's voice deriding me, telling me I'm a nothing, not worthy of the family name. A loser. Undeserving of love.

I stride into the library and grab the portrait she's painting of me. It is three-quarters completed. Earlier today I loved the picture; now I hate it. Has she been mocking me all of this time? I search for the letter opener. I can visualise it. It was Father's: silver and long with a dagger-like point. When did I last use it? Last week or last month? I will rip the painting, slash it into a million pieces, and then she will have to start painting all over again. I pull out the drawers of the built-in cupboards, grab books off the shelves and chuck them onto the floor. It is here; I can't remember when I last saw it, but I'm sure it's here. When I'm ankle deep in antique books, I let out a scream and sink into the chair and sob. Yes, it's pathetic, but if one's dreams are shattered, surely that is acceptable.

I hear a car door slam and an engine starting. It must be the caterers leaving, the stupid cow's tyres making a skidding noise as she pulls away too quickly. And then I realise. My hot head has made me arrive at totally the wrong conclusion. Like the wheels of that car, I went too quickly. Of course I did. Just because I have been passionately in love with Charlotte since the first moment I set eyes on her picture, does not mean that she is able to reciprocate in the same way. I've known her for nearly eighteen months, but she has only known me for a week. That is nothing. Love at first sight is a fairy-tale fallacy. Of course she needs more time to love me back.

I curse. In my eagerness I will have scared her away. I need to backtrack, say sorry. Explain that I was too impulsive, that it is one of my many failings to charge ahead without the requisite thinking. I mustn't slash the painting; I must praise her work, beg her for forgiveness, humbly acknowledge my idiocy. Ask to reset the clock.

Hurriedly I put the books back on the shelves, careless as to their order. I can fix that tomorrow. And when I am fully calm again, I stride up the main staircase and stand outside Charlotte's bedroom door. I rap my knuckles against the door.

There is no answer.

And then the panic returns. What if it wasn't the caterers who left by car? What if it was Charlotte, my love, the owner of my heart, who has fled never to return? My own heart feels as if it might explode out of my chest. I knock again, one fierce bang on the door, and once more there is no answer. I grab the handle and fling open the door. The room is in darkness. Holding my breath, I flip on the light.

And there she is.

My sweetheart is lying in bed, huddled under the covers.

What is that noise? Is she crying?

She looks at me over the top of the eiderdown. Her eyes are red and sore; tears snake down her cheeks.

I fall to my knees at the side of the bed, bringing my palms together in the pose of prayer. And indeed I am praying, thanking the Lord that Charlotte, the owner of my heart, is still in my home. In my life.

'I am so sorry, my darling,' I whisper. 'Please forgive me for my hasty proposal. Way too soon, I realise now. You hardly know me. It was impetuous, naive and thoughtless of me to put you on the spot like that. I am hopeless at relationships, as I'm sure you realise. Quite hopeless. Just because I fell in love with you almost instantaneously, it was wrong of me to assume the feeling was reciprocated. Please, Charlotte, forgive me.'

I wait for her to say something, but other than a delicate sniff, she is silent. I will her to look at me, but she doesn't. Her eyes are fixed on something behind me. I turn to look, but there is nothing there. I must take a different tack. Joviality perhaps? Humility?

'Charlotte, you are so very beautiful. I know I am not worthy of you and that my looks fall so far short of the masculine equivalent of yours, but I hope you will see beyond the surface of my skin and realise how much I have to give. Want to give. Not just the material things that come along with this house and the funds invested in stocks and shares and my cash in the bank and the beautiful jewels, but the truly important things such as love, affection, kindness and companionship. I have those in abundance and I want to shower them on you.'

Surely she must understand that sometimes we are gripped by such overwhelming emotions, no amount of reason, logic and decorum will suppress them? I try to recall what all my relationship books advise. Self-deprecation, humour, asking questions. Oh Lord, I am struggling here. She is still not looking at me and I don't understand why. I *am* good looking. When I visited Dr Talpade for my final check-up, he said I was his greatest success story. He pulled up all of the before and after photographs, and even I, who look at myself in the mirror every day, could see how great the transformation is. He called in his assistant, an attractive young, newly qualified doctor of Indian extraction called Amrita Hathimare.

'Dr Hathimare,' he said, his hands behind his head, 'I challenge you to list the surgical procedures I have carried out on my esteemed patient here.' He turned to me. 'Sir Rupert, could I trouble you to disrobe?'

Two years ago I would have blushed with mortification at the prospect of undressing in front of an unknown woman (or indeed any woman). All my liaisons took place in the dark. But that day I happily stood in front of them both and peeled my clothes off so that I stood there proudly in my navy and white striped boxer shorts. I enjoyed the way her eyes roamed every inch of my face and body, appraising and evaluating.

'Augmented jawline, rhinoplasty and possibly gynecomastia,' she said, 'although if you have done that, the lack of scarring is very impressive.'

Dr Talpade's eyes gleamed and he clapped his hands together. 'Would it surprise you Dr Hathimare, to learn that my handsome patient here has undergone forehead augmentation to widen his forehead and increase the prominence of his brows, cheek augmentation resulting in these angular, razor-sharp cheekbones, mentoplasty to recontour his chin, BSSO bilateral sagittal split osteotomy to widen his jaw and, as you correctly deduced, rhinoplasty to alter the shape of his nose.'

Young Dr Hathimare's eyes widened. 'Yes, it does surprise me.'

'And now let's look at his body. We have lower rhytidectomy – the neck lift, shoulder widening, deltoid and quadriceps implants, gynecomastia to remove his male breasts and considerable liposuction.'

'That's very impressive,' she said.

'And last but certainly not least, we have the impressive package in Sir Rupert's underpants. Would you mind showing my colleague?'

I blushed. However good my surgeon's work was, it was hardly normal for me to display his handiwork to strange women. She picked up on my hesitation.

'It's quite alright,' she reassured me. 'I don't need to see.'

But actually I wanted her to. I dropped my boxer shorts and displayed the results of my testicular enlargement and penoplasty. She nodded admiringly while Dr Talpade stood there, his arms crossed, a proud expression on his face. 'You see now why he is my most esteemed patient?'

'Yes, I certainly do,' the female doctor said.

I pulled up my boxer shorts and put my clothes back on.

Dr Amrita Hathimare was the first woman to see and admire the results of my procedures, but I walked out of their consulting rooms determined that I should share my assets with many more women.

Surgery had become a bit of a habit. I first went to see Dr Talpade on London's Harley Street to request a nose job. I showed him a photograph of my father. 'I want to look more like him,' I explained. Dr Talpade dissected the photograph, explaining all the procedures he would need to undertake to morph my face and body into the clone of my father's. It was worth every penny and every moment of pain.

And now here I am, wanting to give all of that to Charlotte. But she will not look at me, will not see how very much I have gone through to achieve this and, most importantly, how much I have to offer her.

'I am wealthy,' I say, willing her to turn her head just an inch so as to meet my gaze. 'I can provide well for a wife. I couldn't help but fall in love with you. You are so beautiful.'

And then she turns her head, and her sore eyes meet mine.

'I'm going home.' Her voice cracks with emotion.

'But you are at home,' I say.

'I don't want to offend you, but your feelings are not reciprocated, and they never will be. I think it's better for both of us if I finish your portrait at my home in Macclesfield, and I'll ship it to you when it's ready. I am really grateful for your hospitality and for everything you've done for me, but I am going home in the morning. Please can you leave my room now.'

'What?' I am uncomprehending.

'Please can you go and leave me to sleep. I'm tired.'

I stand up then and slowly back away to the door. I hold it open and look at her again, but she has shut her eyes now. As I switch off the light with my left hand, I drop my right hand into her handbag that she has left lying open on the chair.

What have you done, my beautiful Charlotte? What have you done?

16

SIMONE, END OF AUGUST 1994

Oswald took me to his bed the night of the summer ball. He made love to me as if I were the most beautiful woman he had ever laid eyes upon, which I know isn't true because his dead wife was stunning. He made me feel like a true woman, a grown-up with powers I didn't know I possessed. Most nights since, he has come to my room. We make passionate love, and then in the middle of the night, well before the sun starts to rise, he tiptoes back to his master suite, leaving me to slumber in that wonderful, satiated afterglow.

But tonight when he comes to my bed, I can't relax.

'What is it, little one?' he asks, stroking my hair. 'Is it because you return to France in a week?'

I shake my head and then I blurt it out. 'I'm pregnant.'

He freezes.

'What?'

He sits upright in bed and shifts away from me.

'I did a pregnancy test this morning,' I say, breaking the long silence.

'Have you seen a doctor?'

I shake my head.

'You will have to get rid of it.'

'What? No! I'm Catholic. I don't believe in abortion!' I start crying then, silent sobs, as I bite my lip and try to quell the bitter disappointment.

'Don't cry, my love,' he says, pulling me towards him.

'I thought you loved me,' I whisper into his shoulder.

'I do. But what will people say if they know I got a nineteen-year-old girl pregnant?' He shakes his head. 'I can't. If you insist on having this baby, then you will have to put him up for adoption. I don't want another child.'

'Please,' I beg quietly.

'No, it's out of the question. I will make all the arrangements.'

'I don't want to go back to France.'

'You won't have to. I will find you somewhere to live in London; get you a job, something suitable like a shop assistant at Harrods. You can have the baby, and then we will take stock.'

'You're ashamed of me?' I exclaim through my sobs.

'No, Simone. I'm ashamed of myself.'

THE NEXT MORNING Mrs Cherry knocks on my door shortly before 8 a.m. She is holding a tray laden with breakfast things.

'Sir Oswald has organised for you to go to London. The car will be ready in one hour.'

'What?'

'I am to help you pack, and I have prepared a sandwich for your lunch. I will return in twenty minutes with your suitcase.' She places the tray on the dressing table.

'But...'

Mrs Cherry walks out of the door and lets it slam behind her before I can say another word.

I hurry to get ready. I need to talk to Oswald and find out

what's happening. Why is he banishing me so quickly? But it's Mrs Cherry who returns exactly twenty minutes later. It's Mrs Cherry who packs up my belongings and insists on carrying my suitcase, and when we descend the stairs, she ushers me forwards.

'The car is waiting,' she says.

'I want to say goodbye to Oswald and Rupert.'

'Sir Oswald is already out, and he has taken Rupert with him.'

So I do as I'm instructed. I get in the Rolls Royce and Arthur drives me all the way to London, the place that will become my new home.

17

CHARLOTTE

As soon as Rupert leaves, I jump out of bed and carry the upright chair to the door. I wedge the high back underneath the door handle, hoping it will prevent him from coming in again. I don't sense that Rupert is dangerous, after all he has had plenty of opportunity to attack me should he have wished to, but I am certainly not about to take any risks. I wish I could go downstairs, drink a litre of water and make myself a double espresso. Then perhaps I would be sober enough to drive home. But I'm too tired, too dizzy and now a little bit scared of Rupert. I must wait until morning.

As I lie in bed, I plot what I'm going to say to him tomorrow. I don't want to be cruel, but I certainly don't wish him to become my stalker. Frankly, I can't understand why he thinks he has any chance of a relationship with me. I haven't flirted with him, and although I can accept that some women might find him attractive, I don't. Anyway, I'm not ready for another relationship. Perhaps I never will be.

'Oh, Matthew,' I murmur as I hug one of the pillows to my stomach. I toss and turn for hours, but at some point, I drift off to sleep.

When I wake, sunlight is pouring through the sides of the curtains. The chair is still wedged up against the door handle, and I'm relieved that Rupert didn't try to come in again. After a quick wash, I place my suitcase on the bed. I grab all of my clothes and toiletries, placing them on the bed, folding my clothes neatly and packing them into my case. I check that I have removed everything from the wardrobe and the chests of drawers, that I haven't left anything behind in the bathroom. The last thing I want is for Rupert to hang on to any of my belongings. When the suitcase is full, I zip it up and lift it onto the floor. I then strip the sheets off the bed and place my damp towels on top of the pile of used bed linen.

I can't wait to go home, back to the safety of the flat, back to my happy memories of Matthew. Although the small unkempt apartment was meant to have been our temporary abode, it feels like home. It is cosy and all mine – so long as I continue paying the rent. I would hate to live in a big house like this one. It's too grandiose, formal, keeping up appearances as opposed to being homely and comforting. I take one last look around the bathroom and the bedroom to check I've got everything, and then, letting out a sigh of relief, I move the chair away from the door and turn the door handle.

Nothing happens.

I try it again, pulling it towards me. It stays firmly closed.

What the hell!

Once more I tug at the handle, moving it upwards and downwards. Nothing.

Is it locked? There is a keyhole but no key on the inside. Has Rupert locked me in?

My gut clenches and my heart is ramming against my ribcage. What has he done? I bang on the door, firstly rapping my knuckles on it and then slamming my palms against it.

'Let me out! Let me out!'

Still feeling hungover, I think I'm going to be sick.

I am met with silence.

I try to inhale slowly, but it's hard to control my ragged breathing and my pounding heart. I peer through the keyhole, and it certainly looks as if the cylinder is bolted across. *Stop panicking.* I have my phone. All I need to do is call the police and tell them this maniac has locked me in. But where the hell did I put it?

I fumble in my handbag, my fingers searching for the smooth case of my mobile phone. I tip the contents of my handbag onto the floor. My multicoloured, multi-pocket wallet is there, as are my car keys, an almost empty lipstick, my house keys and a packet of tissues. Where the hell is my phone? Did I put it in my suitcase by mistake? I unzip the case, getting the zip stuck. Shit! I tug it harder and it slides undone. I tip everything out of my case, but it's not in there either, so I chuck all my belongings back inside it, not caring that they are unfolded and haphazard. I have to sit on the case to close it again. Could I have left it in my coat pocket?

I'm in danger of hyperventilating now. I force myself to breathe more slowly and to think back to last night. After Rupert made his ridiculous proposition, I came back here, to my bedroom. I got ready for bed and then I texted Jodi. I remember now. So the phone was in here. I am sure I put it back in my handbag, but it is definitely not there now. I look behind the furniture and am crouched on the floor, peering under the bed, when I hear footsteps. I jump up. There is the sound of a key in the door and then it opens. Rupert walks in carrying a breakfast tray, with a plastic bag dangling from his wrist. In a flash, he places the tray on the chair next to the door, he deposits the plastic bag on the floor, and then he calmly turns around and locks the door from the inside, slipping the key into his trouser pocket.

'Let me out!' I scream at him.

'Calm down, Charlotte. There is no reason to get worked

up. I brought you a delicious cooked breakfast, your egg sunny side up, just how you like it. And here's a coffee with a smidgeon of milk in it. I'll put it all on the dressing table so you can sit down properly to eat. The eggs will congeal and be revolting if you let it get cold.'

'You're out of your mind!'

'No, Charlotte, I'm not. But you're right. We do need to talk.'

I am not sure what to do. Should I try to attack him? But he's fit. Very fit, and he told me he was an expert in that Israeli self-defense technique. There's no point in trying to hurt him – he'll overpower me instantly. I will just have to make him see reason.

'Sit,' he says, pulling out the chair for me.

I stand quivering near the door.

'Oh, Charlotte, my Charlotte, please don't be afraid of me. I'm not going to hurt you. I owe you an apology, but first sit down.'

Reluctantly, I do as he says, and sit at the dressing table. But I'm not going to eat the breakfast. What if he's poisoned it with something?

He picks up the plastic bag, and it makes a metallic jangling sound as he sits down on the end of the bed. He places the bag on the bed behind him. He then turns and faces me, his hands on his knees.

'Please accept my apologies for last night. I was wrong on many levels. I should not have proposed to you so soon, and I shouldn't have come into your room without your permission.'

'I want to go home,' I say, making as if to stand up again.

'No, Charlotte. You will not be going home. I don't want you to go. Not yet.'

'What do you want from me? I can finish the painting from home. I won't compromise on quality or likeness. I'll work from photos.'

He shakes his head slowly. 'That is not going to happen,' he says, a doleful expression on his face.

'I don't understand!' I say. 'Why can't I finish painting the portrait at my house?'

'Because I need you to stay here. I want you to love me in the way that I love you. I want you to be my wife and the mother of my children. It's obvious, isn't it?'

'You're out of your mind!' I scream. 'That is never going to happen.'

'Never is a very long time,' he says. 'You will love me, of course you will. But perhaps it will take time.'

'I want to go home!' Tears are flowing down my cheeks as desperation eats at me from the inside. 'What are you going to do to me?'

'I'm going to keep you safe, well and happy, of course. I will treat you better than anyone has ever treated you.'

'But Jodi knows where I am. My friends and my mum know I'm here. You'll get caught and it will ruin your life. You won't be able to be a magistrate anymore. Let me go and I won't tell anyone what you tried to do. You can still get out of this. It's not too late.'

'My lovely Charlotte, you may be naive, but I'm not. Of course I'm not going to let you go. Why would I do that?'

I jump up then and start to kick him, bashing my fists into his torso, but all he does is twist away, laughing.

'There is no one here, Charlotte. No one is going to hear you. No one is going to miss you. And you, my delicate little flower, can't possibly hurt me.'

'But you're wrong! I've got people who–'

And then to my utter horror, he reaches into the plastic bag and produces a pair of antique handcuffs made from heavy, rusting iron. He holds them up, right in front of my face.

'Put these on, Charlotte.'

'No!' I kick him with my right foot, but just manage to jab

him in the shin. I shove my fists into his face, but he simply grasps my right wrist and turns it, all the while pulling my arm behind me. I scream out a string of words that don't make much sense.

'Charlotte, darling, I am very strong. Do not make me hurt you.'

My arm is twisted around my back. I am hysterical now and I try everything, kicking out at any angle, elbowing him with my left arm in the stomach, screaming as loudly as I can, but it's as if he is impervious to every move I make.

'If you don't put the manacles on, you will force me to do something very bad. I might have to break your wrist, and I really don't want to. I love you. You are perfect and it would be such a tragedy to scar you or worse. But if need be...' His voice is low and menacing and he lets the words fade away. I feel such terror, it's as if my limbs have frozen solid. All of the fight leaves my body.

'Good girl,' he says as he brings my right wrist forwards. When the heavy, cold metal clasp goes over my wrist and clicks with a loud metallic crack, I have another quick burst of energy.

'No!' I yell as I try to jab his eyes with the fingers of my left hand. He's too quick for me. He twists my arm behind my back, and I let out another loud yowl.

'Darling, I'm very powerful. The only person you will hurt is yourself, and that would be a tragedy. Now relax and hold out your left hand, and let's link them together.'

He releases my arm and I let it fall to my side. I glance around the room, desperately looking for something I can use to hurt him with. But it's as if he can read my mind.

'Do you want me to hurt you?' His face is just centimetres from mine, the warm, stinking coffee breath making me recoil. His strong fingers grasp my left shoulder so strongly, I know they will leave bruises. 'You're not a masochist, are you, Charlotte?'

I hold both my hands out in front of me as my body trembles from head to foot.

'Now there's a good girl.' He takes the handcuffs and clasps the second cuff around my left wrist. My hands are now tightly bound together, the cold metal eating into my skin.

'I love you, Charlotte. I want to keep you safe. You'll want for nothing, but you need to calm down; otherwise I might end up unwittingly hurting you. I don't want to do that, and I'm sure you don't want that either.' He talks to me in the tone a father would speak to his misbehaving toddler.

'Come along. It's good you've packed up because I'm moving you to another room where you'll be safer.'

'Please let me go.' My voice is a rasping whisper.

'No, my darling. You're coming with me.'

18

RUPERT

I spent the night preparing the old punishment room. I've maintained the space over the years, so it's perfectly habitable although necessarily basic; otherwise it would no longer remain a punishment room. Whenever I am feeling in a quandary or if I have done something I know Father wouldn't approve of, I go down to the basement and sit on the bare mattress, cogitating. Some people might think it's my meditation room, but it isn't. I never feel calm there; it's more like my confession booth. And then when I leave the room, sometimes after a few minutes, most usually after several hours – and once, earlier this year, after three days – I feel light and repentant.

And thank goodness I have looked after the room because now I need it.

There are several adjoining rooms in the basement of the house. Father chose this room as the punishment room because it is the furthest away from the main house, and as loudly as I screamed and shouted, no one could hear me. It is also the most secure room. The only light comes from a window about twenty feet above the concrete floor. It is non-opening and has metal bars across it. The heavy door is secured with two five-lever mortice locks and bolts at the top and bottom. When Father locked me in, I couldn't get out, and I was much larger and stronger than my fragile Charlotte. She will be safe and secure here.

But I couldn't keep it so bare and minimalistic; after all I don't want to punish Charlotte. I just need her to see the light – a dreadful cliché. So I take hours transforming the room. I vacuum and wash the concrete floor and then spray some after-shave around the room to eliminate the odour of dampness. I make up the bed with the finest antique Irish linen and place a fawn and cream tartan cashmere blanket over the bed. I try out all of the pillows in the house and select two of the very softest, made from goose down. I take the flower arrangement from the ballroom and place that on a small side table. And then I go to the study and carry Charlotte's easel and all of her painting paraphernalia down to the basement, carefully setting it up again, so she can continue painting.

I then focus on the very basic adjoining bathroom. I think Mrs Cherry made Father install it all of those years ago. She didn't approve of Father's punishment methods, but then she didn't come from a long lineage where tradition matters. One day, a few months after Mother died, he locked me in and didn't come and get me for over twenty-four hours. I can't even remember what misdemeanor I was meant to have carried out. But when he released me, it was Mrs Cherry who was called upon to clean up the mess I left behind. I overheard her heated words with Father. 'He's a boy, Sir Oswald, not a feral animal. It isn't for me to tell you how to raise your son, but please don't expect me to pick up the pieces.' A few days later, workmen were called in, and a simple shower, a small sink and a toilet were installed.

Now they are old and crusted with limescale. I do my best to scrub the gunge away, but there is little I can do. Instead I find a sweet-smelling soap and the very fluffiest, softest towels I own, and put them in the bathroom, ready for Charlotte's use.

It is 4 a.m. by the time I finish installing the technology and making sure the space is as comfortable as possible. The very final thing I do is put the black silk negligee on a cardboard coat hanger and hang it from a hook on the wall. Sadly, I can't risk leaving anything made from sharp wire. The negligee is so beautiful, and I know it will fit Charlotte perfectly. I spent about an hour in the shop trying to select the perfect garment for Charlotte to wear during our first night together. I bury my face in the black silk. She should be dressed in this right now, lying by my side in our marital bed. But although I am impatient, the silk negligee will wait.

I AM NOT STUPID. I knew Charlotte would be upset when she discovered her door was locked and that I intended to keep her prisoner, but really there is no choice. I tried to come up with alternatives all night long, but there is no other option. Without a doubt, if Charlotte leaves now, we will never get the opportunity to fulfil our destiny. I just need to make her see the light and shower her with so much love that she will be unable to resist loving me back. Between 5 and 6 a.m. this morning, I researched Stockholm syndrome. Obviously it's not my first choice of methods for getting her to love me, but just think of Patty Hearst and Natascha Kampusch, both held against their will, both eventually falling for their captors. Unlike those kidnappers, I am a good man with genuine feelings. I love Charlotte. There is no way I can let her go.

And now I am dragging her downstairs. It is every bit as difficult as I feared it might be. I am having to forcibly pull her along the corridor and down the stairs to the basement, and into the punishment room. I hate that I am hurting her.

'Give me your wrists,' I say when we are safely inside. She

holds out her hands and I unlock the manacles. And then she goes berserk again, kicking me and screaming and crying.

'Charlotte, I love you. I don't want to hurt you. Sit down and pull yourself together.'

I use the tone of voice that Father used to speak to me. Deep, menacing, quiet. It worked on me, and unsurprisingly, it works on Charlotte. She crumples onto the bed.

'I'm sorry, love, that the light isn't so good in here. I suppose it will make painting harder, but if you need me to purchase some daylight lamps, I will happily do so.'

'You're crazy!' she says, spitting the words at me.

'My dear Charlotte, I have tried to make it as comfortable as possible for you down here. I've put a mattress topper on the bed to make it wonderfully soft, and this blanket is pure cashmere. Is there anything else you need?'

She is crying now, her body racked with sobs.

'What would you like to eat over the next few days? I can get you anything. A nice lamb stew for supper perhaps, and a bacon, lettuce and tomato sandwich for lunch? Or would you prefer a soup?'

She doesn't answer.

'Don't be sad,' I say, kneeling in front of her. This supplicant position seems to be my default pose these days, but I don't mind. It makes me look subservient to her. 'I've loved you ever since I set eyes upon you.'

'What, for all of two weeks?' she asks sarcastically, sniffing loudly.

'No, no. I saw you for the first time two years ago.'

'Where? When?'

'You were featured in that artist's magazine *Artist's Weekly*. "Charlotte Aldridge – one to watch". They featured the triptych you did of the Highland cows and they wrote a short biography on you. It was your photograph that made my heart jump. It wasn't difficult to track you down thereafter.'

'What is it about me? Why me?'

I move to stroke her hair, but she flinches away from me.

I sigh. 'You are the spitting image of Simone, my first love. I suppose it's true that we men choose a type. I have tried other women, but it simply hasn't worked. And then when I saw your face, I knew God had sent you to me.'

'But it's not just about looks!' she exclaims.

'Of course not. Looks are just one part of the equation. But when I realised you have the sweetest personality, that you are a woman with extraordinary gifts, and that you have suffered heartache and loss, just as I have, I knew that you and I are meant to belong together.' There is more, of course, but my lips are sealed forever.

'But that's crazy! Totally nonsensical.' She jumps up off the bed and starts screaming at me, kicking and scratching again. 'Let me out!'

I grab her wrists to try to still her, and now I can feel my temper fraying. Even my perfect Charlotte is capable of pushing me to my limits.

'What's the problem?' I say. 'I'll give you everything you need. I'm doing all of this for you.'

'Please let me go!' she yells.

'Calm down! If you don't, I will hurt you.' I let go of her wrists and she sinks back onto the mattress. I stare at her, and she does calm down. She covers her face with her hands. I decide now is the time to leave. She must pull herself together, just as I did all of those times in this punishment room. And when she has composed herself fully, we can have another conversation and discuss our future.

19

SIMONE, AUGUST 1995

I t was a difficult year. How is it possible that one can live in such a large city, be surrounded by so many people, yet suffer from such a profound loneliness that it makes your heart break?

Oswald gave me a small flat located just off Sloane Street, within walking distance of Harrods, where I had a part-time job in the handbag department. The apartment block had a twenty-four-hour concierge, and every morning I would stop and chat with the porters. They were my only friends. The other girls at Harrods made an effort, inviting me out for drinks after work, but I declined. I wasn't like them. After a while they gave up. Once a month, Oswald came to visit. He would call me just hours before he arrived, and then he would let himself into the flat, handing me a bunch of flowers or a box of biscuits from Fortnum and Mason. He never stayed. We never made love.

I begged him to let me go home to France to have the baby there, but he said he would stop my allowance and we would never see each other again if I left. All provisions had been made for the year of my gestation, the birth itself, the adoption, and then I would be allowed to return to Sesame Hall. It was the thought of returning to him at Sesame Hall that kept me going. I saw an obstetrician every few weeks on Harley Street and had regular scans, not that the results were ever shared with me. Three days before my due date, the concierge rang to say I had a visitor. My heart leaped as I waddled towards the door. When I opened it, my heart sank.

'I'm here to be your birthing partner and to make sure everything goes smoothly.' Mrs Cherry placed her small suitcase in the hallway and took off her raincoat. 'You're very lucky Sir Oswald didn't turf you out. Instead you're here in the lap of luxury.'

I never found out if Mrs Cherry knew I was carrying Oswald's baby, because that very night, I went into labour. A taxi rushed both of us to The Portland Hospital, where I gave birth in a private room.

I never saw my baby.

My heart broke.

When they let me out of hospital, I returned to the small flat, where I stayed for a further three months. Oswald visited me weekly then, but still he only kissed me on my forehead. It was summer and my body had more or less returned to its pre-pregnancy state and I suppose that if you looked at me, you would never know what I had been through. But inside, I was a totally different person.

By early July, Oswald looked different too. Thinner, paler, older. I still loved him.

'Come here,' he said, opening his arms to me. I threw myself into his hug. He kissed me then, the first time he had laid his lips on mine in nearly a year. And then we made love, gently at first and then with a ferocious passion.

'Can I come back to Sesame Hall with you?' I asked.

'Yes, my love. You can. But Rupert knows nothing, so for now, you will still be the au pair. When you are twenty-one, then we can declare our love for each other. I will make you my wife.'

I shed tears of joy.

AND NOW, here I am, back in my bedroom at Sesame Hall, unpacking my belongings, when Rupert storms in.

'Why did you leave without telling me?' His voice has broken, but he is still as overweight as last year, and his acne hasn't improved.

'I'm sorry, I just—'

'Have you remembered your promise? You ran away before you could do it last year, but this summer you will sleep with me, won't you?'

'No, Rupert. I can't. You don't understand.'

'Oh yes, I understand all too well.' He storms out of the room, slamming the door behind him.

LATER, at dinner, I try to break the silence. 'How was your school year?' I ask Rupert.

He carries on eating, refusing to meet my eyes or answer my question.

'Answer, boy,' Oswald says. But his voice is quieter than normal, and I get the feeling he is distracted. He drops his napkin, and when he bends down, he winces with pain. It is not normal. After all, Oswald is still a young man, only in his early forties, just two decades older than me.

I excuse myself straight after dinner, take a bath and prepare myself for my first night back in my lover's arms. I am desperate to feel his bare skin against mine. So just before midnight, I decide to go to him rather than wait for him to come to me. As I'm wrapping a thin cardigan around myself, I consider why it was that last year, he preferred to come to my room. I assume that he was still not ready to make love to another woman in the bed he shared with his wife. But the present and the future are him and me. She is dead, never forgotten, but all the same gone forever.

I knock gently on his bedroom door and, holding my breath, turn the door handle. His curtains are open and he is lying on his bed with his hands behind his head, moonlight catching on the curls on his chest. He turns his head towards me and smiles. My heart melts.

'Beautiful girl,' he murmurs as I let my cardigan and night-gown fall to the carpet. I walk towards the bed, climb up and straddle him. He pulls my face towards his and kisses me. His passion and urgency leave me breathless and panting.

'I am so happy to be back here,' I murmur, my lips nibbling his earlobe.

'Me too,' he says as he flips me over onto my back. He groans with pleasure or perhaps it's with pain. I can't tell; all I know is that I am filled with the most unbelievable delight, such joy that I never want this to end.

'I've missed you, Simone,' he says.

I am unsure whether to laugh or cry with joy. My insides are an emotional whirlpool. I open my eyes then, wanting to look at his face, to gauge if he really means it.

I still for a moment as I look over Oswald's back.

'What is it?' he murmurs.

'Nothing. Nothing.'

But it isn't nothing. Rupert is standing at the foot of the bed, his jaw hanging open. It's the perfect opportunity to show him that I am a woman making love to his father, that I belong to Oswald, and that he loves me back. And that I will never be interested in a boy like Rupert.

Oswald continues ravaging my body. I smile at Rupert as he watches us. I arch my body, and my moans become louder and louder. Rupert needs to see how it should be done. And then it's all over and Oswald collapses on top of me. When he rolls over, he opens his eyes and sees his son.

'What the hell are you doing here?' Oswald asks, propping himself up on his elbows. He sounds amused rather than angry. I tug the sheet over me.

Rupert is wearing the same pyjamas he wore when he broke into my room last year, but now they are at least two inches too short. He is holding a large box of chocolates and a bunch of flowers. He lets the flowers tumble to the floor.

Oswald bursts out laughing. 'Who are you? The Milk Tray Man?'

Oswald is laughing so much, tears come to his eyes. The bed is shaking. 'Ow, it hurts to laugh so much.' He grabs his side and I bring my hand up to meet his.

'What is the Milk Tray Man?' I ask. His laughter is so infectious it is causing me to giggle too.

'You're both too young to remember.' He chuckles. 'It was an advert for Cadbury's Milk Tray chocolates. So are those gifts for me, son?'

Rupert opens his mouth, but at first no words come out.

I stifle another giggle.

'You're a bastard!' Rupert says, jabbing his finger towards his father. His eyes are watery with unshed tears.

'No,' Oswald says languidly, his face creased with amusement. 'I'm being a man, making love to a woman. Not that you would understand that.'

Rupert is stomping around the room now, waving the box of chocolates in the air. 'She's mine!' he mutters under his breath.

'Come on, Rupert. I told you I'm not interested,' I say, pouting just a little as I run my index finger along Oswald's jawline. 'He came to my room last summer,' I say, murmuring the words into Oswald's ear. 'I sent him packing.'

'My son, my son,' Oswald purrs. 'What you must understand is that a woman is not a possession; she gives herself willingly to a man.'

I place my hand on his chest.

Rupert hurls the box of chocolates at Oswald, who deftly catches it with his right hand.

'Thank you, Rupert. We will enjoy these, won't we, Simone, my darling?'

I love the way he says my name, gently curling his tongue around the *o*, as if he is moaning for me. But I feel sorry for Rupert. He looks utterly distraught.

He is quivering and tears are smarting his eyes. He looks lost and pathetic. If it wasn't for his size, I would imagine he was much younger than his years. He lets out a sob and then turns around and runs out the door, slamming it hard behind him.

Oswald lies back down again in bed, leans on his side, and traces his finger from my neck, down between my breasts to my stomach. 'I am sorry for the behaviour of my son. The boy never learns. I will have to punish him yet again.'

'Punish?'

'Mmm. You are delicious.' His tongue follows the same path as his fingers. 'You help me forget.'

'Oswald?' I murmur.

'Yes.' He doesn't look up.

'I love you.'

20

CHARLOTTE

He is a crazy maniac. I am being held captive by a madman. Hasn't life been cruel enough to me already? For about five minutes, I sob and scream. I kick the wall and hammer my fists on the door. Why me? Why the hell is this happening to me? And then, as if I have been injected with a massive dose of energy, I feel fury flood my veins. To hell with him. I am resourceful. I will get out of here!

When all is silent, I study the room. There must be a way. The floor is concrete, but he has put down a cheap-looking rug next to the bed. I lift it up. There is nothing beneath it. The walls are brick and unpainted, and the ceiling slopes from the end where the window is down to a normal-height room. There is a metal ring attached to the wall on the narrow end of the room, and I don't know what it's for. I tug at it, but it's cemented into the brickwork and doesn't budge. There is a small window, but it is so high up, it's impossible for me to reach. Besides, there are three metal bars across it. The door is solid, it has no handle on the inside, and anyway, I heard him lock and bolt it.

And then I notice the cameras. Two small black cameras blinking at me, positioned in opposite corners of the room, perfectly positioned so that he has a perpetual view of me. The bastard isn't even affording me any privacy. I stick my middle finger up at them, hoping he is watching me.

The room is about twenty feet square. Sizeable enough but cold and damp smelling. I shiver and pull the blanket around myself like a shawl. The mattress is wedged up against a wall constructed from bare breeze blocks; clearly a partition wall that was built more recently. There is an opening in the wall that leads into a small, very basic bathroom with a toilet, a sink with cracks in the basin, and a showerhead positioned over a plastic tray but no walls or curtains. There are two white fluffy towels balanced on the side of the sink and a soap wrapped in mauve floral paper that smells of violets. I look around, praying he hasn't installed any cameras in here, or if he has, that I can rip them from the wall. But no. There is nothing that resembles a spying eye. At least he is granting me some privacy.

The room looks horribly secure. My only way out will be to hurt Rupert. But how? I don't have enough physical strength, so I'll need to use an implement. He's put my paintbrushes in a plastic pot, but what the hell can I do with those? Stab his eye with a pointed end? It makes me feel nauseous just at the thought of it. I pace around and around the room, the blanket wrapped around me, trying to think. Jodi will miss me. If I don't return her calls and don't appear back home, she will definitely come looking for me. She'll alert the police. Why hasn't he thought that through? Rupert is an idiot. He might be able to keep me here for a day or so, but certainly no more than that.

I sit on the edge of the mattress and try to tune into Jodi's mind. They say siblings who are as close as Jodi and I have a telepathy. We used to attempt to read each other's thoughts when we were kids, but we never had any success. Perhaps it's because we're not even real sisters. But we're in touch every day, and she's expecting me home for my birthday, so really I just have to hold on for another twenty-four hours, or forty-eight max. I can see the headlines. *Aristocrat holds painter captive for love.* I wonder if Rupert will go to prison.

I visualise Jodi and try to imagine there are strings between our heads. I send her an SOS message. Come and get me, sis! And then I hear footsteps and the jangling of locks, the undoing of bolts, and I tremble. Jodi can't have come already. The bastard must be back.

Rupert enters my cell carrying a tray piled high with food, two glasses and a bottle of wine. He really is an idiot. He places the tray on the floor, then locks the door behind him. I am tempted to kick him and try to run out, but I miss the moment. I think I need to be more strategic. He picks the tray up and places it on a small wooden table.

'Come and sit down. I've made you some lunch.' He pulls out the chair for me. I don't move. He disgusts me.

'If you prefer to eat with a tray on your lap whilst you're sitting on the bed, that is your choice,' he says, scowling. 'It was not how I was brought up, but I suppose I need to make some allowances for you.' He unscrews the bottle and pours white wine into two plastic glasses, leaving them on the table. He walks to the wall and fingers the silky fabric of the nightdress.

'I bought this for you to wear when we consummate our love.'

I cannot believe he said that. I lose it. I totally lose it. I grab a glass full of wine and chuck it in Rupert's face. If he rapes me, I swear I will kill him.

'What the hell!' he exclaims as white wine drips down his face, down the front of his pale blue shirt, and puddles at his feet. I then grab one of the knives, a silver knife with a serrated edge, and point it at him.

'If you touch me, I'll kill you.'

He laughs. He bloody well laughs! 'Oh my dearest, how I adore your passion. I love feistiness in a woman. Simone had it and you have it too. Our life together will never be boring. You have nothing to fear. I won't touch you until you're ready, until the moment when you reach for me voluntarily, unable to resist our love.'

'Who the hell is this Simone?' I jab the knife forwards as if I'm about to attack him.

He doesn't answer me and doesn't even flinch.

I am panting hard. I want to shove the knife into his chest, to make him scream with pain, but I'm not sure if I can do it. Am I strong enough? Perhaps I could break the bottle on his head and use the sharp edge to cut him? But I hesitate just for a second, and Rupert steps towards me, shaking the wine off his body like a dog. I hold the knife out in front of me, both hands around the silver handle. I am shaking.

'Don't come any nearer,' I yell.

But he does. He grabs my right wrist and twists it, and I scream and let the knife fall with a clatter to the concrete floor. He puts his arm around my torso, pinning my arms to my sides. I try to kick him, but he is too strong. I don't know who I'm more angry with. Him for doing this to me, or myself for being too weak to defend myself.

'Charlotte, my darling,' he purrs, 'I know this is hard for you, that perhaps you don't understand why I am doing this, but you must trust me. You will see that it is for the best. I won't hurt you, I love you too much to hurt you. Believe me, I understand that you may need more time to think about everything, but I will wait for you as long as it takes. A lifetime, if need be. We are soulmates, and as your soulmate, all I want is for you to be as happy as I am.'

'I will never be your soulmate!' I scream. 'My soulmate is dead. Matthew is dead.'

He shakes his head and releases me. I stumble towards the mattress and sink onto it, sobbing uncontrollably.

'I am so sorry I upset you, my darling. All I want to do is ensure you are safe and happy.'

'And you think by having cameras spying on me, that will make me happy? And you think that keeping me locked up in a dungeon is a surefire way for me to fall in love with you?'

'My dear, the cameras are here to keep you safe. I need to make sure you are alright at all times. When I go out, I need to check that you are well and content. How can I do that without cameras? No one will hear you or find you down here, so if you fell sick or something happened to you, no one would know. It is one hundred percent for your safety and well-being.'

'You need to let me go!' I make a lunge for the bottle of wine, but he is nearer to it and quicker than me. He grabs the bottle and holds it up high in the air.

'Do not push me, Charlotte. I don't want to hurt you.'

Physical violence is not going to get me what I want. I try to stifle a sob as I look away from him. I never want to set eyes on him ever again. He disgusts me.

'If I may, I would like to tell you a story.' He holds the bottle behind his back.

I don't answer. How can he talk to me as if everything were perfectly normal?

'My dearest mother died when I was twelve years old. I was her only child and the apple of her eye. Everything changed when she passed away. I was sent to boarding school, where I was bullied mercilessly. My solace was food, at school and at home. Thank goodness for Mrs Cherry, because Father had no idea how to express affection. His only experience of child-rearing was that which he had experienced himself, so he drew upon what he knew. When I misbehaved, he brought me down here, and with these very manacles, he attached me to that ring that you see on the wall over there. It was where I spent a lot of time as a boy. It is a special place. A place that forces you to look at the reality of your behaviour. A place that allows your mind to unfurl and realise your true destiny. A place where one can repent without distraction.

'In the early days I screamed and shouted, but no one could hear me. I tried to rebel against Father, against all authority. And then I fell in love. She was my French au pair. A beautiful girl. Alas, Simone wasn't all that she appeared. Father got her pregnant and we all suffered from that. But this isn't about Simone, this is about you, my Charlotte.

'Dearest Charlotte, please view this place as your sanctuary. A place to heal and a secure place within which we can nurture our love. Do not be afraid. I will give you whatever you need.'

He walks over to the table and puts all the food and drink back on the tray. He carries the tray to the door, placing it on the floor whilst he unlocks the door. I suppose he is going to leave me to starve too, not that I'm hungry. But he needn't worry about me. I don't have the energy to attack him again. I just watch him leave, and then I let the misery take hold.

21

RUPERT

I would be lying to say that I'm not disappointed in Charlotte's irrational behaviour. I walk somewhat dejectedly back to the kitchen and transfer her food onto paper plates. I find some disposable plastic cutlery at the back of a cupboard. I cannot trust her with china and glass and proper cutlery. Not yet. It is a shame.

Of course, her upbringing will have been very different to my own. She won't have been steeped with English traditions or had the origins of manners explained to her. Perhaps she has never even heard of Debrett's. I doubt she appreciates the difference between eating with stainless-steel implements and solid silver. There will be a great deal that I shall have to teach her, but I am sure she will be a quick learner. I don't suppose she acquired much resilience either. No doubt she went to a local comprehensive school or possibly a minor public school, but she will have had her sister at her side, the two of them looking out for each other. I wonder if Charlotte has ever had to truly stand on her own two feet? That could explain her current behaviour.

Clearly the adjustment period is going to be much longer

than I had anticipated. It is hard enough to change behaviour patterns when one is a child, let alone as a fully fledged adult. So I promise myself that I will be patient, that I will think through all of my actions, that I will consider things from her perspective as well as my own. It will be worth it.

I carry the tray back to the punishment room, and I am saddened that Charlotte is still huddled on the bed.

'I'm leaving your food here,' I say, and then immediately depart, locking the room behind me.

As I walk up the stairs, I fast-forward a couple of years and see Charlotte at my side, both sets of our hands laid across her distended, pregnant belly. Perhaps we will be expecting twins, a boy and a girl. We will laugh about these initial relationship hiccups when we look back to these, our early days. We won't care about what people think, the idle gossip of the chattering classes.

Lost in my thoughts, I meander upstairs to Charlotte's bedroom. Her handbag is lying on a chair, and her packed suitcase is standing next to the bed. I lift the suitcase up and lay it on the collapsible luggage rack. I would never put a dirty bag or case on a bed. I unzip it slowly, my nose close to the inside of the case so I can inhale the scents that will inevitably permeate up and out of the suitcase. Heavenly.

Goodness, but what a mess! She has literally shoved all of her belongings into the case, everything crumpled together. What a disappointment. I can't abide slovenliness. I remove all of her clothes, handling each piece carefully and laying them out on the bed. When my fingers find her underwear, I hesitate. I am not a pervert, so I pick them up gingerly. Oh, Charlotte. I really do need to buy you some new clothes. Cheap fabrics don't last. After I have folded up most of her belongings, I create two piles. One for the items that will go back into the suitcase and the other comprising the clothes that I will give her to wear on a daily basis.

Pleased that I have made order out of chaos, I pick up her beige leather handbag and walk back downstairs. The bag is scuffed, and I fear it may be made of plastic rather than real leather. I will buy her a Mulberry or a Launer bag. Something classic. Launer would be best. If it's good enough for our Queen Elizabeth of England, it's good enough for the future Lady Charlotte Baskerville. I take out my keys again and let myself into my office.

It is the only room in the house that I keep locked, at least when there are other people around. That was before I set up the punishment room, of course.

Many people think the library was my father's study, but it wasn't. This room was. It is lined with walnut bookcases, and his large twin-pedestal desk – inlaid with walnut, sterling silver and black leather – still takes pride of place in the centre of the room. When Mother died, Father spent most of his time in here. I don't know what he did. Grieved, I suppose, because in front of everyone else, me included, he barely showed any emotion. Or perhaps he really was emotionless.

I place Charlotte's handbag on a chair and open up the cupboard behind my desk, and the two monitors flicker to life. The left monitor is split into two, one half for each of the cameras I have set up in the punishment room. Charlotte is still huddled on the bed. Her food will be cold by now and quite unpleasant. The right monitor is split into four, and it streams the live feeds from the other security cameras I have set up around the Hall. This house and I may be steeped in tradition, but we integrate very well with the latest technology.

I swivel the chair around so I can watch the monitors, but then there is an unusual pinging sound. I pick up my mobile phone, but there are no alerts. It takes me a moment to work out where it is coming from. At first I think it must be coming from Charlotte's bag, but then I remember that I took her mobile phone last night and deposited it in here before retiring for the night. It is lying on the side of Father's desk. I pick it up and see that a text message has arrived from Jodi.

Her phone is locked with a code, as most phones are these days. Frustrating but not an insurmountable problem. I am good with technology, and there's nothing I enjoy more than a supposedly insurmountable technological challenge. I try the obvious codes, such as her and her sister's birthdays and the birthday of her dead fiancé, but none of those work. I will have to do a little online research. It takes me about half an hour, but I find an app that simply removes the passcode from her phone. After plugging it into my computer and following the app's instructions, which are unnecessarily complicated, I disable the passcode and I'm in.

I scroll through her messages, and to my dismay, I see that she has told Jodi that she will be coming home. Damnation. The sister is going to start looking for her sooner than I had anticipated. The clock is ticking and I need to get moving. Of course I have thought through the repercussions of Charlotte disappearing, but now I need to formulate an action plan and implement it quickly. And I certainly must not have Charlotte's very inferior sister coming over here, sticking her nose into things.

I sit quietly for a long time, but it isn't hard to work out what I need to do.

'CHARLOTTE, PLEASE TALK TO ME.'

She is still huddled on the bed.

'Charlotte!' I speak more gruffly now, as if I were speaking to an ill-behaved mongrel.

She sits up. Her eyes are red. My poor love.

I crouch down next to her. It pains me to see her so unhappy.

'I have to go away for the rest of the day, but please don't worry. You will be perfectly safe. I can see you on my phone via an app. It links into these cameras. I will check on you regularly. I have brought you a plate of freshly made sandwiches and some fruit, which you can have for supper. There are also some biscuits and a yoghurt, so hopefully you won't go hungry. There are two thermos flasks. One filled with tea, the other with iced water.' I point to the paper plates and plastic cutlery. I doubt she can do much damage with those. 'Oh, and I nearly forgot. There is a bar of fine dark chocolate should you want a little pick-me-up. I'll be back very late, so please don't wait up for me.'

Charlotte lets out an unpleasant harrumph.

'May I suggest you use the time wisely. Why don't you carry on with the portrait? I know the lighting isn't so good in here, but hopefully it will be adequate. I have lots of ideas for your painting career and can't wait to support you in your exciting artistic journey. We can talk about it when I'm back.'

She turns her head away from me. I stand up. Beautiful Charlotte is trying my patience, and it's vital I leave before I lose any control.

I wish I could take her into my arms and kiss her goodbye, but now is not the time. Instead, I stand up, nod at her and leave the room, carefully bolting it behind me.

22

SIMONE, AUGUST 1995

'I can't breathe!' I'm not even sure if my words are audible. The pain is unlike anything I have experienced, searing, burning my throat, my gut, my stomach, eating my innards from the inside out. I think I'm screaming, but I'm not sure if I am making any sound. It was one drink, one small sip after dinner, and now I am collapsed on the antique Persian rug in the drawing room. Poisoned. I know I have been poisoned because what else could cause this agony, this terror?

'Help me!' I gasp. I am writhing now, my fingers desperately clutching for anything, anybody. 'Help! I've been poisoned!'

I lose track of how long I am on the floor drifting in and out of consciousness. I hear footsteps and voices. Loud, angry voices. I see Rupert and Oswald and then Oswald and Rupert, and I can't work out which is which until I feel warm hands stroking my hair, and I realise that it is Oswald. He puts my head in his lap, cradling me like a baby. He is keening, backwards and forwards. 'Stay with me, Simone! Stay with me, my darling.'

I feel a blackness descend as my body disintegrates.

'Someone – call an ambulance!' he shouts.

'I'm dying,' I murmur.

'No! Wake up.' He is shaking me now. 'Wake up, Simone! Wake up!'

I can feel the foam coming out of my mouth. Blood is filling every orifice. Please let me go now, into the abyss. I need to feel nothing.

I open my eyes for the last time, and I see Rupert standing there in the doorway, staring at me and his father.

'Don't just fucking well stand there!' Oswald screams. 'Call for an ambulance. Now!'

But it is too late. Much too late.

23

RUPERT

I nitially I thought the text Charlotte sent to Jodi saying she was coming home presented me with a major problem. On further reflection, it opened up an opportunity that sent shards of excitement through me. I am going on an adventure.

After leaving Charlotte in the punishment room, I climb upstairs and pull down the ladder that gives access to the Hall's substantial loft space. In here are many boxes of belongings left behind by my parents. Over the years, I have attempted to create a semblance of order, but invariably emotions get the better of me, and I have to descend to the basement and the punishment room in order to calm down. Although I have made a half-hearted attempt to create two piles – one for keeping, the other for giving to charity – I have never been able to bring myself to dispose of anything. Fortunately one of the earlier boxes I went through had some rather bizarre dressing-up accoutrements, such as masks, fancy dress gear and wigs. I don't recall my parents hosting fancy dress parties, but based on the amount of garbage I found in the attic, I assume they must have had a penchant for them. I switch on the light, and the single light bulb illuminates a complex maze of cobwebs lacing between the rafters. I make my way to the box I have marked *Fancy Dress Clothes* and rifle inside it. There are three ladies' wigs. I select the blonde one. The hair is synthetic and bears little resemblance to Charlotte's blonde tresses, but it will have to do.

I collect Charlotte's handbag and suitcase and carry them to the back door. After ensuring the Hall is locked up, I pull on a pair of leather gloves, stride to Charlotte's car, find her car keys and open the car. I have never driven something quite as basic as this little Fiat. And it is so dirty on the inside. There are chocolate wrappers on the floor and a couple of empty Coke cans. Very disheveled and unpleasant. I pull the wig over my head, tucking any of my dark hairs away underneath it. It is itchy and hot, but there is no gain without pain. I then put a baseball hat over the wig, pulling the cap down quite low, ensuring I don't impair my vision. I wonder if I should swipe my lips with a slash of Charlotte's lipstick, but I am unable to bring myself to do that. I stare at my face in the rear-view mirror and barely recognise myself; it is quite amusing.

Fortunately, the car fires up immediately. Blowing a quick kiss to my love in the basement, I drive away calmly and steadily.

It is a long drive, onto the M25, past Heathrow and then onto the M40. The Fiat feels insignificant and rather unsafe. It is vital that I don't draw attention to myself, so I plod along between sixty and seventy miles per hour. Shortly after joining the M6, I pull off the motorway and go into some anonymous town to fill up with petrol and get a drink, taking off the ridiculous wig first, of course. I daren't stop at any motorway service stations for fear of being spotted by surveillance cameras.

It is dark by the time I see the sign to Macclesfield. My heart jumps with joy. Coming off the M6 at Knutsford, I pull over into a lay-by and call Charlotte's home telephone. I must be absolutely sure that no one is there. Receiving no answer, I carry on driving. Now my excitement is palpable. I hum under my breath and tap my fingers against the steering wheel. I have input Charlotte's address into the satnav app on my phone, and the female voice calms my nerves. Eventually I turn onto her street.

If I hadn't already done my research into Charlotte and where she lived, I would have been bitterly disappointed. It is an ordinary street: a row of semi-detached houses that could be found in any shabby town in England. She lives in number 41b. Frankly the houses don't look big enough to split into two. Poor Charlotte. She deserves so much more than this. I drive very slowly and am fortunate to find a parking space just a few doors down, so I pull up and sit in the car for a moment. I try calling her landline once more. One can never be too careful. It rings and rings.

Now is my time.

With the wig firmly on and the baseball cap pulled down low, I grab her suitcase and a plastic bag in which I have placed her handbag, put her easel under my armpit, and palm her keys. I lock the car and stride purposefully towards her front door. Fortunately, the street is deserted. Nevertheless, I have watched enough movies to know that confidence in gestures is of vital importance. I slide the key into the front door and it opens easily. It is a communal entrance area for both flats, flat A being downstairs and flat B upstairs. Charlotte's post is piled up on a narrow table in the entrance hall, so I collect it, shove it in her bag and stride upstairs. I knock gently on her front door just to be absolutely positive no one is there. It would be horrendous to come face-to-face with Jodi. But once again, there is silence. Even so, my heart is thudding as I open up.

The lights are off and the flat is cold. Slipping my shoes off in the entrance hall, I switch the lights on and close the door behind myself.

So this is where Charlotte calls home. Why oh why would she choose to live here when she could be with me at Sesame Hall?

This is a pokey little flat with zero character. The small hall leads into a living room to the left that houses a two-seater sofa covered with a cotton throw with a garish print in reds and yellows. There are two sagging armchairs – one is grey, the other is red – and a large television. A small table that could possibly seat four is positioned to one side of the room. I wonder where Charlotte paints. There are no paintings lying around, although there are several hanging on the walls, all pictures of animals and birds, signed by Charlotte of course. I decide to place her easel by the window where there is the most light. I run my gloved fingers over it before walking out of the living room and into a kitchenette. It is clean and tidy but very dated.

I pace back to the hall and find the only bedroom. I inhale deeply. This is more my Charlotte's taste. The bed looks comfortable and is neatly covered with a mohair throw. I place her suitcase on the ground and unzip it. I place all her belongings on the bed and then work out where she stores what. I hang up her blouses and trousers and put away her underwear and jumpers. I then go into her bathroom. There is a half-opened bottle of bath oil. I pick it up and smell it. Glorious. I will take it home as a little memento. In fact, I may take several things home.

I return to the bedroom, delighted with the opportunity I have to look through her things, to try to get inside the head of my beloved. What a shame that I have to wear gloves. I cannot risk touching her belongings with my bare skin. But then, shoved at the back of a drawer, I find the most exquisite silk camisole with matching knickers. They are wrapped in tissue paper. A knot of jealousy curdles in my stomach. Did Matthew give her these, or did she buy them herself? Was she keeping them for her wedding night? I have to touch them. I remove one glove and the fabric is beautifully smooth and cool under my touch. I hold them up to my nose and inhale. No. They haven't been worn by Charlotte. She was clearly keeping them for a special occasion. I take them back into the living room and, along with the bath oil, drop them into my plastic bag. I slip the glove back onto my hand.

There are a number of photographs placed around the flat that make me unhappy. Very unhappy. Charlotte has her arms around Matthew. He is kissing her cheek. They are holding hands and jumping up in the air. Oh, Charlotte, you will never move on if you leave out all these mementos. I rifle through the drawers of the armoire in the living room, and there I find a photograph of Charlotte in a passionate embrace with Matthew. This is too much. Simply too much. I have no choice but to rip it in two, and then into four and finally into the tiniest little fragments of paper that I can manage with my gloved hands. I stuff the torn photograph into my jacket pocket for disposal later.

I place Charlotte's handbag on a chair and leave her wallet, phone, car and house keys on the table. Fanning the envelopes I found downstairs, I decide to open them. Oh dear. *What a mess you have got yourself into, my love.* These are all final demands and bank statements. How could she be so very care-less with money? I pace backwards and forwards. I would dearly love to pay off these debts, after all it is small change to me, but frustratingly I don't suppose I should. Undoubtedly, the money would be traced back to me, and that would place me in a very precarious position. But I remind myself that as soon as Charlotte accepts my hand in marriage, I will make sure that everyone she owes money to is paid immediately, with interest. I take a couple of the invoices and put them in my bag.

Sighing, I glance at my watch. It is time for me to leave. I switch off all the lights, tug off the wig, placing it into a carrier bag, put on my shoes, and pull the door closed behind me. I hesitate on the stairs, straining my ears to hear whether there is anyone in the building. I do not want to be accosted by the residents of flat A on my way down. Holding my breath, I race down the stairs and out of the building. I walk along several streets, my eyes straight ahead, before I hit a main road. Now I need to find a taxi that will take me to Macclesfield station.

After climbing onto the fast train to London, I breathe a sigh of relief as I recline in my first-class seat. That little exercise went swimmingly. I turn on my phone and log in to the security app. There she is, my gorgeous Charlotte, lying on the bed, motionless. The light is low and I can't tell if she is asleep or awake. Never mind, I can still watch her. A smile creeps over my face. How much I love this woman!

I doze contentedly until I am awoken by the train pulling into London Euston. I hurry off the train and catch a taxi to Selfridges. How fortunate that the shop doesn't close until 10 p.m. It is my love's birthday tomorrow and she deserves some fabulous gifts.

Thirty minutes later I have an array of gifts neatly wrapped, all in the distinctive yellow Selfridges bag. I am sure she will love them, but perhaps the Montblanc pen and leather-bound notebook will be the pièce de résistance. And then I change my mind. The cashmere jumper is rather fabulous and the Tiffany necklace with the interlocking hearts very simple but stylish and, of course, imbued with meaning. As I am in another taxi on my way back to London's Victoria station, I curse. Damnation. I meant to buy her a new handbag. I grind my teeth. It will have to wait. I must catch the last train to Pulborough.

24

JODI

I wake up and stretch. It's Charlotte's birthday today. We have a tradition. I organise the celebrations for her birthday, and she does the same for mine, although normally, if it's a stay-at-home celebration, we split the cooking. I glance at my phone. There's a message from Mum saying she hasn't been able to get hold of Charlie. I'm too tired to work out what the time is in New Zealand. Is it even the same day?

I call Charlie, but after several rings, the phone goes to voicemail.

'Hey, sis. Happy birthday! Hope you got home ok. Give me a call when you're awake or leave me a message. Supper is at 7 p.m. at mine. Stay the night with me. Food's all sorted and the normal gang will be here. I'm on a short shift at the hospital from 8 a.m. until 3 p.m. The girls are covering for me later. Leave me a message. Have a happy day. Love you.'

I hurry to get ready for work. It's frustrating having to work today when I'll be cooking for a dinner party tonight, but we're short-staffed at the hospital, so needs must. Then again, we're always short-staffed.

It's one of those crazy hectic days when it seems as if every mother in the north-west has decided to go into labour at the same time, and I don't have a second to think about myself or my plans for this evening. I feel bad because I don't even have a moment to check my phone. By 3 p.m., I am exhausted, not helped by the fact I didn't even have time for lunch.

On the way out of the hospital, I stuff a sandwich into my mouth and simultaneously fumble in my bag for my phone. I'm multidexterous, but then you have to be in my job. I have a message from a mutual friend of Charlie and mine asking what she can bring tonight, and a message from Rohan, who may or may not after tonight officially become my boyfriend. I smile. He's cute and kind and we have, very tentatively, been spending more and more time together. Unfortunately those times are short, snatched moments because he's a doctor and his shifts rarely coincide with mine. He has, however, promised me that he'll come for supper tonight, with the caveat that he has no idea what time he will be able to arrive.

But in the meantime I have lots to do, not least to buy the food for our meal. I nip to my favourite shop: all vegan, fantastic choice and way too expensive for my modest salary. Nevertheless, I max out my credit card. It's a special occasion tonight, and I can't wait to see Charlie and find out more about that creepy aristocrat. Which reminds me; I still haven't heard from her. Weighed down by heavy shopping bags, I wedge my mobile phone between my cheek and shoulder and ring her again. This time it sounds as if the phone is off, as it goes to voicemail immediately.

'Call me, Charlie. Want to discuss plans for tonight. Love you!'

Charlotte is a much better chef than me, and it would be quite easy for me to leave all the cooking to her, but over the years our roles have split. I do the mains; she does the puddings and the birthday cake. She's renowned for her baking skills and particularly cake decorating. Her designs have ranged from an artist's easel, palette and brushes to a full-blown Noah's Ark with animals. Last year it was two islands, each with palm trees, a turquoise sea between them and a zip line connecting them both, the seashores lined with shells. But that was before Matthew's death, and this year I haven't even mentioned a cake. I wonder if I should pick something up from Sainsbury's.

By five p.m., the table is laid and my vegetarian curried stew is under control. And I still haven't heard from Charlie. This is weird. We have spent every one of our birthdays together, and even if we don't get to see each other until the evening, we always speak during the day. I check the last message from her. Yes, she said she would definitely be home for her birthday. There's not even anyone I can call, as she's distanced herself from most of her friends since Matthew died. Mum and I are her only crutches. I'd lay my life down for Charlie, but still it's quite a responsibility.

I run a bath and soak away the day in a mountain of rose-scented bubbles. After washing my hair, I am wrapped in a towel when the doorbell goes. It's just before 6 p.m. Relieved that it must be Charlie, I press the door buzzer release button without asking who's there. Then I leave my front door button slightly ajar.

'Hello! Jodi?'

Oh shit, it's Rohan, and I'm not even dressed.

I shout from the bedroom, 'I'll be out in a sec. Help yourself to a drink.' Rohan and I haven't slept together, and we're still at that early stage of tiptoeing around and pretending to be cool. Ridiculous at our age, but hopefully tonight that will all change. I grab a wraparound dress from my wardrobe, fling it on and rush out of the bedroom, still towel drying my hair.

'Whoops. Sorry, I'm obviously too early!' He is holding an enormous bouquet of flowers and a bottle of champagne. He proffers both.

'That's so kind, thank you!' I say, kissing him on the cheek and accepting the gifts.

'What can I do to help?' he asks. He looks a bit awkward, as if he is too large for my flat.

'You can help yourself to a beer from the fridge and pour me a glass of wine.'

He grins.

I dump the wet towel in the bathroom, put on some mascara and lipstick, and pad back to my living room.

'Who's coming tonight?' he asks, handing me a glass.

'There'll be eleven of us.' I wish I could persuade Charlie to consider dating again, but I know it's too soon. Where the hell is she?

I try her phone again, but it still goes straight to voicemail.

Rohan must notice the frown on my face. 'Everything ok?'

I shake my head. 'My sister, Charlie, whom you'll meet tonight, she hasn't been in contact all day, and it's really not like her. I'm getting a bit worried.'

'When did you last speak to her?'

'I had a text from her last night saying she was coming home today. She's been in Sussex painting someone's portrait.'

I can tell from Rohan's expression that he's thinking the same as me. When you work in a hospital, you tend to think the worst. Accident. Illness. But then again, if something had happened, I'm her next of kin and would be the first to be told.

'Maybe she's just going to surprise you. What time have you invited the others?'

'Seven p.m.' I don't tell him that Charlie never liked surprises, and after the horrific shock of Matthew's death, surprise is no longer in our vocabulary. I busy myself with finishing off the supper, and before I know it, the doorbell is ringing.

It isn't Charlotte.

By 7.15 p.m. I am unable to concentrate. I am in my galley

kitchen staring at my mobile phone when Rohan walks in. He puts his arms around me.

'If you're worried about your sister, why don't we go around to her house and check that she's alright?'

'But everyone's here and Charlie lives in Macclesfield.'

'If this bunch are good friends of hers, they'll understand.'

I nod.

'Guys,' I say, 'I'm really sorry, but I'm worried about Charlie. She's been out of contact, and what with everything that's happened this year...' They all make sounds of sympathy. 'Rohan has offered to drive me over to Macclesfield. We shouldn't be more than an hour or so at this time of night. Gail, can you take charge of the food?'

'Of course, babe,' my best friend says.

'Eat, drink and we'll be back as soon as we can.'

The noise levels drop as I scurry back to my bedroom to find my handbag and a thick jumper.

My foot is bouncing up and down as Rohan drives us out of Manchester towards Macclesfield.

'It'll be fine,' he says, laying a warm, brown hand on my knee.

He's a lovely man, and I wish he had a brother whom we could match with Charlie. Rohan wouldn't be driving me to Macc if he wasn't interested in me, would he?

'Charlie's text said Sir Rupert Baskerville asked her to marry him. That's weird, isn't it? They barely know each other.'

'What a name!' Rohan smirks. 'I know it's easy for me to say, but try to stop worrying, Jodi. We're nearly in Macclesfield.'

Even so, the journey seems to take forever. When we pull up into Charlie's street, cars are parked on both sides, and there is nowhere for Rohan to park.

'That's Charlie's car!' I say, pointing at the little white Fiat.

'Good news. It means she must be home, or perhaps she's even at yours by now.'

'No. Gail would have rung me.' I put my hand on the car door. 'Would you mind dropping me here, and I'll come out and find you when I'm done. You might be able to park on the next street over.'

'Don't you want to wait for me to come in with you?' he asks, his eyebrows knotted together with concern. He doesn't need to say I'm a doctor, and if you're about to face a terrible scene, I want to be there to support you. I can't think that, so I just say, 'Thanks, but I won't be two ticks.'

I hop out of the car and stride back towards number 41. I ring the doorbell on flat B, but there's no answer. Shit! In the rush, I didn't even bring my set of Charlie's keys. I am so bloody stupid. I push flat A's bell and press it long and hard. Eventually a male voice asks, 'Who's there?'

'It's Jodi. Charlotte's sister. Have you seen her?'

I've met the occupant of the flat on a couple of occasions. He's a miserable man, mid-thirties, lives alone, works in IT or something and is forever complaining about the noise coming from the piano teacher's house next door. But he's quiet and keeps himself to himself, so Charlie doesn't mind him.

'Nope. Thought she'd gone away?'

'Yes, she had, but she came back today.'

'Heard some footsteps earlier, but I haven't seen her.'

'Can you let me in?'

The door buzzes and I push it open. I stride up the stairs and knock on Charlie's door. There's no answer. What if she's locked herself in and has done something awful? I turn the handle and, to my surprise, the door's unlocked.

'Charlie, are you here?' I switch the light on and walk into the living room. Her keys and wallet are on the table, and her handbag is on a chair. Shit. She is here. I feel nauseous as I walk towards her bedroom. The door is slightly ajar, but the lights are off. I exhale with relief. She's not here. Her suitcase is neatly placed against the wall, next to her chest of drawers. I lift it up and note that it's empty, so she must have unpacked. Just one more room to check: the bathroom. I take a deep breath and push open the door. She's not there either.

What the hell?

Her belongings are here, but she's not. So where is she?

I walk back to the living room and see that her phone is on the table. I pick it up. It's powered off and I wonder if it's run out of battery, but no. It turns itself back on. I put in her passcode and scroll through her caller list. The only person she's called in the past week is me. The same with her texts. The last one was the text she sent me yesterday saying she was coming home. None of this makes sense. And her post. It's all opened and left on the table.

Could she have nipped out somewhere? Surely not. She wouldn't leave her wallet, keys and phone behind. I'm getting a really bad feeling. My breath is catching in my throat.

I find a pen and scribble a note on the back of an envelope.

Call me as soon as you read this, Jx

I'm going to have to leave her flat unlocked, the way I found it. Feeling very uneasy, I go back down the stairs and rap on flat A's door again.

'Yeah.' He's wearing a torn T-shirt and black jeans. His hair is on end.

'What time did you hear footsteps upstairs?'

'Dunno.' He yawns. 'Sometime this afternoon. I didn't wake up until about one-ish.'

'I think something has happened to my sister. Can I take your mobile number, and will you check if she's home later?'

'S'ppose so,' he says, rubbing his eyes. There's a smell of weed coming from his flat, and it turns my stomach. We swap numbers, but I don't have any confidence in him.

Charlie, I think, *where the hell are you?*

. . .

Rohan's car is hovering a few metres down the road, so I run towards it. He turns towards me, his kindly dark eyes looking at me questioningly.

'She's not there. But all her stuff is. The flat was open, and her wallet and phone were on the table. It doesn't make sense.'

'What do you want to do?'

'Call the police.'

He nods. 'I'll find a parking space.'

But I don't wait. I call 999. 'I'm reporting a missing person.'

The policeman asks for my name and address, and I give him Charlie's details.

'How long has she been missing?' His voice is kindly.

I do a quick mental calculation. If Charlie's dopey neighbour heard footsteps this afternoon, she's probably only been missing seven hours maximum.

'I'm sorry, ma'am, but we only consider an adult a missing person if they have been out of contact for twenty-four hours or longer.'

'But Charlie would never just disappear or miss her birthday!' I exclaim.

'I'm sorry, but I suggest you call us back tomorrow in the unlikely event that your sister hasn't turned up.'

I hang up and let out a scream.

Rohan strokes my arm. 'What would you like to do?'

I sigh. 'Go back to Chorlton, I suppose.'

He nods and starts the car engine. We're just pulling onto the A523 to head back north when Rohan says, 'The man she was painting. Why don't you call him to find out what time your sister left Sussex?'

'Good idea,' I say, bringing up the search engine on my phone. I put in Sir Rupert Baskerville, and up comes his address of Sesame Hall, but nowhere can I find his phone number. I ring directory enquiries.

'I'm sorry, but that number is ex-directory.'

I end the call and yell, 'Of course it's bloody ex-directory!'

Rohan throws me a sympathetic glance. If he's not put off me by all of this, he must be a good man. Tears smart my eyes.

I can't even find an email address for him. What the hell should I do now?

We are back at my flat shortly after 8 p.m. Our friends all look up at me when Rohan and I walk through the door.

'Is she here?' I ask Gail, but from the looks on their faces, I already know the answer.

Charlie, where the hell are you?

25

CHARLOTTE

Why oh why didn't I listen to my gut? I knew that Rupert was a weirdo the first time we met at The Titanium Gallery. Why is this happening to me? What have I done to deserve so much misery and heartache?

I have lost track of how long I have been curled up on the mattress, sobbing. I didn't hear Rupert come back last night, but he obviously did, because this morning he came into my room, or to call it by its proper name, my prison cell. Rupert was all spritely and bouncy as if our situation were perfectly normal. He brought me another cooked breakfast and a hot cup of tea. But he's obviously a bit wary of me, because he didn't hang around. He just dumped the tray, wished me a good morning and locked me back up again. The bastard.

Even though I don't feel like it, I eat the eggs and bacon. Matthew would tell me to eat it, to keep up my strength. *Oh, Matthew, why have you gone?* And why haven't the police come to rescue me? How long will it be until Jodi tells them I've gone missing. She will contact them when she can't get hold of me and when I'm not home for my birthday. I've just got to hang on in here. Another day and night, max.

But time goes so very slowly.

I have nothing to do in this place other than indulge in my memories, and it's nigh impossible to keep out the bad ones. Why is it that terrible memories are so vivid, yet happy ones fade?

Matthew had promised me he would be home before midnight. He was a man who always did what he said he was going to do. Reliable, trustworthy but never dull. And so I went to sleep expecting to wake up as he slipped into bed and wrapped his arms around me. Except at about 2 a.m. the doorbell rang. Twice. I fumbled to switch on the lights, and when I saw that Matthew's side of the bed was empty, I suppose I knew. I ran to the door and then I hesitated. I didn't want to know. I still don't.

When the police man and woman scooped me up off the floor and sat me on the sofa with a cup of tea, and my hysteria and shaking had diminished just a little, and they knew that Mum and Jodi were on their way over, they asked me if Matthew habitually drank a lot.

'What?' I couldn't compute the question. 'He's a pilot. He drinks, but never before flying. Why are you asking?'

'We are investigating whether he might have got involved in a drunken brawl,' the policewoman said gently.

I stood up then, spilling the tea all over the floor. 'Oh, thank God! You've got the wrong person. There must be another Matthew Shuttleslowe. You've got the wrong man! Matthew would never have got involved in a fight, and he wouldn't have had more than one beer. He's flying tomorrow.'

They looked at each other, frowning.

'We have identified him via a receipt in his inside jacket pocket.'

'But you said his wallet was stolen, so how do you know it was him? And his phone. Where is his phone?'

'It appears to have been stolen too because we didn't find a mobile phone.'

'So you don't know that it's my Matthew?'

I started pacing around the room. But then my memory goes hazy because they told me that they had verified his pilot ID and checked his credit card against the receipt for perfume bought at Geneva airport, and that I was mistaken because it definitely was him. I started screaming again, and I think Mum arrived at some point and Jodi too, and then I was back in bed and then...

I'm back in this bloody cell. I need to go to the loo. That's what tea does to me. I stand and hold my middle finger up in front of one of the cameras. I hope the bastard is watching. I walk around the partition and sit on the loo. I sit for a long while, and then it strikes me, the damp smell is worse in here. I bend down and touch the wall next to the cistern and behind the toilet. The bricks feel wet. I scrape a fingernail down the line of mortar between a couple of the bricks, and little lumps come away.

I feel a flicker of hope. Maybe I won't need to be rescued. Maybe I can get out by myself. I look around again for cameras, but I think Rupert was being truthful when he said there are none here in the bathroom. I flush the loo and then kneel down in front of the wall. The mortar is soft, but it'll take me forever to flick it away with my fingernails, and I'll probably break them all in the process. What can I use instead?

I stand up and walk back into the cell. I glance at the easel. My painting of Rupert is turned to the wall so I don't have to look at it. And then I remember. I wonder if he brought all of my paints and brushes or whether he carefully sorted through the box. Hurriedly I position the box so that my body is blocking it from the cameras. I rifle through my brushes and there it is. My palette knife. It's not sharp and it's not strong, but it will be a darn sight better than using my nails to scrape away the mortar. I slip it up my sleeve. Then I take one of the brushes, turn the painting around – even though it repulses me – and stand in front of it, paintbrush held out in front of me. There is no bloody way I will be painting a single stroke onto that canvas. But let him think I'm considering it. After a couple of moments, I chuck the paintbrush into the air and let it tumble to the floor. It rolls across the concrete floor, collecting dust in its hairs.

I lie on the bed for ten minutes, but I'm too eager to get going on the bricks, so I hurry back to the loo. I don't want him to get suspicious, so I'll pretend I've got an upset stomach if he asks. Let him think his cooking is to blame.

I turn the palette knife over and over in my hands. Is it strong enough? Could I cause Rupert any damage with it if I attack him? Probably not. He's so much bigger and stronger than me. I kneel down in front of the toilet and start hacking away the mortar around a brick. It comes away surprisingly easily. After about fifteen minutes, I have removed a whole brick and I'm elated. I don't know what's behind the wall, but now there is a possibility of escape. There is a problem though. When I put the brick back in its place, it's obvious the mortar has been removed. I will need to use my paints to create an optical illusion, as if the mortar still surrounds each brick.

My knees creak as I stand up. I will chisel away at night so that he doesn't get suspicious of me spending so much time in here. Stretching, I wash my hands and am about to walk back into the cell when I hear footsteps and then the unbolting of the door. I shove the palette knife between the folds of my towel and am lying back on the bed, with my back to the door, when Rupert enters.

'Charlotte, love, are you alright? I noticed you were in the bathroom for a considerable time.'

'I've got a stomach upset,' I mumble. What is he doing? Sitting there watching me all day?

'That is such a shame, my dear. And on your birthday.'

I tremble. How the hell does he know it's my birthday?

'Turn around, my dear. I have some gifts for you.'

I debate ignoring his request, but I don't want to anger him, so I do as I'm told. He is holding a large bag from Selfridges.

'These are just a few modest tokens of my affection for you.' He takes out three wrapped gifts and places them on my bed.

'I don't want them,' I say, pushing them back towards him.

'Darling Charlotte, you mustn't see your stay in this room as a punishment. It is for your own well-being, and it certainly won't stop us from celebrating your birthday. I have a lovely breast of duck cooking in the oven and a fine bottle of champagne—'

'I don't want your bloody gifts or your birthday wishes. I've got no desire to celebrate it with you! You need to let me go. Let me go home!'

'Oh, Charlotte!' He tilts his head to one side and looks at me pityingly.

'My family will be looking for me, and the police will be arriving at any time. Don't you think Jodi will wonder why I haven't arrived home? Why I'm not there to celebrate my birthday with her, as I do every year?'

Rupert goes very pale and then his face is flooded with redness. His nostrils flare and his eyeballs look as if they might pop out of his skull. His lips flatten. He clenches his fingers up into tight fists, and for a moment I fear he is going to hit me. I quiver on the bed. But then he takes a deep breath and roars.

'I've gone to all of this trouble to cook you duck breast just how you like it, slightly pink on the inside! I've brought up the best bottle of champagne from the cellar, and I went especially to Selfridges to buy you presents that I know you will love! Just have the courtesy of opening them and you'll realise how considerate I have been. How dare you accuse me of being anything but kind! You can be a right little bitch!'

And with that he storms out of the room, slamming the door behind him. The bolts sound like they are being hammered into place. And once again I am terrified. For the first time, I wonder, if I don't comply with his crazy demands, will he kill me?

I lie with my hands over my head and the blanket wrapped tightly around me. I just want to go to sleep and wake up tomorrow when the police will arrive to rescue me. But a mere five minutes later, the footsteps are back and the bolts are being undone, and terror grips my throat.

'Turn around,' Rupert orders. I ignore him and he bellows at me, leaning right over my head. I do as he says, and he steps backwards, his arms crossed over his chest, regarding me as if I am a scientific specimen. Perhaps I am.

'I have a few things for you,' he says, a sardonic smile creeping across his face. He puts his hands into a plastic bag.

'Some of your post. You really do need to start paying your bills, Charlotte. Debts can get you into all sorts of trouble. The silk garments I suspect you were planning on wearing the night of your wedding. I found them shoved at the back of your underwear drawer, which incidentally is a disgrace. And here is the half-opened bottle of bath oil, which you left quite messily on the side of your bath. It's a sad little flat you live in, isn't it, Charlotte?'

I go berserk. I try to kick and punch him. I call him all sorts of names. I swear. I spit.

But then he grabs me in some sort of karate grip, and I know he is much too strong. I can't even move. He whispers in my ear, 'I thought you'd be grateful that I collected some of your things, that I checked on your post and watered your plants. Is this how you show gratitude, Charlotte?'

I whimper. I would like to be strong, but it's so hard when his arm is gripped around my neck and his foul breath is blowing on my face.

'Do you really think anyone is going to come looking for you here when they think you've gone back home? When Jodi sees your car parked outside and your keys, phone and wallet on the table, what do you think she'll do?' It's a rhetorical question because he continues. 'If your friends and family think you've returned to Macclesfield, they'll hardly come looking for you in Sussex, will they?'

He lets go of me suddenly and I stumble. I fall onto the mattress. He strides towards me and I cower, up against the wall. I wait for him to reach out, to hit me or worse. But he doesn't. He puts his hands in his pockets, and he just stares at me, his green eyes affixed on mine, gazing, cold, invasive. I don't understand what he wants. Why me? Why has he chosen me? And then to my horror, it's as if he has read my mind.

'I can't possibly hope that you will understand right now, but in the long run you'll realise that I have acted to secure our future happiness. All I want is for you to love me. Just a little bit at first. Is that so hard, Charlotte? Really?' He shakes his head slowly as if the concept of me hating rather than loving him is totally impossible to grasp, and then he sweeps my belongings into a plastic bag and leaves the room, bolting the door again behind him.

26

RUPERT, 1997

'Rupert, how are you, young man?'

I stand up as Harold Browne enters the waiting room. We shake hands and I follow him back into his office. He is wearing a green tweed jacket and a red bow tie. His white hair is too long and too wild and gives him the appearance of a mad professor rather than a country solicitor. His room smells and looks like a gentlemen's club, with dark green armchairs and the scent of tobacco. Legal tomes line the top shelves on his bookcase. A complete set of Wisden lines the bottom shelf. I have little doubt that Harold Browne knows more about cricket than he does about the law.

When Father went away, Harold Browne became my legal guardian. He arranged for Mrs Cherry to stay on at Sesame Hall and for Arthur to collect me from school during my exeats and to ferry me around during the holidays. He does the best he can to make life as smooth for me as possible. On the whole, I like him. He doesn't have any of his own children, so he talks to me as an adult, and I have always appreciated that.

'Once again, my sincerest condolences, Rupert,' he says as he sits heavily on his chair. It creaks ominously. As I have shed weight over the past two years, Harold has gained it. I suspect his portliness and bon vivant living has largely been funded thanks to Father. 'How are you bearing up, young man?'

'I am well, thank you, now that the shock of losing Father has sunk in.'

'Indeed. Indeed.' He shuffles some papers on his desk and then puts on his gold-framed reading glasses, leaning forwards towards me.

'As you know, I am the executor of your father's will, and as such, it is my responsibility to ensure that his final wishes are fulfilled. I have the will here.'

I grip the arms of the chair. I never saw Father again. Not since that horrendous day at the end of August three years ago. I tried. Oh yes, I tried. But they wouldn't let me in. And then Father wrote to me begging me to stay away, to start afresh. There is every possibility that Father might have cut me out of his will, and then I would be a pauper and a nobody. During the past three weeks, I have had too many sleepless nights mooting that possibility.

I think back to when I found out. Father's death came as a horrible shock. I was in my last term at school and had my own study room. It was 8 p.m. and there was a loud knock on my door.

'Baskerville, Mr Carruthers wants to see you. Now.'

When one is called to see the house master, it never bodes well. I thought back over the past couple of days and was sure that I had not infringed any regulations. It had been quite an ordinary week so far. I strode briskly along the corridor, down three flights of steps and rapped on Mr Carruthers's door.

'Come in!'

My heart was pounding. I might be an adult myself, about to leave school and launch myself into the world, but this tyrant of a man still had the ability to put fear into me.

'Have a seat, Baskerville.' He motioned to the upright

wooden chair in front of his desk. I'm not sure he ever asked me to have a seat before.

'I'm afraid I have some difficult news. Your father passed away last night.'

I sat there, motionless. It was if my brain had frozen and my limbs turned into stone. Father is dead. Father is dead. The words didn't make any sense.

'Your guardian, Harold Browne, will be arriving later today to collect you.'

'No,' I said, my fingers gripping my knees. 'I want to stay here. Please, sir, let me stay at school.'

And amazingly they did. I attended Father's funeral, of course. It was a private, dignified affair, conducted by an anonymous vicar that Harold found somewhere. At Harold's suggestion, Father was cremated, and his death was not publicised in the newspapers. The only people present were Harold and Marjorie Browne, Mrs Cherry and Arthur Stone. For that, I was very glad. I wanted the world to remember Father as the man he was, not the felon he had become.

'Rupert.' Harold tugs me back into the moment. 'As your father's only son, I can confirm that you will be inheriting everything.'

I let out a long whistle. Thank God.

'You seem surprised.' Harold stares at me, his spectacles slipping off his long nose.

'Not really. Father was a wonderful man, and I hope that I will be able to carry on doing his good works and maintaining the family name.'

Harold splutters. 'I trust you mean that you will reinstate the honour of your family name?'

'Indeed.'

'Have you thought about changing it? It might free you from the stigma of what–'

I stand up and lean my hands on his desk, my face just a foot away from his. 'I have nothing to be ashamed of. My father did what my father did, but the son should not be chastised for the sins of his father.'

Harold blinks rapidly. 'Quite so. Quite so. But the unfortunate circumstances surrounding the events of three years ago...' He lets his words fade away.

'Have been forgotten.' I sit down again.

Harold raises his bushy eyebrows. He is annoying me. He clears his throat, picks up the papers, and puts his glasses on again, pushing them back up his nose. 'Anyway, there are a few codicils to the will. Namely Mrs Cherry has been left ten thousand pounds, Arthur Stone has been left five thousand pounds, and I have been left twenty thousand pounds. The family of Simone Durand have been left thirty thousand pounds.'

'What!' I explode. 'No, that can't be right. I thought that was all done and dusted. It's blood money!' I stand up and start pacing around the room.

'Please, Rupert, relax. Sit down. Let me explain. Your father called me in to see him, some two and a half years ago now. Prior to then, he was talking about leaving his entire estate to a horse welfare charity. I persuaded him otherwise.' He pauses as if he wants that statement to sink in, as if I should somehow be grateful to him for Father's change of heart.

I scowl.

'At the time of the trial, your father knew he was dying.'

'What!' I exclaim. How can that be so? I stand stock-still and stare at Harold.

'Your father was diagnosed with cancer shortly before the unfortunate incident with the Frenchwoman. We had hoped that the judge might be lenient with his sentencing as a result of that, but it wasn't so. As you know, your father was sentenced to life in prison. Tragically, his remaining life was very short. He was adamant that you were not to be told that he was dying.'

'But why?' I gasp.

Harold shrugs his shoulders.

I feel tears smart my eyes. My father was a truly extraordinary man. So stoic, so generous, so able, so handsome. 'I hope that I will be like Father,' I murmur.

'Rupert, surely not!' Harold splutters. 'For all of his wonderful qualities, your father was still a convicted murderer.'

'The jury was wrong,' I say, jutting my chin forwards. 'It was an accident. A horrible accident.'

'Rupert, denying it–'

I cut him off again. 'May I remind you, Harold, as to who is paying your bills.'

Harold's eyebrows shoot up to meet his fuzzy hairline. He coughs and takes a sip from a flask, which I assume holds whiskey rather than water. I sit down again.

'And may I ask, what will you do now?'

'I have a place to read land management at Cirencester. I will complete my degree there, and then I shall move back to Sesame Hall and manage the estate. Exactly as my parents would have wished me to do.'

'Very good. Well done.' He looks away from me. 'I suppose my words about your father were perhaps a little harsh.'

I narrow my eyes at him. Nothing like backtracking when the damage has already been done.

'Other than the obvious aberration of murdering the au pair in a moment of passion, Sir Oswald was indeed a good man. And I am sure that you, Rupert–'

I butt in again. 'It's Sir Rupert now.'

'Indeed. Sir Rupert, that you will carry on the fine qualities and actions of your forefathers.'

'I have every intention of doing so,' I say, standing up and striding towards the door. With one hand on the door handle, I look back at him. 'Incidentally, Harold, once probate has been completed, you are fired.'

I smirk as I watch his face fall. I might have liked Harold Browne when I walked into his office, but now I'm leaving it, I realise that he is a sycophant. I am an adult now, with money and responsibilities. People who fawn and patronise have no place in my life.

27

RUPERT

Charlotte's behaviour shocked me, and I wonder if I've been a tad naive. I am certainly going to have to work harder than I anticipated to get her to love me. Perhaps it was unfair of me to quash her hopes of being rescued, to show her the items that I took from her flat. On the other hand, I find the fire in her belly very attractive. She has sparks and passion, and I cannot wait until we have a true lovers' tiff, and then we make up, clawing at each other, just as you see in films, collapsing into bed and making love with an intensity I can't even begin to imagine.

I am up early. I have been very distracted over the past week or so with Charlotte, and I have let my work slip. I cancelled a couple of meetings I was due to have with my tenant farmers, and I need to use the day wisely, to get up to date with my paperwork and ensure that everything is in order on the estate.

After Charlotte's shocking behaviour, she does not deserve a cooked breakfast. I consider starving her, but that certainly won't facilitate her falling in love with me. No. I shall do as Father did. A mixture of a strong hand and loving considera-tion. Be cruel to be kind. It worked for me. I make her a boiled egg, a piece of toast lightly buttered, and a cup of tea. I open the door with a degree of trepidation. But I have no need to be worried.

My Charlotte is back. She is sitting on the chair at the little table, her paints and brushes in front of her.

'How are you this morning?' I ask brightly.

'Fine, thank you. And you?'

'I slept very well. I hope you enjoy your breakfast. Let me know if you'd like another egg.'

'This is enough. Thank you.'

She doesn't look at me when she speaks, but her voice is calm. It was amazing what a firm hand and a good night's sleep can achieve. I place a pile of her clean clothes on the bed.

'Would you like me to bring you something to read, or will you do some painting today?' I ask.

She shrugs her shoulders. Perhaps she hasn't decided, as of yet. I don't push it.

'I have quite a busy day ahead, so I might be gone for a few hours. Will you be alright?'

I don't get a response, but this time it doesn't aggravate me. I remember that we are in this for the long game, Charlotte and I. Things that are worthwhile need to be worked at.

As I wander back upstairs, I imagine our wedding.

Charlotte will wear my mother's wedding dress, with her hair held up in a chignon and the long lacey veil stretched out behind her. Mother's sapphire engagement ring will be on her left ring finger. Her make-up will be minimal, just enough to enhance her natural beauty. I can't abide women who cake on artificial colours. I will be waiting in St Peter's Church, the beautiful little stone chapel in the village. The pews will be filled with guests, mainly villagers. Everyone will gasp at Charlotte's beauty as she walks down the aisle, alone, as her father is deceased, and I will be the proudest man on the planet as she takes my outstretched hand and smiles coyly beneath her veil. I will read her a poem I have written, even though it is years since I have put pen to paper. When the vicar declares us man and wife, she will swoon as I plant my lips on hers, and then she will grasp my hand as we walk together back down the aisle and out into the glorious sunshine.

Our honeymoon will be on Italy's Amalfi Coast. We will drive there in the Rolls Royce. There is nowhere more beautiful, more romantic, with fine food and wines, and that unsurpassed combination of rich history, breathtaking landscapes and exquisite architecture. Charlotte will spend her days painting and I will read, from time to time glancing up to enjoy my new wife's loveliness.

And then, joy of all joys. A couple of months after returning from our honeymoon, I will come home from work to a beautifully laid table with flowers and candles and champagne, and Charlotte will announce that she has something to tell me. My eyes will well up with unbridled joy as she says that we are expecting our first child. We will go together to the hospital for her scan, and I will overcome my distaste for all things medical. I will need to go, just to be sure. But then I will quickly realise that the worries for my love were all for nothing. The sonographer will turn to us with a wide smile and say, 'Congratulations, Sir Rupert and Lady Baskerville. You are expecting healthy twins. A boy and a girl.' We will dance out of there, and Charlotte will glide through the next seven months, blooming beautifully. Every night, I will lay my hands on her expanding belly and feel the kicking of our children. And when they are born, I will pace the corridor outside her hospital room until a nurse pokes her head around the door and says, 'You are the father of the most beautiful babies I have ever seen.'

I am sitting at my desk now, lost in my imaginings, when I am jolted back to the present by the ringing of the telephone.

'Sir Rupert, it's Charles Withyfield. Did you still want to walk the fences today?'

'Oh, Charles, I've been a little distracted with other matters. What's the time?' I glance at my watch and am shocked to discover that a whole hour has slipped by. 'I'll meet you by the front gates in ten minutes.'

I hurry to the cloakroom and put on my Barbour and boots. This is what Charlotte is doing to me. She has taken my mind hostage. It seems that I can think of no one or nothing else. It is just as well the estate is a well-oiled machine that can run largely without my daily input.

Charles Withyfield is my tenant farmer, the one who has the largest acreage. His father farmed the land before him and worked with my father. Charles is an equally hard worker, and despite the doldrums in agriculture, a result of poor politics and the interference by Europe, Charles manages to turn a solid profit, which benefits us both. Once every two months, we walk the land.

'How are things with you, Charles?'

He is a very tall man and I have to walk quickly to keep up with his lengthy strides.

'Very good, sir. And yourself?'

'Likewise.' I would love to tell him. I know the locals would like me to find a wife. But it's too soon.

We walk down towards the river. 'What measures are you putting in place to stop flooding this year, Charlotte?'

He throws me the strangest glance, his ruddy face and bright blue eyes crinkling like crepe paper. For a moment I'm not sure why, and then I realise I've just called him Charlotte instead of Charles.

'Apologies,' I bluster. 'I've just had my portrait painted by a charming woman called Charlotte.'

'Oh yes. When will we see it?'

'When it's completed, I shall hang it in the grand hall.' I need to change the subject, so we start talking about the price of sheep and his plans for the flock, and I concentrate carefully when calling him by his name.

I'm not back at Sesame Hall until gone 2 p.m., and I'm very concerned that I haven't given Charlotte any lunch. I would have liked to have cooked her a roast, but instead I have to make her some sandwiches.

I've missed her during the four hours I have been out with Charles. I couldn't even watch her on my phone. I turn the app on as I'm lathering butter onto bread. Where is she? The room is empty. For a horrible moment, I think she might have escaped, but then I laugh out loud. There is no possibility of escaping from the punishment room. I know that for a fact. Year after year, I sought a means of escape and failed. Not that it did me any harm. She must be in the bathroom. I slap a piece of ham onto the bread and cut up a few slices of cucumber and tomato.

Hurrying downstairs, I unlock the door, and there she is. My beautiful love, sitting on her bed, clutching her knees.

'My sincerest apologies for the tardiness of lunch,' I say.

She shrugs her shoulders.

'I was in a hurry to get it to you, but later I'll bring you some books to read. How are you getting on with the painting?'

I turn the easel around, and my portrait looks exactly the same as it did yesterday. I am disappointed, but this time I don't say anything. I turn and leave.

THE PHONE RINGS again in the evening.

'Good evening. Can I speak to Sir Rupert Baskerville?'

'This is he.'

'My name is Detective Sergeant Timothy Black. We are investigating the disappearance of Charlotte Aldridge. I understand that she was staying with you.'

I nearly drop the blasted phone. Damnation. I didn't expect

that the police would be in touch quite so soon. I need to think quickly.

'Sorry, I'm not following you. Did you say that Charlotte has disappeared?'

'Yes, sir.'

'How terrible. Where has she disappeared from?'

'Can you confirm that she was staying with you?'

'Yes, she did stay with me. Charlotte is an artist, and I commissioned her to paint me. She left Sesame Hall on Friday. I'm afraid that was the last contact I had with her. What has happened?'

'We are still investigating, sir. She has been reported as missing.'

'Might she have had an accident on her way back to Cheshire? Goodness, that would be terrible.'

'No, sir. Her car is parked outside her home.'

'Could she have gone to stay with friends or her sister?' I ask.

'We are investigating, but it appears not.'

'Would you like me to organise a search here in Sussex? Would that be of help?'

'No, sir. We believe that she has gone missing in or around her hometown of Macclesfield. Her essential belongings seem to be there.'

'This is terrible news. Charlotte is such a delightful person. I had a very enjoyable time with her whilst she was here.'

'Did she express any concerns at all?'

I pause. 'I understand her fiancé died tragically some months ago. I got the feeling that she is still grieving.'

'Indeed. But there was nothing else out of the ordinary?'

'I don't think so. Of course, I don't know her well. We only met for the first time a fortnight or so ago.'

'Thank you for your time. If you think of anything that might be relevant, please let me know.'

'And likewise. I would be very grateful if you could notify me when she reappears. I have a lot of respect for her.'

I put the phone down, lift my arms above my head and let out a very long exhale. *So, my little Charlotte, your friends and family must love you very much if they're already on to the police.* That doesn't surprise me. She is indeed loveable. But it means I will have to be extra careful. But after a while, I discount my concern. No one thinks she's here. I have covered my tracks carefully. Even so, I pour myself a small glass of whiskey and it's well before my drinking hour of 6 p.m.

28

JODI

Rohan doesn't stay the night. I think he would have liked to, but I wasn't in the mood. How can I enjoy a dinner when Charlotte isn't there? Call it telepathy or whatever you like, but I have a sixth sense that something is seriously wrong. I promised Rohan that we would go out for dinner as soon as Charlie was home and life was back on an even keel. I don't want to lose my chance with him, but Charlie is my sister, and no one will ever be more important than her.

I sleep fitfully, leaving my mobile phone on, with the volume turned up high, and placed on the pillow next to me. I wake at 4 a.m. There are no missed calls, no text messages. I try her landline and her mobile again but, as before, get her answer phone. I am sick with worry.

At 6.30 a.m. I must have dozed off because I wake with a start. My phone is still silent, but a thought has hit me. Where is the portrait of Sir Rupert? Charlie expressly said that she would bring it home with her to finish off, but unless she has hidden it somewhere, it was not in her flat and certainly wasn't on her easel, which is where she normally leaves her current project.

I wait until 8 a.m. and then call the police station again.

'I reported my sister missing yesterday. The thing is, she told me that she was bringing a painting home with her, and it's not in her flat.'

'Please, miss, start at the beginning.'

So I do. I repeat what I told the policeman yesterday, that she was staying at Sir Rupert Baskerville's house to paint his portrait, and that it looks as if she's come home, but she hasn't brought the portrait with her, and that doesn't make sense.

'Perhaps she changed her mind?' the policeman suggests.

'No.'

'You say she drove home and her car is outside her house?'

'Yes.'

'Could the painting still be in the car? Perhaps in the boot?'

Of course it could be. I didn't check. I'm furious with myself, but I'm not letting my concerns go.

'And the other thing is, Sir Rupert asked her to marry him. He really creeped her out. They'd only known each other for just over a week, and it wasn't as if she was in a relationship with him. It's weird.'

'Do you have reason to believe that your sister is at risk of harm?'

'No,' I say reluctantly. I know that Charlie is still heart-broken from Matthew's death, but I don't think she's suicidal. 'But this is totally out of character and I'm worried sick. We're sisters. She would never miss her birthday party or not contact me.'

He asks me some more questions about Charlie and then gives me a police reference number. He tells me to call back if I hear from Charlotte.

'Please, can you speak to Sir Rupert Baskerville? He was the last person to talk to Charlotte.'

'We will do our best.'

I don't know if he will.

I feel thoroughly disillusioned by the time I put the phone down. I don't feel as if the policeman took Charlie's disappearance seriously. Yes, he asked all the right questions, but there was a weariness to his voice, as if a grown woman going missing was very far down on their list of priorities.

After drinking a cup of tea, I find my knackered, old laptop and fire it up. I go online and search for Sir Rupert. Up comes everything that Charlie discovered. He's a magistrate, the owner of a large estate, he supports all sorts of charities, and the locals think he's a bloody saint. I look for information on his family. An only child. His mother died when he was a kid, and his father, Sir Oswald, died in 1997. I do a search for the father and then, bloody hell, I see a news headline. I am positive that Charlie didn't find this.

Baronet Convicted of Killing French Au Pair

Sir Rupert's father was a murderer! The article doesn't tell me much, just that a twenty-one-year old girl, Simone Durand, was found dead on the living room floor of Sesame Hall. Sir Oswald admitted murdering her by feeding her with rat poison combined with some long-worded drug that I've never heard of. What a scandal.

It's not surprising Rupert is odd with those tragedies in his childhood. How awful to lose your mother to cancer and then for your father to be convicted of murder. I note that he didn't last two years in prison. There is no mention as to the cause of Sir Oswald's death. I wonder if he was beaten to death in prison for being a privileged toff.

But just because his father killed the au pair doesn't mean that Sir Rupert has harmed Charlie. The thing that doesn't make sense to me is the portrait. I decide to go back to Charlie's flat in Macclesfield, and if I can't find it, then I will investigate myself. I have today and tomorrow off work, and if I need to take Charlie's car and drive down to Sussex, I will do.

But first I call every single friend of Charlie's whom I have the number for. Unsurprisingly, no one has seen or spoken to her for about a fortnight.

I DON'T HAVE A CAR. Driving and parking are hopeless in south Manchester, and I get to work easily on a bike. The downside is that I have to take the train to Macclesfield, and by the time I'm back outside Charlie's flat, it's nearly noon. With an overnight bag over my shoulder, I hold my breath as I put my finger on the buzzer. There's no answer. I take my keys and let myself in, and it's exactly as I found it last night. Charlie's belongings are all there, but she's not. Nor is the unfinished painting of Sir Rupert.

I look at the photos of Charlie and Matthew. They were so happy together. The golden couple. I can't imagine Matthew getting into a fight; he was such a gentle man. But as the months have passed and the police enquiry into his death has stalled, I have begun to question things. Perhaps he had been drinking. Perhaps it wasn't just a random act of violence. Perhaps he provoked someone. It's possible.

Sighing, I pick up Charlie's car keys. I nip downstairs and out to the road and open the boot to Charlie's car. It is empty. The painting isn't there. Locking the car again, I race back up to the flat and leave her a note on the table. *I've taken your car. Call me the second you read this! Jx*

I decide to lock the flat this time. I can't risk anyone breaking in, and if Charlie finds herself locked out, I'll be the first person she contacts. Besides, the idiot downstairs will tell her I'm looking for her. I will drive her car to Sussex and look Sir Rupert in the eyes.

29

CHARLOTTE

After Rupert made it clear that he went into my flat and stole some of my belongings, I am filled with a terrifying fury. I know, without a shadow of doubt, that if I had a knife or a gun, I would kill him. That scares me, as I have never been inclined to violence, or even joked about it in a flippant way. But now, I honestly think I could kill Rupert, and what is even worse, I might take pleasure in it. Surely that makes me a wicked person, as bad as the drug dealer who murdered Matthew? But then I remind myself that I am acting in self-defense. If Rupert wasn't keeping me hostage, it would never cross my mind to harm him. Obviously Rupert is mentally sick, but now I wonder if he's more than that. Surely only an evil person would drive halfway across the country to cover his tracks? He professes to love me, but I doubt he knows what love is.

At least my anger fuels action. I spend every moment I can in the bathroom. I turn the shower on to make noise, and I gouge at the mortar with an intense ferocity.

This morning, when Rupert brought me breakfast, I told him that the bathroom is my sanctuary, the only place I can go for privacy, somewhere away from the cameras and his prying eyes. I hope he believed me. Even so, I am careful. I spend fifteen minutes in there, digging, gouging, and then wait at least an hour before returning for more.

But now I am feeling some hope. After I removed the first brick, it exposed another brick behind it, and as I remove the mortar, I am sure I can see daylight. I go faster and faster and then kneel forwards. Ouch. I scrape my knuckle on the pile of mortar I've flicked on to the floor. My right hand is bleeding, a trickle of blood making its way down to my wrist. I wipe it with a piece of toilet paper. I must carry on. My fingers are aching and sore. It's hard work using this little palette knife, especially as the second layer of bricks is less damp and the mortar is more solid. But still I can't stop.

As I remove each brick, my hope increases and I celebrate, just a little. The hole is getting bigger and bigger. I can flick the mortar through to the other side now. I mix up my acrylic paint to match the colour of the mortar and blend it into some of the mortar fragments and dust that I have chiseled away. I use this mixture to create fake mortar around all of the bricks that I have loosened. The beige colour matches perfectly, but the lines of mortar are a little thinner than elsewhere. I hope I don't run out of paint. But the effect is good. Only if someone carefully inspected it could you tell that the mortar is fake and nothing is cementing the bricks together.

I have removed seven bricks. Two on top, three underneath and two behind, and it won't be long before the hole is large enough for me to crawl through. But I only leave a gap of one brick at a time. I can't take the risk of Rupert being in the adjacent room and seeing the hole. I have had a good peek through to the other side, and it looks as if the room is empty: just another space, similar to my cell, with a concrete floor and exposed brick walls, and a high-level window. A duplicate cell with nothing in it.

And then I hear footsteps and I need to hurry. I shove the bricks back and slide my tools and paints under my towel, but I don't have time to evaluate my handiwork. What is Rupert doing visiting me now? It's 11.15 a.m. and normally he restricts his visits to mealtimes. I jump up and race into the bedroom just as he opens the door. He stands there holding a large carrier bag, and he stares at me, his eyes moving slowly down my legs.

I follow his gaze to my knees and see the dust and cobwebs and flecks of mortar on my trousers. My heart sinks.

'What have you been doing?' Rupert asks coldly.

'The sink was blocked. I tried to unblock it.'

'I'll have a look.'

I step in front of him to try to stop his path to the bathroom. 'It's fine. I sorted it. It's full of caked-up limescale. It's probably because it hasn't been used much until now.'

But my blustering doesn't stop Rupert. He steps around me and walks behind the partition wall. I feel sick, unsure whether to follow him, or just to await my fate. What will he do to me? Have I just blown my sole chance of escape?

I hold my breath as my heart hammers hard and my gut clenches. I hear him turn the tap on and off again. And then two footsteps and he is back from the partition and standing in front of me. His face is expressionless.

'I can't see anything amiss,' he says.

'I told you I fixed it,' I say. 'I used the wooden end of my long paintbrush to dislodge the gunge.'

He nods, but again he stares at my knees. I wipe the debris off my trousers and then wonder if he noticed my sore knuckles. But his eyes are now on my face.

'I have something for you.' He turns to the table and I think now. Now is the time I can punch him, shove my fingers in his eyes, and I lift my arm ready to swing it. But he turns. A frown on his face.

I let my arm drop to my side. It is futile. I already know how strong he is. The only way I can hurt him is if I get hold of an implement. Something more ferocious than my paints and palette knife.

He holds out a large plastic bag with the name of a famous art supplies store on the side.

'I have bought you some new paints.'

'I've already got paints.'

'Indeed. But insufficient. If you need any more, just let me know and I'll buy them. I have also purchased some new brushes. Please, take the bag.'

I accept it gladly, but not for the reason Rupert thinks. My fake mortar uses a lot of materials, and I am running out of paint. I follow his eyes and I see that he has noticed my sore knuckle. He sucks in his breath but doesn't say anything. I turn around and empty the bag onto the table. Good heavens! He has spent hundreds of pounds on paints and brushes. There are numerous Winsor and Newton professional-grade paint tubes and kolinsky sable brushes in a wide selection of sizes and shapes.

'There's enough paint here to fill a gallery with canvases,' I exclaim. If I weren't being held a prisoner by a demented man, I would be overjoyed to be given so many expensive paints and fine quality brushes.

'And indeed, that is the plan. You need to start painting again. I have the most exciting opportunity for you. I have arranged for you to have an exhibition at a famous gallery in Mayfair, London. It's run by an old friend of mine, and I showed him pictures of your work, and he's agreed to hold a solo exhibition for you. Isn't that marvelous?' He claps his hands together and his eyes are bright.

This seems absurd. He is keeping me prisoner, but at the same time he is promising me an exhibition in London. I am wary. Where is he going with this?

'You will need to prepare fifteen paintings over the next three months. I want three of those paintings to be self-portraits. The rest can be of any subject matter of your choice, so long as animals or people feature in them. If you tell me what size canvases you would like, I will get them for you.' He is pacing around the cell, excitedly now, rubbing his hands together. I don't react. He steps towards me and puts a hand on my shoulder.

'Aren't you happy, Charlotte? This is a phenomenal opportunity for you. A dream come true. You'll get the fame and fortune you deserve, and I will be your manager, making sure that we secure the very best deals.'

'Will I be allowed out of here? You can't expect me to paint in this dungeon!' I feel a glimmer of hope.

'Of course, my darling. I want the world to know about you.'

'So you'll let me out today, and then I can start painting?'

'No, Charlotte. That's not what I said. When you love me, I'll let you go. And I mean true love. I will know when that happens. For now, you will paint in here. You need to earn my trust, to show me that your emotions are as genuine as mine and that you are ready to accept my hand in marriage. Then you will be free to come and go as you wish because I will know that your heart is mine and mine is yours.'

The hope fades.

'So you'll start painting?' he asks, his pupils wide and the cleft in his chin pulsating as if a nerve has got stuck in it.

I shrug my shoulders. Painting is the last thing I feel like doing.

'What sized canvases should I get you?'

I shrug my shoulders again. Who cares? I won't be painting.

His eyes narrow. 'Finish my portrait, and I will bring you a selection of canvases tomorrow.'

I turn away from him. I hear him unlock the door, then bolt

it again behind himself. He can shove the canvases where the sun doesn't shine.

I lie on the mattress and listen to his footsteps fade away upstairs, and then about five minutes later I hear a car starting up, and the roar of its engine fades away into the distance. I wait another five minutes and then walk to the bathroom.

Two more bricks. Just two more bricks and I'll be through. I don't care about my painful knees where I've been kneeling for too long, or the stinging from my bloodied knuckles. I am so nearly there. I dig the palette knife hard into the mortar on the last remaining brick, and just when I'm nearly there, the palette knife snaps.

'Shit!' I yell.

I scratch at it with my fingernails, I kick it with my foot. Perspiration is dripping down my forehead, my top is wet with sweat, but I don't care. I am so nearly there. And then one final shove, and the brick tumbles out into the other side, into the empty room. The hole is big enough for me to climb through. I push my head in first and wriggle my shoulders. It's tight, and my shoulders and upper arms are scraped raw, even through the cotton of my top. But once my shoulders are through, I can wriggle the rest of my body through. I yelp as a large splinter digs into the palm of my left hand. But it doesn't matter because I can breathe freedom. My legs tumble through the hole, and I lie panting on my back, so relieved to be out.

Catching my breath, I stand up and look around. It is an identical room to my cell, and I just have to pray that the door isn't locked. I am hopeful because this door actually has a handle. I walk across the empty room.

I am going to have to move so quickly because if Rupert has his cameras rigged up to his phone, then he will see me dashing through the house, running as fast as I can down the drive. I just have to pray that he is far away, that I can reach freedom before he returns to Sesame Hall. I take a few deep breaths to ready myself. I say a silent prayer that this door isn't locked. Closing my eyes briefly, I inhale as I slowly turn the handle. It moves easily. I push the door, just a little, and I want to jump for joy. It opens. It creaks, but I push it a little harder now. I count down from three, so I am fully ready to run as fast as I can, opening the door as I do so. Three. Two. One. I inhale, ready to go, and then I scream.

Rupert is standing there, his legs planted wide, a look of terrible fury on his face.

30

RUPERT

She must take me for a bloody idiot. There she was, trying to look all innocent with dust and rubble on her trousers and scratches on her hands. I bought her excuse to begin with, as it's hard for me to think of Charlotte as anything but perfect. All I want is to make her happy. I almost grabbed her sore hand and brought it to my lips, in an effort to kiss it better, but I knew she wouldn't have appreciated that. Not yet, anyway. So I left her. I got back into the Aston Martin and took off down the drive. I had a meeting with my accountant, but it's not possible to concentrate on tax returns when your ideal partner is waiting for you in your house. So I stopped at the gates to get a quick fix from looking at my love on the app on my phone. And once again, she wasn't there.

Charlotte was spending too much time in the bathroom. I don't like to think the worst of her, but my suspicions were raised. I turned the car around and drove back up the drive, approaching as quietly as possible. I didn't park around the back of the Hall as I normally do, because the roar of my engine and the crunch of my tyres can be heard from the punishment room. I know that because I used to listen to

Father drive away, leaving me sobbing pathetically. Instead, I drove to the front of the Hall and got out of the car, shutting the door as gently as I could. I opened the front door, removed my leather shoes and tiptoed in my socks downstairs.

And then I heard a crashing sound. It didn't take much imagination to work out what was going on. Charlotte underestimated my knowledge of Sesame Hall. I have lived here all my life and know every nook and cranny, which floorboards creak, which doors stick and which rooms have rising damp. I rushed to the room next to the punishment room, and then she flung open the door, and here I am, standing in front of her, disappointment rushing through my veins like the spring meltwater from a glacier.

I honestly thought that Charlotte was becoming more malleable and more loving. She seemed delighted with the new paints and brushes and over the last twenty-four hours hasn't been averse to communicating with me. Two days ago, she wouldn't look me in the eye. Today I have got lost in the depths of her soulful blue eyes, as blue as the azure Tyrrhenian Sea that laps the rocks of the Amalfi Coast, where Charlotte and I will be spending our honeymoon. But now I know the truth. She hasn't been more loving; she has been conning me and planning her escape.

Charlotte lied to me, and now she must be punished. I have tried to be gentle with her, but my methods have failed. It is clear that I will have to grind her down, break her in like a young filly. It will be hard for me to be forceful with my love, but I know I must. I suppose that is how Father felt when he punished me. I know he loved me, his only son. And I know that he tried to hide his feelings because that is what we upper-class British do. A stiff upper lip and all that. It has served us well throughout history: hiding our emotions, thinking rationally, conquering the empire. And I must learn from that. However painful it will be for me and for Charlotte, I can see now that the only way I will get her to respect me is to use the stick. The carrot has failed.

She tries to push past me, but I grab her, clutching her upper arms so hard, I know my fingers will leave raw purple bruises.

'I am so disappointed in you,' I say, my voice low and quiet. I use the tone that Father used when admonishing me, and I am startled at how similar my voice sounds to his.

She kicks me hard in the shin, so I wrench her arms behind her back, clasping her wrists together. They are so fragile and slender I fear they will snap in my hands.

'Stop it!' I order.

She screams. I have three options. Ignore her. Slap her in the face. Kiss her lips. The latter is the most attractive and perhaps she will succumb, but then I don't want her to think I would rape her, because I would never do anything like that. I am not naturally a violent man. So I ignore her. I am the bigger person, as Father used to say about himself, and I drag her back to the punishment room, her feet scraping across the floor, her screams piercing my eardrums.

When we are safely inside, with the door locked, I release my grip on her wrists, and she comes for me, attacking me like a wild animal. She kicks and spits at me, calling me names, and I can feel the anger rising and rising within me. With a roar, I swing my hand at her, slapping her cheek.

'I am giving you just one warning,' I say. 'If you don't stop, I will hit you. Not a stinging smack like that, but a proper wallop. And it will hurt very much. I don't want to hurt you, but I will.'

And it works, she shrinks away from me, curling back onto the bed in a foetal position.

'I have tried the loving approach, Charlotte, but it's clear that has failed. It spears my heart, but it is evident that you react better to the stick approach. I will break your spirit and rebuild you again. You will appreciate it. You will emerge a better, stronger, more loving person. You will thank me.'

When Father betrayed me with Simone, he broke my spirit. But then I forgave him and I emerged a superior man. It will work for Charlotte too.

Now I need to remove all of the creature comforts that I so carefully put into the punishment room to make it feel more homely, but first I need to secure the hole in the wall.

'If you try to escape again, Charlotte, I will hurt you so badly, you will scream for mercy. It will break my heart to have to do that, so I suggest that you stay here and ruminate on what you have done.'

I lock the door behind me and go in search of my toolkit. I find a piece of plywood in the shed adjacent to the garages and carry that through to the cellar next to the punishment room. I screw the wood to the wall and then place a heavy-duty lock on the door along with some bolt locks, just in case. Then I find a couple of those collapsible plastic crates and go back into Charlotte's room.

'Get up!' I order her. She ignores me, so I lean over her on the bed and raise my hand. She trembles. My love trembles. But the threat works. She scrambles off the mattress and cowers in the corner of the room. I strip the bed and fold the blanket and duvet and pillowcase. Then I go into the bathroom and remove her towels, her toiletries and her clothes. I leave her toothbrush and toothpaste but nothing else. I take out the table and chair, the flowers in the plastic pot. I vacillate as to whether I should leave her painting equipment or not, and decide for now to remove it. She should have no pleasures. It is imperative that Charlotte is left to cogitate on what she has done, what she has brought upon herself.

Locking her in again, I go in search of items to put in her room. I bring her a bar of cheap soap and one small towel.

'These are so you can wash yourself.' I drop them on the

mattress. I have left the bottom fitted sheet, but no covers. She will be cold in here and that makes me sad. Oh, Charlotte, why have you done this? It breaks my heart that I need to punish you.

It is clear that I will need to watch her all the time, now she has shown herself to be so untrustworthy, so I fix another camera in the corner of the bathroom.

'What are you doing in there?' she asks.

'Obviously I regret removing all your privacy, but you have forced me into it. As I can't trust you, I need to have the facility of watching you at all times.'

'You're disgusting! A pervert!' she cries. The high-pitched tone goes right through me.

'No, Charlotte, I am not. I have no desire to watch you doing your ablutions. You have brought this all upon yourself.'

'You're a monster! How can you do this to me? Please, please let me go home. I will never tell anyone, and we can both get on with our lives.'

'No!' I roar. I don't want to lose my temper, but she is pushing me so, so hard. Charlotte quivers; her back is against the wall, her arms in front of her head, as if she thinks I am going to hit her and she needs to protect herself. I have to take myself out of the room; otherwise I will hurt her. I stride to the door, slam it shut behind me and lock her in.

Charlotte, oh Charlotte. I didn't want to use the methods of my father, but you have given me no choice. I climb back upstairs, along the corridor and unlock my study. Father kept the leather belt in the top drawer of his desk. I didn't know that when I was young and only found it when he was sent to prison. I remember the poignant moment when I pulled open that drawer and there it lay, all supple and innocent. I took it out and ran it through my fingers. How could something so innocuous looking inflict so much pain? I drew it back and it whistled through the air, and when it hit the desk, a book flew off it. I needed to know what it felt like to use it on a living being, but I'm no masochist. The only living thing was my father's old mongrel, who hadn't stopped moping around since Father went away. When it came limping into the study, I drew the belt back and whipped it down on the dog's back. It yelped and ran away with the speed of a dog ten years younger. It never came back.

And now Charlotte is forcing me to use it on her. It saddens me, for Charlotte is, in so many ways, perfect. I won't give her as many lashes as Father used to give me. She is so slender and fragile. Half as many. No, a third perhaps. I need to think about where I will lash her. Father used to alternate between my hands, my back, my thighs and my backside. It is unthinkable to whip Charlotte's hands, those magical fingers, which she uses to paint with and which will, in due course, caress my skin. Her legs are so shapely and it appalls me to think that they might be covered in red welts. Besides, I need her to be strong on her legs; otherwise she won't be able to wear high heels. And her back, well, her back may also be visible if she wears backless dresses or a bikini. When we are sunbathing in Amalfi, of course she will wear a bikini. It leaves me with only one option. Her pert little backside. I would so much prefer to be running my hands over her rear end, but it is the only part of her body that will not be visible, and goodness, does it hurt. I recall all of those long summer days when I couldn't bear to sit down because of the pain, when I tried to put a book down my trousers, but Father realised and gave me twice as many lashes as a double punishment.

It worked. Father always knew what was best for me, and I know what is best for Charlotte. My darling Charlotte.

31

JODI

I
t's a long way to West Sussex. I'm not used to driving and have to concentrate extra hard. It struck me halfway down the M6 that I'm not even sure if I'm insured to drive Charlie's car. So then I slowed down even more and crawled along in the slow lane, wedged between vast articulated lorries. When I stop off for a sandwich and coffee in a service station, I do an online search for somewhere to stay. There is a pub with rooms and a bed and breakfast just outside the local village. If they are full, there's a proper hotel in Pulborough and a few properties listed on Airbnb. It's not as if it's a busy time of year, so I'm hopeful I won't struggle to find a cheap room. I decide to head to the pub first, as it's the nearest and not too expensive.

It's dark by the time I arrive. The pub is attractive. An olde worlde building with low black beams interspersed with white walls. There are a couple of elderly men sitting up at the bar, and a woman, not much older than me, with frizzy black hair and a large mole on her right cheek is wiping down glasses.

'Do you have a free room for tonight?' I ask, trying to stifle my yawn. The two old men look up and stare at me. I stare right back.

'Sure,' she says, putting the glasses down and grabbing a large leather book. She takes my details and hands me a wrought-iron key with a red tassel attached to it.

'It's up the stairs, second room on the left. Would you like a table for supper?'

'I'll just grab some sandwiches later, if I may.'

'Of course. Enjoy your stay.'

The room is small, with a low ceiling, but it is clean and warm. I am so exhausted I collapse on the bed. When I wake up, it is 9 p.m. and too late to trek over to Sesame Hall. I want to be alert and refreshed before confronting Sir Rupert. I splash my face with water, straighten my clothes and go downstairs to the bar. I don't feel like sitting at a table by myself in the restaurant or bar, so I bring my plate with a BLT and chips and a glass of orange juice up to my room. By 10 p.m., I am fast asleep.

THE MORNING IS grey and far from the sunny Sussex that I was expecting. I try Charlotte's home and mobile numbers for about the hundredth time. Still no answer. After a strong cup of coffee and several pieces of toast, I reckon now is as good a time as any.

I pack up and check out.

There is a different woman on duty, older with equally frizzy hair and a face lined with as many wrinkles as a walnut. I assume she is the landlady, and perhaps the woman serving last night is her daughter.

'Please can you give me directions to Sesame Hall?' I ask, after I have paid.

'Of course. Turn left out of the village, carry on for about two miles, and you'll see a sign to the Hall just after the letterbox on the right-hand side. Such a nice man, Sir Rupert.'

I nod my thanks and leave. I doubt I'll ever become a member of the Sir Rupert fan club.

Sesame Hall is exactly as Charlie described it – a red-brick monstrosity. Well, perhaps that's a bit strong, but it certainly isn't a beautiful stately home. I walk up the wide steps and ring the brass doorbell. When there's no answer, I ring it again, and then I hear footsteps and the door is flung open.

Sir Rupert is tongue-tied. I thought he might not recognise me, after all we only met the once, and I don't look anything like Charlie. But he does.

'W-w-what are you doing here?'

'I need to talk to you,' I say, staring at him. He looks away, his eyes darting everywhere except in my direction, his fingers clenching and unclenching. 'Are you going to let me in?' I ask after a long silence. It's as if a switch has been flipped in his brain because then he becomes Sir Charming.

'Yes, yes! How rude of me. It is lovely to see you, Jodi. Please come in.' He stands to one side, and I walk past him into the dark hallway stuffed full of terrifying paintings and medieval armour. 'I am so distressed that Charlotte has gone missing. I had a phone call from the police. Please tell me you have brought good news.'

'She's still missing,' I say curtly.

'That's terrible. I became very fond of Charlotte.'

So fond that you asked her to marry you, I want to say. But I hold my tongue. I need to get more information out of this man before I antagonise him.

'What can I do to help?' He frowns and shifts uneasily from foot to foot.

'I've got a few questions.'

'Yes, yes. Of course you will have. Please come in. Would you like a coffee?'

'Thank you,' I say.

'Come through to the drawing room.'

I follow him along the dark corridor into the vast living room. I look around and wonder which chair Charlie sat in.

Did she paint him in here? I am relieved that the police have taken Charlotte's disappearance sufficiently seriously to have telephoned Sir Rupert.

Rupert sits down on a high-backed chair covered in loose green covers. 'I told the gentleman on the phone that Charlotte left here on Friday. I offered to undertake a search; however, he told me that her car was parked outside her home and that she has gone missing in Macclesfield.'

'Mmm,' I say, sitting in a floral chintz-covered chair.

'Anyway,' he says in a chirpy voice, standing up again, 'how do you take your coffee?'

'White, no sugar, please.'

'Coming right up!'

I am surprised that living in a house as grandiose as this, Sir Rupert doesn't have staff. Perhaps all the money has run out and they're asset rich and cash poor. I wander around the room, picking up trinkets from the mantelpiece and examining them: silver dishes, china statues of animals and women in strange poses from bygone ages. I shiver as I look at the stuffed boar's head on the wall and the taxidermy owl stuck for eternity in a glass dome. I am standing in front of a detailed painting, men seated around a fire, smoking, women hauling bales of hay on their backs, when Sir Rupert creeps back into the room. He startles me.

'Do you have a similar appreciation of art to your sister?' he asks as he places a tray on a glass side table.

'No, I haven't got a clue about paintings.' I sit back down.

My eyes widen as I watch him pour coffee from a very ornate silver coffee pot.

'I can't stand those modern coffee machines that seem to be everywhere these days. Real coffee needs to be ground and poured from a silver pot.'

I don't say anything but think, *You pretentious git.*

He hands me a small porcelain cup, in cream with a gold band around the rim. Then he sits down opposite me.

'How can I help, Jodi?'

'Can I see the painting that Charlie made of you?'

'Regrettably not. I haven't got it. Your sister took it home to finish off.'

I lean forwards, my hands on my knees, my eyes trained on his face. 'That's strange, because it's not there. It's not in Charlie's flat nor in her car. Are you sure it's not still here?'

His eyes narrow. 'I am absolutely certain it is not here. What are you suggesting?'

'I don't know. What do you think?'

Sir Rupert stands up and then immediately sits down again.

'I gather you asked Charlie to marry you?' I say.

He licks his lips and tugs his ear. 'It was a bit of banter. We get on very well together, and I understand that your sister lost her fiancé and is feeling somewhat lonely. I offered to marry her should she not get a better proposition. Not, of course, that this is any business of yours.'

'Everything to do with Charlie is my business,' I say, abruptly standing up.

'Quite so. Indeed. She is your sister. But you are nothing like each other, are you? You don't look like each other. You don't act like each other.'

'No. I am not nearly as trusting or as nice a person as Charlie.' I have no intention of explaining our family make-up to this man.

He stands up now too. He is breathing very quickly and clenching his fists by his sides.

'It's time for you to go, Jodi,' he says, walking to the door and holding it open for me.

'With pleasure,' I say, striding past him along the corridor and back out into the hall, my trainers squeaking on the wooden floor. I open the front door before he can get to it.

'It was good to meet you again, and I sincerely hope that Charlotte turns up soon.' There is an insincerity to the tone of his voice, and it fills me with dread.

Now it's my turn to narrow my eyes at him. 'You'll be hearing from me and from the police,' I say. I bolt out of the front door, run down the steps to Charlie's car, and start it up as quickly as I can. As I'm driving away, I glance in the rear-view mirror. Sir Rupert is standing on the steps, his arms crossed, watching me go.

ON THE FACE OF IT, there was nothing that Sir Rupert said that suggests he is anything but innocent. The trouble is, I don't believe him. Call it a sixth sense or just a gut feeling, but I know he's lying. And I don't know why. If I was being sensible, I would drive straight back north, but I'm not sensible. I'm desperate. I need to find Charlie. I'm staying put.

I head back for the local village and park the car in front of a cute little village shop. There are boxes of vegetables outside. Inside they sell all sorts of day-to-day items typical of a convenience store. There is also a post office counter – a surprise to see when so many post offices have been closed. A man is unpacking a carton of sweets behind the counter.

'Excuse me.'

He turns around to face me. He has a kindly expression at odds with his long beard and T-shirt promoting a heavy metal band.

'I was wondering if you've seen my sister in the local village. She's gone missing. She was painting the portrait of Sir Rupert Baskerville.' I hold out the small photo I keep of Charlie and me in my wallet.

The man's face lights up. 'Sir Rupert,' he murmurs. He peers at the photo. 'Sorry, never seen her. What does Sir Rupert say?'

'That she left.'

He shrugs his shoulders. 'Well, then she left. He's a good man is Sir Rupert. Nothing like his father.'

'You mean his convicted murderer father?' I say with a heavily sarcastic tone.

The man's face hardens. 'Are you looking to buy anything?'

'No. Thanks for your help.'

I leave.

I'm not sure where to go next, so I climb back into the car and shut my eyes. I have two options. Go home and leave the police to search for Charlie or return to Sesame Hall. If I revisit Sir Rupert, I know he won't let me in, so I'll have to break in. And then I remember. Charlie told me that he sits as a magistrate on Wednesdays. If I wait another day, hopefully he will be out of the house, and it will give me an opportunity to find a way into the property.

32

CHARLOTTE

I have been in here for four whole days, and I wonder if I'll ever get out. I was so close. In touching distance of freedom. Now it's worse than ever. He's treating me as if I'm a real prisoner with no creature comforts. How do kidnapped people maintain hope? I simply don't know. All I can hold on to is that Jodi will be looking for me, and the police will have been notified. Surely it won't be that difficult for them to put two and two together. And now, here are his footsteps again, and the clunking of the locks and the metallic jarring of the bolt. I want him to stay away, to leave me alone.

'Charlotte, get up.'

'No.' I huddle closer to the wall.

'Charlotte, do you want me to hurt you?'

'No,' I whisper again. I can feel the heat emanating from his body, and his breath tickles the hairs on my neck. 'Move away and I'll get up.'

'Charlotte, oh, Charlotte, you don't tell me what to do!'

I sit up and he is standing right next to the mattress, wagging his forefinger as if he were a teacher chastising a naughty child. His left hand is clasping something behind his back. As I stand, still shivering because it is so cold in here, he grabs my right hand, and before I can blink, he has snapped the manacle around my wrist.

'No!' I scream, trying to pull my arm away, but the cold, sharp metal painfully chafes my skin.

'Be still and it won't hurt,' he says, snapping the other manacle onto my left wrist. He grabs the chain attached to the centre bar.

'Where are you taking me?'

'Nowhere.'

It doesn't make sense. Why has he manacled me? He tugs me across the room.

'Bend down.'

'What?'

'Get down onto the floor.' His voice is clipped, his vowels short.

I do as I'm told. What choice do I have? And then my gut clenches. I realise what he's doing: he is attaching my manacled wrists to the metal ring that is bolted into the wall.

'No! You can't do this!' My voice is a whimper. 'Are you going to leave me here?'

'Of course not.' His laugh is brittle. 'We'll get this over and done with, and then you can go back to the mattress. Kneel with your face to the wall.'

'Why?' I spit. Is he going to do something in the room that he doesn't want me to see?

'Just do it, Charlotte.'

I shuffle into position, my hands clasped together, attached to the metal ring, my nose almost pressed up against the cold whitewashed wall.

'Lean your forehead against the wall and take a deep breath.'

Before I can ask why, I hear something slicing through the air like a whistle, and then I scream. He has whipped me on my backside, the thin cotton fabric of my twill trousers doing nothing to protect me. Bile rushes up into my throat and I gag. And again, the sound of something flying through the air, splicing downwards and cutting through my trousers. It's even more painful this time, searing hot agony.

'Stop!' I say, but my voice is hoarse and pathetic. Tears pour down my cheeks. 'Please stop.'

'Five times, Charlotte. That's one-third of the number of lashes Father gave me.'

I try to kick back at him, but he is too strong.

'Keep still, Charlotte. I don't want to hurt you. If you keep still, it is better. I should know. Please, my darling, don't make it any worse.'

I glance over my shoulder, the room blurred through my tears, and I see him pull back a long dark brown leather strap, and then it whistles through the air again, hitting me a little higher this time, cutting into the bony section of my lower back. I scream.

'I told you to keep still, Charlotte. I don't want to hurt you.'

He isn't making any sense. How can he say he doesn't want to hurt me, but he is lashing me with a leather strap? And it comes again, and this time my scream sounds strangled, and all I can hear is the blood rushing in my ears, and I want to pass out. Please bring blackness. Please.

'Last one, Charlotte. You are so brave, my darling.'

I am sobbing now, shaking, my brain freezing, but I still tense as the air moves around me and the belt, or strap or whatever it is, sears my backside. The pain is indescribable: burning, blistering, as if someone has plunged a fiery hot dagger into my flesh. I am sure that blood is dripping down the backs of my thighs, that my taupe trousers will be slashed with red.

I hear him lay the strap down. He walks towards the wall, his brown leather brogues level with me, his knees click as he bends down, and then he strokes my hair.

'Beautiful girl, I never want to hurt you.'

I try to shake him off me.

He pushes a small key into the slot of the manacle, releasing my wrists one by one from the metal clamps. 'Don't cry, my love. Please don't cry.'

He grasps my right hand and tries to pull me to my feet, but I am too weak, so he puts his hands under both my armpits and lifts me up, and I am in too much agony to resist him. I hate this man. He is a monster and I am so weak. Every step feels as if a hot poker is jabbing my flesh, and when I collapse onto the bed, I have to lie on my side, facing the wall, but still the pain is so intense, the tears don't stop flowing.

'Forgive me, Charlotte. If only you had succumbed and hadn't tried such a reckless escape, I never would have had reason to punish you. Get some sleep, my love, and I might be back with some food later.'

I listen to his footsteps and hear the bolting of the door and I want to kill this monster. I am coiled up in a tight huddle, trembling and crying, waiting for the pain to subside. I would like to take my trousers and knickers off, to let the air cool my broken skin, but I cannot. The last thing I want is for Rupert to see my naked body. I can't even go to the bathroom to examine myself. Not only is there no mirror, but the camera is there, watching, constantly watching.

I am so cold and hungry and in pain, and I want this all to end. And then I sink into sleep, a blessed, dark sleep. Matthew is lying next to me, his arms around me, stroking my back, making me better. He says I love you and repeats it again and again. I love you. I love you. I will never leave you. And I am crying inconsolably because I know that when I wake up, he will be gone and my heart will break all over again.

A noise awakens me, and I turn over onto my back, crying out with pain as I remember what Rupert did and that Matthew is not here.

But Rupert is. He is sitting on the floor staring at me.

'Hello, darling,' he says as my eyes adjust to the fading light.

'What do you want?'

'What I've always wanted. I have told you so many times. All I wish for is for you to love me in the way that I love you. All I've ever wanted is for you to be my wife and fulfil your dreams as one of England's most acclaimed artists. Come on, darling. It is time for you to start painting again. Look. I have brought you back your easel and paints.'

The easel is standing in the middle of the room. I turn away again, my face to the wall.

'If you finish painting my portrait and are good, I will bring back your creature comforts. You shouldn't have to suffer with cold and hunger and pain. But rest assured, Charlotte darling, if you misbehave, although it will sadden me, I will whip you again.'

I weep, my body racking with uncontrollable sobs. I brace myself to be hit again, but there is silence. I simply can't stop the tears, self-pity mingling with fear, grief conjoining with despair. It would be better to be dead. And then after many long minutes, I hear the quiet click of the door and the gentle sliding of the bolts. I turn around. Rupert has gone.

Carefully, I sit up, but the pain is too much, so I kneel on the bed and wipe my face with the sleeves of my jumper. He has left something by the door. Every movement hurts, but I need to look. I waddle to the other side of the room, and every step, every movement is agony. Very slowly I bend down. It's a pile of six bridal magazines. The man is truly demented. I hurl them across the room and then hobble back to bed. I wait a long time for sleep to claim me.

When I next awake, it is dark and the pain has eased a little. Gingerly, I feel the raw skin on my backside. It's dry. Perhaps the wounds are not as bad as I feared.

I fumble in the dark and shuffle to the bathroom, switching

on the light and blinking hard at the glare from the single bare bulb. It feels like it's the middle of the night, and I'm hoping Rupert will be asleep and not watching me on the video camera. I turn the shower on and let it run until the water is burning hot; then I strip off, keeping my back to the camera, and step underneath the head.

The flow is weak, but it's enough to wash away some of the filth I feel from where Rupert's strap whipped my backside. The water stings terribly, but I don't mind this pain. It's cathartic and helps me mull over my limited options. There are only two stances I can take. Continue to resist him and make life as difficult as possible, or be compliant. It's not in my nature to comply, and I'll be damned if I give in to this bastard. By the time the hot water becomes tepid and then frigid, I have made up my mind. Shivering, I wrap the towel around myself and rub my hair and body dry. I will fight him with every ounce of strength and brain power I've got.

I select two paintbrushes from the plastic pot he has left next to the easel, and again with my back to the blinking cameras, I slide them up my sleeve. I then switch off the light and carefully climb back onto the mattress. Time ticks by slowly, but eventually the darkness begins to fade, and pale grey light illuminates the cell. The house makes creaking and groaning noises as the boiler kicks in, and all the while, I lie there, ready and alert, desperate to end this nightmare.

His footsteps get louder, then he unlocks the door, and I hear him close it behind him. Still I don't turn around.

'Charlotte,' he says, 'how are you this morning?'

I ignore him and pretend I'm asleep, my back to the room. I sense rather than hear him appear next to me. I am nearly positive that he is doing exactly what I hoped he would, bending down next to me, his leather shoes creaking on the floor. I can sense the heat from his body and smell the overbearing scent of his aftershave. I try to control my breathing. Slowly in, hold, slowly out.

'Charlotte,' he whispers again. I can feel the air move above my forehead. He must be millimetres away from me now. I inhale, and then holding the longest of the paintbrushes so that the bristles are in my palm, I sit bolt upright and in one fluid movement turn towards him and lunge forwards, jamming the pointed end of the wooden brush into his face. I wanted to get his eye, but I miss it and it pokes him in the cheek. I jab it towards him again, but he roars as he grabs my wrist.

'You bitch!' he cries. And then he slaps me. I can't help but release my grip on the brushes and he grabs them, and once again, I'm the weaker person kneeling on the bed, and he is standing over me, his eyes narrowed and his teeth bared.

'You must never, ever try to hurt me, Charlotte,' he says. His voice is low and quiet and more menacing than if he were shouting at me. 'You have left me with no choice. Do you understand? No choice.'

He steps away from the bed and paces to the easel. He picks up all the paintbrushes, replacing just one of them back into the plastic pot. The only brush that has a curved end that can't cause any damage. He strides to the door, unlocks it and then turns to me, his right fist holding the brushes, his left fist clenching and unclenching. 'I will be back.'

And once again he is gone.

33

RUPERT

I had honestly thought that whipping Charlotte would have been sufficient to beat her into submission. I was wrong. She has not learned her lesson. She has not succumbed, so she leaves me with no choice.

Father only used the most brutal punishment on me once. I was fourteen years old. Life was pretty unbearable both at school and at home. I had no friends. Even Scummy, as he was nicknamed, had one friend, but I was the lowest of the low. The last to be chosen for games teams, the person no one wanted to sit next to in class or share a dorm with. When I walked into the room, either conversation dried up or I was set upon.

It was an evening in the Michaelmas term. About twenty minutes after lights out, Rump and Rocket came for me. They were the cool boys, the bullies of the bullies. Today Rump is the managing director of a Footsie 100 firm and Rocket is an MP. Say no more. Rump, who was the tallest and strongest boy in our class and the first to hit puberty, grabbed me by the neck, hustled me along the corridor and forced my head into the toilet. Rocket flushed the loo. Twice.

Later that night when they were all sleeping, I found

Rump's little silver lighter that he hid with his Benson & Hedges cigarettes at the bottom of his wardrobe. I flicked it open and held the flame against the fabric of his duvet cover, down by his feet. I watched as the flame took hold of the synthetic fabric, dropped the lighter onto the floor next to his bed, and then I tiptoed back across the dorm and slipped into my bunk.

A minute or so later, Rump woke up and screamed, and an almighty panic took hold. The whole school was evacuated. The fire brigade arrived. Rump was rushed to hospital. Rocket blamed me, saying I had forced Rump's head down the toilet and then set his duvet alight. All the other boys concurred. I suppose the housemaster, Mr Carruthers, must have had his doubts because I was suspended for a week rather than being expelled. But Father, he was incandescent with rage.

At first I lied and told Father that I was the scapegoat, that it wasn't me who had set the duvet alight. I thought Father would take pity and let me have a week of lounging around in my bedroom. I was wrong.

'If you are that pathetic and can't stand up for yourself, you disgust me,' he said. 'Go to the punishment room.'

'But I'm not pathetic,' I said, tears welling in my eyes. 'I admit that I did set the duvet alight, but it's only because they were bullying me. Rump picks on me all the time, and he forced my head down the toilet. I did it to get my own back.'

'And you think that makes it alright?' Father said scornfully.

An hour later he whipped me fourteen times. One for each year of my life. And something broke inside me. I couldn't do anything right in Father's eyes. As he turned to coil up the strap, I took my fist and punched him in the sternum. Father didn't say a word. He didn't try to fight back. He turned and walked out of the room, locking the door behind him. Later that night, the sound of the locks being unbolted woke me, but the room remained dark, and I couldn't see anything.

'Who's there?' I called out, my heart thumping.

No one answered. And then it sounded as if the door was being locked again. I lay on the mattress, wondering if Father or Mrs Cherry had come down to check up on me, but then a few moments later I heard the scurrying of little feet. I screamed. I wet the bed. I wrapped the single sheet tightly around me in the hope that it would give me some protection.

At the end of the week when it was time to return to school, Father asked me what lessons I had learned.

'To stand up for myself without hurting other people.'

He nodded slowly and placed a hand on my shoulder. That was one of the only times I had his approval.

It worked for me, and now it must work for Charlotte.

It's 7 p.m. and I haven't given her any food all day. I spread butter on three pieces of toast and put them, an apple and a thermos flask of water on a tray. I take the tray downstairs and leave it outside the door to the punishment room. Then I return and collect the items for her punishment. Perfect.

I open the door and carry in the food. I place the tray on the bed.

'Eat,' I say, standing there with my arms crossed across my chest. She ignores me. I take a step closer to her and she quivers. 'Do what I say.'

She picks up the toast and eats it, hungrily stuffing it into her mouth, and I wait until it is all gone. I can't decide. Should I do it now whilst it's light or wait until it's dark?

'If you behave badly, I will whip you again. I may have to hurt you more than last time. It's not what I want, but you leave me no choice. Do you understand?'

She nods but doesn't look at me.

'You will be punished again. A particularly unpleasant experience, but it will teach you a lesson.'

I leave the room, locking it behind me. I hurry to my study to do a little more research into Stockholm syndrome. I had hoped that Charlotte would succumb quickly and develop positive feelings for me, but it seems that, once again, I am being impatient. In the meantime, I will take another leaf out of Father's book. I will unleash this punishment in the dark, just as he did to me.

My little Charlotte, you have no idea what's coming.

34

CHARLOTTE

I lie on the mattress and talk to Jodi. 'Please come and get me!' I whisper. I visualise her walking through the front door of Sesame Hall and then striding along the down-stairs corridor towards the kitchen, and down the flight of stairs to the cellars and along to the punishment room. In my mind's eye, Jodi is holding Rupert's set of keys and opening the door, several uniformed police officers standing behind her. We fall into each other's arms. 'Where's Rupert?' I ask. 'In custody,' one of the police officers says. 'He'll be sent away for life.'

I drift off into an uneasy sleep, and then I'm startled awake. What the hell is that? My eyes are wide open, but it's pitch black. It sounds like scratching, the patter of little feet. My heart pounds. Is it mice? I don't like mice, but I remind myself that they're harmless, and I'm sure I'll survive. Gingerly, I swing my feet out of the bed, and holding onto the edge of the mattress, I make my way towards the bathroom and the light switch.

And then it's as if little pinpricks go over my right foot. I scream. I lurch for the light, and when it illuminates the room, I scream even louder. There are rats scuttling across the floor, ranging in size from about four to eight inches long. One of them has climbed up onto my mattress and is burying its nose into the single sheet. I hop back towards the bed, swipe at it, and it opens its mouth, exposing sharp little fangs. I scream again. It scurries down the side of the mattress and onto the floor. I jump onto the bed.

'No!' How can the bastard do this to me? And then, as if the rats weren't bad enough, I see the largest, hairiest spider I have ever seen in my life – the sort of thing you see on wildlife programmes set in the Amazon – creep across the floor towards the table adjacent to the bed. It is about twenty centimetres in diameter, brown and hairy. I am standing on the mattress, my back to the wall, shaking in terror. What the hell is Rupert thinking? Is the spider poisonous, and could it kill me? I wonder if I should try to kill it first. Tip the table on top of it and hope that it gets crushed? But I reckon it will be too quick. No. Surely Rupert is just trying to scare me. I remember now I told him that I was scared of rodents and spiders. I dig my fingernails into the palms of my hand.

'Oh, Matthew!' I whisper under my breath. It's as if I hear his voice, because suddenly I know what I need to do. Acquiesce. Rupert wants me to love him. He has said that time and time again. Of course I can't love him, but all I need to do is pretend. And if I do that, then perhaps I will have the chance to escape. If I have to sleep with him, I will. It will be prostituting myself, but that is better than death and better than a lifetime locked away in here. I will not be able to sleep tonight, knowing that these creatures are roaming my cell, but if I can control my fear of them and act calmly, then perhaps Rupert will remove them in the morning.

I wrap the single sheet tightly around my body and sit on my mattress in the corner of the room. I watch the rats investigate the room, their black beady eyes darting from side to side as they scavenge for non-existent food. I kick outwards, ignoring the pain, when a rat attempts to climb up the side of the mattress. The spider moves surprisingly slowly across the floor. And then to my utter horror, the spider makes a hissing noise and pounces on the smallest of the rats. I can't watch. The spider eats the rat. I have to fight down the nausea.

'Please take them away,' I whisper out loud again and again. I'm not sure what terrifies me more. That tarantula or Rupert. I have to leave the light on and stay awake all night, watching them, making sure none of them come too close to me. The minutes and the hours tick by interminably. I count from one to a thousand and then lose my place and start all over again. It feels like days until I hear footsteps and keys in the locks and there he is. It is still dark outside.

'How are you enjoying my friends?' he asks as he stands against the door, wearing a navy dressing gown with striped pyjamas tucked into black wellington boots.

'I'm sorry,' I say quietly.

'Sorry for what, Charlotte?'

'For disobeying you. For acting violently. For not doing what you want me to do.'

He tilts his head on one side. 'How do I know whether you are truly remorseful?'

'I am. I really am.' I let the tears flow. 'Please, will you take them away?'

He doesn't answer. I glance up at him, and he is staring at me as if he can't decide what to do.

'Please,' I whisper again.

'But I went to such an effort to get them for you. The manager of the local pet shop is such an unsavoury-looking chap, with long straggly hair and a lisp. He chose these rats especially for us. And do you realise how special that spider is? And how expensive he was?'

I shake my head.

'It's a Guyana goliath bird-eater, very rare and requires a lot of looking after. He eats like a horse. Insects, frogs, snakes, rats, you name it. As you might have gathered, he gives a nasty, painful bite, and if you touch him, he'll cause serious irritation to the skin, hence my wellington boots.' He kicks out his right foot.

I shiver.

Rupert peers at me. 'I will remove these vermin, Charlotte, as you are clearly very distressed. Would you like to be comforted?'

I freeze for a moment. What is worse? The spider, the rats or Rupert? And then I remember my earlier decision. Acquiesce.

'Yes, please,' I say.

He walks quickly over to the bed, kicking out at a rat that gets a little too close to his boot, and pulls me into a bear hug. My face is wedged against his chest, and his face is buried in my hair. Eventually he lets go.

'I'll remove them for tonight. But if you try any more funny business, I will whip you again and these pets will live here permanently.'

'I will behave,' I promise.

Rupert struggles to catch the rats. The spider he scoops up with a net, and it hisses as he drops it into a plastic box, but the rats just scurry all over the place. If I wasn't in such a horrific situation, I would laugh. It's almost comedic. Eventually he captures them and drops them into small cardboard boxes. He piles all of the boxes one on top of the other, on the far side of the door, and then turns towards me. For a horrendous moment, I wonder if he is going to force himself on me. We are both static, staring at each other. And then he smiles.

'Goodnight, my love.' He turns and locks the door behind him.

WHEN THE HOUSE IS QUIET, I shuffle back to the bathroom. I sit down on the toilet seat and the pain makes me gasp. As I am stumbling back into the bedroom, I glance up at the shape of the negligee that is still hanging on the wall. He wants me to wear that, so I shall.

As the pale light of day banishes the darkness, I stand up and walk over to the wall. I take the silken nightdress. I then stand in front of the camera, brazen, uncaring, and strip off my clothes, dropping each item onto the floor. I am freezing cold, standing there naked. Then I slip on the negligee, the smooth silk doing nothing to warm me up, and I wait. I have no idea how long, but it seems like a short time. I hear his footsteps, then the unbolting of the door and the turning of the locks, and he steps inside, a look of wonder on his face.

'I thought I might be imagining it,' he says, stepping towards me. He is carrying a breakfast tray with freshly squeezed orange juice, a teapot, a plastic cup and a plate underneath a silver dome. He places the tray on the floor and then lifts off the dome, and there is a full English breakfast – bacon, sausage, eggs, tomato, mushrooms and toast – and my stomach gurgles in anticipation.

Standing up, he stares at me. 'You are the most beautiful woman I have ever seen.'

I force myself to keep my eyes on his face. I allow them to glaze over, and I pretend I am looking at Matthew.

He steps towards me and gently lifts my chin. I quiver. I don't know if I can do this. I find him so repulsive.

'By wearing this nightdress, is this what I think it is?'

'Yes,' I whisper, although I don't know what he is suggesting.

'You agree to allow me to make love to you?'

I shut my eyes and nod. If it buys me my freedom, I will do it.

'My darling, I am speechless. I knew my father's tactics would work, but this quickly. I hope you are being truthful and this isn't one of your tricks, because you know the consequences if it is. Are you being honest, Charlotte? Look me in the eyes.'

I look straight into those green eyes, darker now in the dim light, and I force myself to find the good things about them. That they are clear, and his lashes are well defined, and they are too close together, and he's an evil bastard. I don't know if I can do this. Yes, I must.

'Are you being straight with me?'

I nod, knowing my voice will betray me. He runs his fingers down my cheek and whispers hoarsely, 'Tonight, my love. Tonight.'

35

JODI

I rang work yesterday late afternoon and spoke to my manager. Candice is a joy to work with; I couldn't ask for a better boss. She's calm, fair and has a wicked sense of humour, which is a must in our line of work. Other than six months ago after Matthew died, I haven't had an unscheduled day off during the past four years. I don't have to lie to Candice.

'My sister has gone missing. I know it's the last thing you need, but could I have a couple of days off?'

'Of course. You'll be no good here, delivering babies, when your mind is on Charlotte, will you?' It's a rhetorical question. 'We'll have a shuffle around of shifts, and don't you worry about us. Just find that lovely sister of yours. Keep me posted, Jodi.'

'I will. And thank you.'

Candice knows what a terrible time our family has had over the past six months. Her heart is truly filled with gold.

I slept badly, and now I've awoken to a pale light and it's time for me to get up. I pray that Sir Rupert will be out of the house today.

I'm the first person in the pub's breakfast room at 6.30 a.m., but the landlady is there, bustling away, all chirpy despite the early hour.

'What can I get you, love?'

'Just a coffee and some toast, please.'

She brings it over. 'And how was Sir Rupert yesterday?' she asks as she pours the coffee.

'He was fine. I've only met him a couple of times,' I explain.

'Such a lovely man and all alone in that great big house. I don't know what we'd do without him in this community. He's forever putting his hand in his pocket. If it wasn't for Sir Rupert, we wouldn't have a playground or a cricket pavilion, and goodness, I remember now, when there was a threat we'd lose the vicar, it was Sir Rupert who promised to help with his salary. He's a true saviour.'

'Not like his father, then?' I say, watching the landlady carefully. She twitches and frowns but doesn't say anything. 'I gather Sir Oswald was convicted of murdering the au pair.'

Her mouth flattens. She reaches over to the adjacent table and puts a plate full of little jams in front of me. 'Are you sure you wouldn't like a cooked breakfast? We've got some fine sausages.'

'I'm certain, thank you.' I debate asking more about Sir Oswald, but I don't want to alienate her. 'I don't suppose you have seen my sister, Charlotte Aldridge, have you? She was staying with Sir Rupert.'

'I can't say I have. I didn't know that Sir Rupert had a guest. Any wedding bells in the near future?'

'No, definitely not,' I snap.

'Sorry, didn't mean to offend,' she says, and scuttles towards the kitchen.

By 7.30 a.m. I am loading my bag back into the car, having paid and checked out. I want to be at Sesame Hall to watch Sir Rupert leave and be sure that no one is there before I have a good snoop around. I decide to walk. The last thing I can risk is parking up somewhere and Sir Rupert spotting Charlie's car. I'm wearing a thick grey wool jumper and my parka, which fortuitously is khaki green and should provide camouflage, along with black jeans and trainers. I've pulled a black beanie low over my hair. A couple of muesli bars are stuffed in my pocket, and my hands are toasty in gloves. I walk briskly along the grassy verge next to the country lane, my head down and looking away from the occasional car that passes.

Half an hour later, I am warmed up and turn into Sesame Hall's driveway. There is a dense hedge on the left-hand side of the drive, with trees set behind it. I wriggle my way through a hole in the hedge, scratching my hand, and crouch down. I am sure that I can't be seen, but I do have a good view of the drive. I have no idea how long I'll have to wait, but I don't care. I'll sit here all day if need be.

Time goes so slowly when you're watching it. Although I can't be sure that Sir Rupert is a magistrate in the courts at Brighton, I assume he must sit there, because that's the nearest court to where he lives. Unsurprisingly, the courts website does not list the names of their magistrates. By my reckoning, it will take him about forty-five minutes to drive there, so he should be leaving any time soon. By 8.30 a.m. my legs are feeling cramped, so I stand up and shake them out. It's cold too. I debate chewing one of my bars but decide to hold off for another half an hour.

And then at 8.40 a.m. I hear the deep roar of a car. Holding my breath, I press my body up against the tree and peek through the gap in the hedge. The car's wheels spray up little stones as it goes past. It's a pale blue Aston Martin and the driver is unmistakably Sir Rupert. I watch the car indicate to the left, and then wait until the sound of the engine fades into the distance. Yes. He's gone.

I creep along the side of the hedge, but then the hedgerow gives way to a metal fence, and there is nothing for me to hide behind. I am going to have to brave it and walk up the drive. So long as I'm not visible from the front entrance where I saw that camera, I hope I'll be fine. As I approach the house, I climb over the fence and walk through long grass up the side of the house. It's all overgrown now, but there is a dilapidated green-house and raised beds, suggesting this was the vegetable garden in Sesame Hall's heyday. I pass a number of outbuild-ings, each with large wooden doors. They were probably the stables in years gone by. I peer in through a glass window, but it's hard to make out what's inside. A car perhaps?

My heart is thumping as I move nearer to the house. What if there are security cameras or sensors? I glance around, but I can't see or hear anything except the faint whistle of the wind as it sways the branches of the nearly bare trees. There are no cars parked around the house. I hold my breath as I tiptoe across a courtyard at the back of the main building. It has the same crunchy gravel as at the front, and it's almost impossible to walk silently.

I make a beeline for a white painted door with a small window in its upper half. There are three windows adjacent to the door, each with white frames. I stand with my back to the wall and peer in, as spies do in the movies. I almost topple over in the process and have to bite the inside of my cheek to stop myself from giggling out loud. But then I think of Charlie and remember that this is far from funny. It's the gravest situation I have ever faced, and in my line of work I've faced a fair few. But then I was with strangers, trying to help them, to save lives. But this involves my sister, the person I love the most in the whole wide world.

With my face up against the glass, I can make out various coats hanging from pegs and boots lined up on wooden slatted shelves. I shift to the next window along. It looks into a utility room with an industrial-sized washing machine and metal shelves that are empty except for a box of washing powder.

Some men's shirts are hanging from a wire that stretches from wall to wall. I edge back to the door and try the handle. Unsurprisingly it is locked. What now?

I am going to have to break in and risk setting off an alarm. But I reckon by the time the police or anyone else turns up, I will be long gone, hidden in the woodland in the distance. There are rocks edging the gravel drive, so I tiptoe over to them and pick up a medium-sized rock the size of my fist. When I am about a metre away from the back door, I hurl the rock at the glass. I was lousy at sports at school, and even this close up, it's a miracle that the stone hits the glass, but it does. The glass shatters and splinters and sounds as loud as a cymbal in a silent auditorium. I hold my breath. If anyone is here, they would definitely have heard that. I wait. One minute. Three minutes. And now I'm confident that no one is coming to investigate, so I put my gloved hand through the broken pane of glass and am surprised that the key is in the lock on the inside. At least I won't have to clamber through the window. I turn the key and open the door, further shards of glass tinkling to the ground.

I tiptoe inside, my trainers squeaking slightly on the terracotta tiled floor. My heart is banging inside my chest, reverberating in my ears, my breath too loud. But I have to do this. I walk out into a corridor, past the utility room and into a large kitchen. The units are made from pine, and the kitchen counters are vinyl, the floor the same terracotta tiles. There is a large Aga and an old-fashioned-looking fridge. There is nothing on the surfaces; everything looks clean and tidy. Back into the corridor I peer into a number of reception rooms, including the living room he took me into yesterday. And then I arrive in the grand hallway. At the far end of the corridor is a large ballroom, empty but for a grand piano. Next to it is a study; I assume it's Rupert's, as a modern laptop lies on his desk. I'll return here later.

Now I tiptoe upstairs, and I lose count of how many

bedrooms and bathrooms there are. One by one, I check each old-fashioned bedroom and bathroom until there is just one bedroom remaining. I am confident that there is no one in the house, so I start shouting. 'Charlotte! Charlie! Are you here?'

I have no reason to think that she is, other than my intuition. And my intuition is rarely wrong.

36

RUPERT

I knew Charlotte would come around, but I hadn't dared to hope that my methods would take effect this quickly. I shouldn't have doubted; after all, Father's disciplinarian approach worked with me. There certainly is no gain without pain. Despite my research, I haven't been able to ascertain how long it takes for Stockholm syndrome to take effect. Natascha Kampusch was held in captivity for eight years, but then she was a child and her kidnapper was a revolting pervert. It is quite a different situation with Charlotte and me. We are adults, we have so much in common, and I love her. Love overcomes everything, and she must realise that all I want is for her to be happy.

When she was standing in the punishment room wearing the black silk negligee, her pale skin dotted with goosebumps, her eyes wide and her lips slightly apart, I thought I was going to combust. Charlotte, the epitome of female beauty, has absolutely no idea the effect she has on me. For a moment, I wondered if I was imagining it, whether she had somehow rigged the camera and created this spectacle. But then she moved and sat on the bed, shivering, and I knew it was for real.

I'm not naive and I did doubt her sincerity, but the longer I stared at her, the more I sensed her feelings were genuine. She was calling me. She was telling me the time has come, that our love is mutual.

I hurried to the kitchen to make Charlotte a full English breakfast. My poor darling must have suffered last night with no food in her delicate belly. I squeezed some oranges and fried up sausages and bacon from the local farm shop. Then I found one of the silver domes that Mrs Cherry used to use when bringing our food from the kitchen to the dining room.

My legs were trembling as I opened the door and walked into the punishment room. She stood up, ready for me. Ready to give herself to me.

I would have liked to have consummated our love there and then. To my delight, Percy was ready. But it was neither the time nor the place. I have to be in court this morning, and to make love on that old mattress, with no comfort around us, seemed all wrong. Instead we will do it tonight. And for the first time ever, Percy will behave.

She is standing at the side of the bed when I enter the room. Her eyes don't leave mine, and eyes don't lie. My guidebooks suggest that a good way to assess if someone likes you is to look at their pupils. If they enlarge, then the signs are positive. Charlotte's pupils are big black holes that draw me inside her, leaving me trembling with joy.

After giving Charlotte her breakfast, I have to force myself to leave the punishment room. Passion is overwhelming and I know that both of us found it exquisitely difficult not to indulge in our mutual carnal desires. But I am strong willed. I am the sort of person who will leave their favourite piece of food on their plate until last. I hurried upstairs to transform my bedroom into a love nest. I put clean sheets on the bed, antique linen with the family crest embroidered onto the sheets and pillowcases. I removed the duvet and replaced it with traditional waffle woolen blankets, and then I made a quick list of the items I need to buy later on, when court is finished.

It is just as well I sit in Brighton, a town full of wonderful shops. Flowers. Perfume. Rose petals. Chocolate. The finest champagne. What else should I put on my list? I debate going into one of those sex shops, but immediately discard the idea. It's tacky and unnecessary. But perhaps I should consider my own clothes. Should I purchase some silk underwear to match my love's? I hope I will have time to do a quick online search for advice. During our lunchtime recess perhaps. And food. Goodness, I nearly forgot about the meal. I will have to put a call into a local caterer in the hope one of the girls can whip something up for us.

By the time I finish preparing the bedroom, I realise with a start that if I don't speed up, I am going to be late for court. I would have liked to have said goodbye to Charlotte, removed her dirty breakfast things and left her a sandwich for lunch, but I haven't got time. At least she's had a hearty breakfast this morning, so it should sustain her through. I have another quick peek of her from my phone. She is eating the breakfast I prepared for her, a look of satiation and enjoyment on her face.

I put on my suit jacket and adjust my tie. I always wear the same things for court. A dark navy, almost black suit, a white shirt and a dark blue tie with pale blue stripes, in the same hue as our family colours. I glance in the mirror and wonder if I have time for a haircut after court. It is a little long.

Collecting my briefcase and overcoat, I hurry out to the garages, get into the Aston Martin and reverse out of the garage. I don't think I have ever felt so happy. And I remember how I told Charlotte when we first met that I was a poet. Surely now would be a good time to try out my creative juices, to pen her a love poem in the manner of Keats or Byron. I murmur a few words out loud: *My darling Charlotte.* But the only word I can come up with that rhymes with Charlotte is harlot and that is totally inappropriate. I give up trying to compose a ditty and switch on the radio. But my normal classical music just isn't appropriate today. I channel hop and choose some lively, upbeat pop music with a tune that is just about discernable, and after thirty seconds of listening, I am able to sing along.

Good heavens! I nearly forgot. I must buy Charlotte some jewellery to mark this, the most auspicious day of our lives. I will have to nip into The Lanes and select a diamond bracelet perhaps from one of the jewellers. Something classic that will stand the test of time; something that will be suitable to pass on to our daughter. I can't imagine Charlotte liking anything too fussy. Simple lines and elegant, that must be the order of the day.

I am at the end of the drive now and, without thinking, indicate to the left and pull out onto the main road. Quite how I will be able to concentrate in court today, I have absolutely no idea. I hope that the cases are interesting, something to grab my intellect, rather than a morning of dull speeding offences and mundane burglaries. What a day!

Ping.

What was that?

Ping.

My head is so full of Charlotte that it takes me a moment to realise that my mobile phone has pinged, the sound indicating that one of the sensors has gone off in the hall.

'Shit,' I say out loud, and swerve the car onto a grassy verge, annoyed that the wheel hubs will have got muddy. I put the handbrake on and grab my mobile phone. Please, please don't let it be Charlotte. If she has tried to escape today, just when everything is going so well, my heart will break. My fingers are trembling slightly as I open the app, which connects to a live feed. Someone is moving around Sesame Hall, but I can't see who it is. The mobile reception is so poor here, there isn't enough connectivity to display a clear picture.

It can't be Charlotte, surely? I think back to the punishment room. I have secured the wall with the decaying bricks. The door is firmly bolted, and it is an impossibility to reach the high-level window. It can't be her. I flip the feed so that I can view the cameras in the punishment room. Thank heavens, Charlotte is still there. She has changed out of the negligee into the clothes I left her yesterday. It's a shame, but my main concern is that my love is safe.

The phone pings again. Another sensor has been set off. There is definitely someone there. I consider calling the police, but I cannot risk them turning up and searching the house.

Damnation. I am going to have to go home. And if I go home, I won't make it to court in time.

With a shaking hand, I call the clerk of the courts. 'Sir Rupert St John Baskerville here. I'm sorry, but I'm going to have to let you down this morning. My car has broken down in the middle of bloody nowhere, and it's going to be a good hour or so until the rescue service arrives. You'll have to do without me.'

The clerk sighs, but my no-show is hardly an insurmountable problem. The ideal is to have three magistrates hear every case, but the courts work perfectly well with two. And besides, we magistrates are unpaid, doing our bit for the British justice system as volunteers. If it's necessary to bail out from time to time, so be it.

I do a three-point turn in the middle of the country lane, and I'm grateful for the horsepower of my car because just three minutes later I'm speeding up the drive to Sesame Hall. Whoever is snooping around won't be for much longer.

37

JODI

My shouts for Charlie echo around the large house, but I don't hear anything. No faint cries, no footsteps. Just a leaden silence. I turn the door handle to the only bedroom I haven't checked, and I grip onto a chest of drawers to stop myself from fainting.

There are photos of Charlotte all over the room. On the mantelpiece, on the chest of drawers, on the bedside tables. There are even A4 printed pictures of her pinned onto the walls. Every spare space has a picture of my sister. Some of the photos are ones I recognise, of her when she was featured in an art magazine, of Charlie at her art exhibition in Alderley Edge. But others I don't recognise, and these are the ones that fill me with horror. She is in a room with bare brick walls, wearing her own clothes, but either sitting or lying on a mattress. Her hair looks unwashed and there are dark circles under her eyes. The pictures are slightly blurry, low resolution. And they are very, very wrong.

I run back downstairs, almost stumbling as I do so, grabbing onto the dark, wooden stair rail.

'Charlie!' I yell over and over again. She is here. I am sure she is here. Those photos suggest she's being held somewhere, but where? The pictures don't show enough of the room to confirm where it might be. I race back to the study, where I saw the MacBook Air. There are a couple of photographs on the desk, next to the laptop, along with a pad of lined paper. I don't know what I'm looking for, but I feel sure that this room might throw up some answers. I pull the handles of the desk drawers, but they're locked, and other than using brute force, I don't know how to open them. Turning so my back is to the window, I am facing a large walnut wood bureau about eight feet in width. Its doors are closed, but the small key is in the lock. I turn the key and open the doors.

'Oh my God!' I whisper as I stare at two large flat computer screens, a small keyboard and a mouse. I move the mouse, and one of the screens springs to life.

And there is Charlie, on a video cam. Is that live?

She is in a dungeon-type room and she is moving. Thank god she's alive. I peer at her. What's she doing? And then she comes more into focus, and I see that she's painting. She must be alright if she's painting. There is a single bare light bulb hanging from the very tall ceiling and a window, so high up. Maybe twenty feet above her.

'Shit!' Charlie says as she drops her paintbrush. I jump with surprise. Not only can I see her, but I can hear her too. It's going to be alright.

'Charlie!' I say, but she doesn't turn around. Clearly she can't hear me. I am so disappointed. But if there is one-way audio, perhaps there is two? Could the microphone be switched off on my end? I press random keys on the keyboard, I move the mouse again, and I have no idea whether this is doing anything. I say her name over and over again. 'Charlie, Charlie.' And then I see another little device with a lit-up LED button on it. I suppose it could be a microphone. I press it and repeat, 'Charlie.'

She freezes. Charlie swivels around and faces first one camera and then the next.

'Jodi?'

'I'm here.'

She bursts into tears.

I keep my finger on the button. 'Charlie, I'm here. I'm going to get you out. I'm going to call the police.'

'Oh, Jodi, I knew you would come!'

'Are you alright? Are you hurt?'

'No, yes. Nothing that won't heal. He's holding me hostage.'

'Why?'

'He's in love with me. It's ridiculous and terrifying. Apparently, I remind him of his first love.'

'You don't have to worry anymore. I'm going to get you out of here, away from this monster. I'm calling the police right now. It won't be long, sis.'

38

RUPERT

Rupert

I have never driven up the drive so quickly. Normally I go cautiously, careful not to allow any of the pesky stones to jump up and scratch or indent the gleaming bodywork of the Aston Martin. But today I don't even think about the car. I just have to get home. I have to make sure that my Charlotte is safe.

And then, maybe one hundred metres from the front door, I slam on the brakes. Why should I alert the bastard inside the Hall that I am here? I will sneak up on him and catch him in the act. I leave the car parked in the middle of the road. It also means that whoever is here won't be able to drive away with my car blocking the drive. I sprint along the verge up to the house and around to the back. The pane of glass in the back door has been smashed. I pause and bring up the app on my phone to check the live camera feeds. My lovely Charlotte is talking to someone, but she's alone in the punishment room. And then I realise. I flip the feed so I can see the camera in my study. And bloody hell. It's Jodi. Her dreadful sister. I should have guessed she would come back.

What the hell am I meant to do now? I clench my teeth so tightly, my jaw aches and my teeth make a cracking sound. I tiptoe in through the open back door, trying to avoid treading on any of the glass shards; then I carry on down the corridor and pause outside my study door.

She's still talking to Charlotte. Telling her that she's going to call the police, that she'll rescue her sister, that I'm a monster.

No, Jodi. You are the monster.

I tiptoe into the room. She has her back to the door.

'It won't be long, sis,' Jodi says.

I can see Charlotte's beautiful face all lit up as she speaks to her sister. She looks so pathetically grateful. My Charlotte was lying to me.

'It'll take the police a while to arrive,' Charlotte says. 'We're out in the sticks here.'

'I know, but just hang on in there,' Jodi says. She takes her finger off the microphone and picks up the phone lying on the counter next to the monitors. How dare she use my phone!

I tiptoe forwards again just as she dials.

I am so close now, just a metre from her back. I hear her inhale as if she is about to speak, and then I pounce on her from behind, my arm snaking around her neck, pulling her away from the screens. The phone clatters to the ground and I kick it away, the plastic casing shattering. With my left hand I slam the door to the cupboard shut. Without a finger depressed on the button, Charlotte won't hear us. I drag Jodi backwards into the room. She tries to hit me, but I tighten my grip around her neck. A photo frame flies off my desk and lands with a clatter on the floor.

'What the hell are you doing here?' I say, allowing my spittle to fly across the room. Fury is burning inside me and it's about to boil over.

'You've got Charlotte. I'm calling the police,' she pants.

'No you're not!'

She struggles, trying to remove my arm from the grip around her neck. She's stronger than Charlotte, much stronger. But I don't care if I hurt this bitch. She bites my arm, but thanks to Father's lashes, my tolerance for pain is high. I tighten my grip further and it sounds as if she is gargling.

I kick her legs, and one of her knees gives way, and I release the grip around her neck just a little.

'The police are looking for Charlie,' she says, her voice croaky. I put more pressure around her neck again, my forearm squeezing her voice box.

'You're not even her sister, are you?' My saliva sprays her cheek. 'You're pretending to be, but you're not related, are you?'

'What?' she wheezes.

How I wish I really did know Krav Maga, as I told Charlie. I could do with it right now. She is wriggling like crazy and manages to elbow me in the sternum. I gasp. I must be strong. I must stay focused. Thanks to all of my workouts, I am much more muscular than her, but I release my grip, just a little, just for a nanosecond, and she manages to get away from me. She can't go. If she escapes, it's all over for Charlotte and me.

'You think I'm so stupid. You think I don't know all about you and Charlotte, where you come from and where she comes from?' I spit as I lurch towards her.

I grab the thing nearest to my right hand. The antique Saint-Louis glass paperweight that has stood on this desk for three generations. The paperweight that was said to have belonged to Queen Victoria. The paperweight that Father forbade me from touching because it was valuable and had an impeccable heritage. The paperweight that is a thing of exquisite beauty, that even as a child, I recognised to be something special. The paperweight that has a dancing devil silhouette cane in its centre.

It is heavy and fits perfectly into the palm of my hand. She is forcing me to do this. It's not that I want to, but she has given me no choice. I sprint towards her, like a jaguar about to pounce on its prey, and I hurl the paperweight at her with all of my strength.

It catches the side of her head, just above her hairline. Her knees give way and she concertinas to the ground, her arms flailing and her head flopping sideways, the back of her skull hitting the edge of the stone fireplace with an ominous crack and thud. And then she is still. I stand above her, shaking. I watch as a small pool of blood starts to spill outwards, creeping along the edge of the fireplace. I place the paperweight back on the desk. Jodi isn't moving.

What has the stupid bitch done? She's ruined everything.

How can I have a happy future with Charlotte if my love blames me for the death of her sister? If I tell her the truth, will she understand?

39

CHARLOTTE

I knew she would come. I knew she would leave no stone unturned. It is what I would do for her if the roles were reversed. Jodi is strong. She doesn't take no for an answer, and Rupert doesn't stand a chance with her. I say a little prayer. She even remembered that today is Wednesday, when Rupert is out for most of the day, sitting as a magistrate.

I perch on the edge of the mattress and cry tears of relief. I won't have to allow Rupert to rape me. I won't have to engineer a way to escape. The police are coming, and he will go to jail for a very long time. This nightmare is over.

I stare at the almost-finished portrait, and I know I must destroy it. No one should have to look at that evil man's face. He took my broken palette knife, but I still have the paintbrushes. I take two of them and, using their pointed ends, gouge at the canvas, digging in harder and harder. The paint has created a strong crust, so it takes a while for me to bend and distort the canvas, but eventually I do. And then I decide to paint over it, a muddy mess of every colour that he gave me. It goes every-where. On the canvas, on the floor, down the front of my clothes. A brown mess. I jab and flick the paint, and with every move, I feel a further degree of relief. I don't care if I don't receive any of the money he promised me. It's only money. My life is what matters.

After a while, the painting is totally destroyed. I place it on the ground and jump on it. It's stupid but so satisfying. I sit again on the mattress, my ears straining to hear a siren. But there is silence. I'm not sure how long has passed since Jodi spoke to me, but it must be fifteen or twenty minutes at least. Why is it taking so long? Surely she should be battering my door by now. I'm only in the basement of the house. I doubt it's that difficult to find. Jodi is resourceful and much more astute than I am.

Sometimes I think that if we were blood sisters, we wouldn't be so close. With barely eleven months between us, we are inseparable. I have always known that I was adopted, and I have always known that Jodi was Mum and Dad's real child, the miracle baby who came along just a few months after they adopted me. Matthew asked me once if I felt jealous that Jodi had their genes and I didn't. The answer is no. I couldn't have asked for a more loving family. They treated us equally. I have always felt loved. Mum says that Jodi and I complement each other, that our differences bring us together. I trust Jodi implicitly, so I must be patient.

I look at the revolting black silk nightdress that I wore like a prostitute earlier this morning. It is crumpled on the end of the mattress. I don't want Jodi to see it. I pick it up, and standing up, I hold one end with each hand and I rip it, enjoying the sound of the tearing silk. But it's strong, and although I've ripped the seams apart, I can't tear the fabric any further. But I don't care. I pick it up and shove it down the toilet. Silly, petty even, but it makes me feel good.

Come on, Jodi. Where are you?

I pace around and around the room like the caged animal that I am. I wish I had a watch or a clock, but it must be half an hour by now. Where are the sounds of voices, of cars? And then I wonder. Is everything alright? Has something happened?

On cue I hear footsteps. Thank heavens. And the turning of the key in the locks.

'Jodi?' I say.

There is no answer. I rush to the door just as the bolts are undone and the door swings open. 'Jodi!' I shout again.

It is Rupert.

I scream, the loudest I have ever screamed. No! This is not meant to have happened! Jodi was getting me out of here. I push Rupert with every iota of strength I possess and manage to slip past him up the stairs.

'Stop!' he shouts, but I am ahead of him, just a few steps, but enough. I can't let him catch me now. I just can't.

'Jodi!' I scream as I run. I skid along the corridor with no idea as to where I'm going. I just need to get out. His footsteps are right behind me, his breath panting and heavy. He is so fast, so nearly on top of me. I can feel the vibrations of his steps, the fetid breath on my neck, and I carry on, straight through an open door, confused as to which rooms lead out to the terrace and which rooms have no external doors. And then I rush into the room that was previously locked. I nearly trip over her.

'No!' I scream so loudly this time, I wonder if I have pierced my own eardrums. Jodi is lying on the floor, motionless. Her legs are bent under her at an unnatural angle, and her head is lying on the edge of the stone fireplace.

I drop down onto the floor next to her.

'Jodi!' I cry, cradling her head. My hands are sticky. Her eyes are closed. She is so heavy, so motionless.

'What have you done to my sister?' I scream at Rupert, who is standing there just staring at us. 'Help her!' I yell.

'No, Charlotte. It is too late for Jodi, but it is not too late for you.'

I can't listen to this evil man. I try to remember the basic first aid that Jodi taught me shortly after she completed her midwifery exams. I turn her onto her side, but that is worse. There is so much blood. Too much blood and she's not moving. I place my cheek on her chest, willing her to move, willing her heart to kick into action and her lungs to draw in breath. But she is still. I put my lips over hers and force air into her mouth, pumping her chest with both my hands, trying to remember how to do mouth-to-mouth resuscitation. *Come on, Jodi. Breathe.*

'Call for an ambulance, you bastard!' I shout.

More compressions: one, two, three, four.

And then Rupert grabs me, pulling me away from my sister.

'Stop it!' he says, shoving me backwards. I can't stop screaming and kicking and clawing at him.

'What have you done? You've killed my sister!' I yell.

He clasps me to him, pinning my arms to my sides, placing his revolting chin on the top of my head. He is too strong, and my beloved sister is just lying there dead. He releases his grip just for a moment, and I slide back down to the floor. I am about to cradle Jodi, when my eyes fall upon a photograph in a broken frame. I lean forwards and pick it up.

The photograph could be of me. She has my blue eyes and broad lips, but her hair is a little blonder and longer, and she's wearing a pink summery dress. I never wear pink. My brain feels sluggish, as if the pieces of a perverse jigsaw puzzle are right here, but I can't slip them into the correct order.

'Who is this?' I shout.

Rupert is standing above me, his arms crossed. He doesn't answer.

A terrible thought strikes me. My voice trembles. 'Is this Simone?'

He narrows his eyes at me. This woman looks like my doppelganger. This woman who Rupert says was his first love, am I related to her?

'Oh my god!' My hand is in front of my mouth as the reali-sation hits me. 'Was Simone my mother?'

I try to remember what Rupert said. My brain is in shock and isn't working quickly enough. And then it comes to me. His father got the au pair pregnant. If Simone was my mother and Rupert's father was my father, that makes Rupert my half-brother.

I scream.

40

RUPERT

'Stop screaming!' I yell at Charlotte.

Everything has gone wrong. Everything. I didn't mean to kill Jodi, of course I didn't. It was her fault for breaking in and trying to defy me. It was self-defense. The stupid cow brought it upon herself. And now Charlotte is distraught, and all our plans for the best day of our lives have been destroyed.

'I didn't do it! If she hadn't broken in and slipped on the floor, she'd still be alive.'

But I don't think Charlotte hears me. She is screaming and sobbing and being totally hysterical. I'm going to have to be harsh with her. It worked before.

'Pull yourself together!' I shout.

She spits at me like a wild animal, her face tear-stained, blood on her jumper and on her hands. 'You're an incestuous murderer!'

'Anyone with sense would accept that Jodi brought this upon herself. She broke in, and I had every right to defend myself and my property. Get back up, Charlotte, and come with me quietly. If you don't, I will hurt you too. Do you hear me? I don't want to harm you; I love you, but if you resist me, you will leave me with no choice.'

'The police are coming.' Her words are hard to make out, and they are spoken with doubt.

'No, they're not. Jodi didn't call the police. Look, I don't want to hurt you, Charlotte. Really I don't. So come with me and we'll sort this all out. I'll arrange for Jodi to have a wonderful funeral, no expenses spared. Stand still, my love, and let's get you clean. You've got blood all over you.'

'No. No!' She is still sobbing, her arms around Jodi, and the sight of them together sickens me. 'You're disgusting! A pervert!'

I wince.

I reach down and grasp Charlotte under the arms, dragging her upwards. She tries to resist me, but I'm too strong. But just as I've got her into the upright position, she stamps her foot hard onto my toes. I cry out with surprise. I didn't know she had the strength to cause me pain. But I remember I'm stronger and bigger than her, and if she makes me harm her, I will. Ideally so long as it's not an outwardly visible injury. I put my arm around her neck and tighten it. She gasps.

'Charlotte, don't make me hurt you,' I say, my lips brushing her hair. And then it's as if all the strength dissipates from her body, and I wonder for one horrific moment if life has left her too. She flops forwards, her legs giving way, a little wheeze coming from her open lips. I think she's fainted. It gives me the chance to pick her up, to put her arm around my neck. She's such a lightweight, fragile thing in comparison to her sister. Just a couple of moments later, she comes to and I nearly drop her, but we're at the top of the stairs to the punishment room now. Her legs fall out of my grip, but I pull her down the stairs, her shoes clattering against the steps.

She has another unexpected burst of energy, and I have to quite literally throw her into the punishment room. My poor

Charlotte lands on the floor with a bump. I hesitate for a moment. Is she alright? But then she opens her eyes and throws me a look of such evil hatred, I gasp. No. It's not meant to be like this. Only a couple of hours ago, Charlotte loved me. She was ready to give me her heart, soul and body, and now her bitch of a sister has ruined everything.

I slam the door to the punishment room and bolt it.

What the hell am I going to do now?

I walk slowly back upstairs. I have a dead body in the study, and although I'm not expecting anyone to visit Sesame Hall, it can't stay here. I remind myself that I have time and I mustn't panic. I thank my blessings that I cancelled the cleaning contract when Charlotte came to stay. At least I won't have any prying eyes noticing the splatters of blood, but I will have to clean it myself.

I walk upstairs and go into my bedroom. This was meant to be the room where rose petals would be scattered and where our love was to be consummated. I remind myself that it still can be, it's just not going to happen tonight.

Sighing, I take off my suit. There are some blood marks on it. I will have to try to remove them before sending the suit to the dry cleaners. I hang it up on the front of the wardrobe. I remove my shirt and underpants, flinging them into the wash basket. I feel dirty, contaminated with Jodi's blood, so I take a quick shower. Afterwards, I throw on my oldest clothes, a pair of frayed corduroys and the navy jumper that dear Mrs Cherry bought me, which is now ridden with holes.

I think of how Mrs Cherry's bony fingers clasped around mine as she lay on her deathbed. How she told me the truth, the information that had been kept from me for all of those years.

'The baby was put up for adoption,' she said in a slow, halting voice. 'Simone was willing to do it for your father. She'd have done anything for that man. And then he killed her.'

I looked away when she said that. Mrs Cherry had to go to her grave believing Father was responsible.

She coughed and carried on talking. 'I organised it all. Simone thought she was having a boy, but she wasn't. It was a bonny, wee girl.'

'I have a sister?' I gasped.

She nodded. 'You might be able to find her. I'll never forget the name of the adoption agency. Busy Bees Adoption Agency.' Mrs Cherry shut her eyes then, and her chest was so still, for a moment I thought she had passed away. But then she spoke again.

'You mustn't live alone in that big house, Rupert. Find yourself a wife.'

An hour later, Mrs Cherry was dead. I made a promise to myself that I would find myself a wife and I would find my half-sister. I never set out with the intention that my wife and my sister would become one. I am, after all, a law-abiding man. A Justice of the Peace, an upholder of the laws of the land.

It wasn't easy to find my sister. I spent three years searching for her, and in the end I found her through not exactly legal means. Charlotte Aldridge. I didn't mean to fall in love with her, I just wanted to share my life with someone who shared my blood, but when I saw her photograph and when I saw her video, I couldn't stop those profound feelings. In the flesh, my feelings for her were simply too powerful. I love this woman. Percy and I felt an overwhelming passion, an irresistible attraction, unlike anything I have felt for anyone else with the exception of Simone. Charlotte's mother. I knew that we were meant to be together, that Charlotte and I couldn't be bound by society's petty rules, for at long last I had found a woman with whom I could truly be a man.

How could I deny myself that?

. . .

I PAD BACK DOWNSTAIRS and into the study. Now I need to move the body. I walk back into the drawing room, and my eyes fall upon the antique Persian rug. It belonged to Mother, one of the few items in the Hall that comes from her side of the family. So much history lies within those silken threads. The times when Mother dressed me up in a turban made out of a large towel and pretended I was Aladdin flying through the air on this magic carpet. Later, when Father told me she had died, I collapsed onto the russet and blue rug, burying my face in the fibres. And then Simone. This is the rug where Simone died, where her soul left her body and went to meet its maker. I shake myself out of the sentimentality. I cannot afford to be nostalgic for times gone by. The rug is the perfect size. About five by seven feet.

I roll it up and drag it out of the drawing room, along the hallway and into my study. After shifting some of the furniture around, I lay it flat next to Jodi. Then gingerly, I roll the body onto the carpet, trying to control my natural impulse of gagging with the stench and the sight of blood and human excrement. And then I roll her over and over so she is fully wrapped in the carpet. What a waste of a beautiful carpet. *Mother, I am sorry.*

On television, they make it look so easy, wrapping a body in a carpet and dragging it out of a house. Believe me, it's not. As I try to drag the carpet, the body starts slipping out of the roll. I leave the large bundle on the floor and hurry to one of the outbuildings to find some rope, a can of lighter fluid and matches. Once I have tied the rope several times around the body, it's easier to move. I drag the carpet roll along the corridor to the back door; the back door that thanks to Jodi is now a gaping hole giving access to the Hall. I will have to take the risk and leave the broken window. I'll fix it later. Then I find the car key to the old farm Defender and stride around to the garages. It takes a couple of attempts to fire up the old motor, but with a belch of black fumes, I reverse it out and park the rear of the car as close to the back door as is possible.

It requires every ounce of my strength to get the large package into the Defender. It's not helpful that the car is so high off the ground, but I'll be damned if I'm putting anything as gross as this in one of my quality cars. I shove the rear door shut and put the lighter fluid and matches on the passenger seat. Now I need to dispose of it all.

Silently, I thank Father for maintaining such a large estate and passing it on to me. I know this land inside out, and because I'm an excellent estate manager, I keep on top of what my tenant farmers are doing. Charles Withyfield farms the largest section of the estate, a little over six hundred acres to the west of Sesame Hall. There is a disused slurry pit on the northern edge of the land next to a derelict farm building that is no use to anyone. We had gypsies living there for a few months, until I managed to persuade the police to see them off. Father pointed out the slurry pit to me years and years ago, and shortly after I took over the estate, I investigated getting planning permission to turn the old shed into an agricultural dwelling. Without road access and over a mile away from the nearest electricity pylon, it made no economic sense, so I shelved the project and have rarely thought about it since. But now, it's exactly what I need.

I drive the Defender along the farm tracks and then, bouncing over the uneven terrain, I hang a sharp left and, with mud splattering up behind us, drive along the side of the hawthorn hedgerow until I come to the slurry pit. It just looks like a large muddy, square pond.

I drag the carpet out of the car and to the edge of the slurry pit. And then, with a scarf around my nose and mouth so as to avoid breathing in any of the toxic fumes, I unwind the rope and the rug and kick the body into the slurry pit. It sinks slowly, with the muddy gunge bubbling up. Slowly, slowly it sinks, and then with a final plop, it's gone.

I would have liked to have kept the rug, but I suspect the dry cleaners may have something to say about the revolting mess of blood and gore dirtying the antique fibres. It is going to have to go. I carry it to the area where the gypsies left a filthy mess. There's a pile of rubbish, including a broken chair and a battered kettle. Initially I am annoyed at Charles, who should have cleared this up, but then I realise it could be a blessing in disguise.

I say a silent apology to Mother. I seem to recall that the rug is worth about twenty-five thousand pounds, but I'm sure she would understand. I chuck the rug onto the pile of filth and pour the lighter fluid all over it. One flick of a match and the whole thing goes up in flames. I don't hang around to watch. Instead, I kick some leaves and branches around to cover up the dragging marks between the car and the pit, jump back in the Defender and drive as quickly as I can back home.

It's only midday, but I need a whiskey. I go to the drawing room, open the cupboard holding the collection of cut-glass tumblers, and from the drinks bar, I pour a large measure of my finest grand vintage malt. I'll have a quiet drink and then will tackle cleaning up the mess in the study. As I relax into my favourite armchair, I choke on the whiskey as the most dreadful realisation hits me.

If Jodi had a mobile phone on her, it may have shown that she came to Sesame Hall. It may even show that she is currently in the slurry pit.

I bang my forehead with my knuckles. I acted too fast without thinking this through. I tip back the whiskey and pour myself another one. What the hell should I do now? As soon as anyone realises that Jodi has also gone missing, this will be the first place they'll visit. And with modern technology being so good, surely the police will be able to locate where she has been just by checking her mobile phone records? I should have gone through her pockets before hastily disposing of her. And how did she get to Sesame Hall? I've walked around the exterior of the property, and there is no car here. A local taxi driver must have dropped her off.

What the hell have I done?

'Father, please help me!' I murmur with my eyes squeezed close. My head is pounding, the blood pumping around my body, banging in my ears. All I want is Charlotte, for me and her to be happy ever after. If her bloody sister hadn't got in the way...

I pace up and down the drawing room, my grip getting tighter and tighter around the glass. And then I've had enough. I hurl it against the wall and the glass shatters. I pick up a solid silver ash tray and chuck that across the room.

'Oh, Father,' I mutter, collapsing onto my knees and clasping my head in my hands. 'Why aren't you here to help me? What should I do now?'

Time is of the essence. How long have I got? I wonder. Hours? A day? Several days? I don't even know if Jodi has a boyfriend or whether she has told anyone she is coming here. She could even have told the police, I suppose. Life is so unfair. I asked for so little. I would happily give up every material asset I own, just to be with Charlotte. And now Jodi has got in the way of that.

I wonder. Could we elope? We could go to South America. I've heard that Paraguay, or is it Uruguay, is a good place to escape to. But how would I get Charlotte to agree to that? And then it is as if Father is speaking directly to me. I hear his voice telling me what to do, and I know he is right. There is a way Charlotte and I can be together for eternity, and no one will be able to stop us.

I close my eyes and feel an unexpected peace descend from the top of my head to my toes. I know exactly what I need to do.

41

CHARLOTTE

My life is no longer worth living. The two people I loved more than anyone else in the world are dead. I thought my heart had been ripped out of my body when Matthew died, but if it's possible, this is even worse. Jodi is my sister. The person I trust with my life, the person who knows what I'm thinking, the person who has been at my side forever, and now she is gone. It's all my fault. If it weren't for me being here, she would never have had to come looking for me, and she would still be alive. Jodi may not be my blood sister, but she and I are closer than any 'real' sisters I know. And that bastard is my half-brother. The disgust burns in my stomach and I have to swallow hard to stop myself from throwing up. Only this morning I was prepared to have sex with this man in order to gain my freedom. My own half-brother. He is profoundly sick and evil. A perverted murderer who didn't just randomly fall in love with me but knowingly sought me out and plotted to make me his wife, knowing that he was committing incest. And now it feels as if my brain and my body are shutting down, and I welcome it.

I suppose I sleep eventually, because when I awake, my cheeks are crusted from tears and I am shivering as if I have a fever. As my eyes adjust to the light, I let out a sob. The memories come cascading back. Rupert. He is a murderer. A degenerate incestophile.

I hear the slamming of a door in the distance and then there are footsteps. Is he coming back to kill me too? It's as if a switch has been flicked in my head. I will not let him get away with it. I could so easily just lie down and die, but I will not. Jodi deserves justice, and it is up to me to make sure Rupert is punished. And what would Mum do if both of us are gone? Rupert is an evil man and I will see him in hell.

He opens the door, steps into the cell, and closes it again behind him. He is carrying a large bag. It's cream and looks like a dress bag. He lays it on the ground. Then he steps towards me and I register that he is wearing a morning suit. What the hell? The trousers are a mid grey, and the black jacket is long at the back, reaching down almost to his knees. He is wearing a periwinkle tie and a matching silk brocade waistcoat, a periwinkle handkerchief peeking out of the top pocket of the jacket.

I look at him with disgust, but as he steps towards me, I cower back against the wall. I know now what this man is capable of.

'What are you going to do to me?' I whisper.

'Nothing, my darling. Don't be afraid.'

He sits down on the mattress next to me. I shuffle up to the end, but he follows, and now I'm wedged in to the corner of the room. He strokes my hair. I try to push him away.

'Everything is going to be fine, Charlotte.'

'How can you say that?' I sob. 'After what you've done to Jodi. You've killed my sister!'

'No, no, you're wrong. We both know she wasn't your real sister. You have pure blood running through your veins.'

He puts his arm around my shoulders and pulls me towards

him. I try to shift away but fail. He is wearing a strong, pungent aftershave with peppery undertones. It revolts me.

I can't think straight. All I see is Jodi lying there on the floor in a pool of blood.

'Jodi died a quick, painless death. You have no need to worry, my love. Calm, calm,' he says, stroking my hair and my forehead. 'She slipped and knocked her head. It was a terrible accident and one for which I will never forgive myself, because I was there, standing right next to her, and I didn't grab her in time before she fell.'

But he is lying. I see how his eyes flicker. Does he think I am that stupid?

'It is so unfortunate that Jodi tried to come between us.'

'She didn't. She tried to save me.'

'No, Charlotte. She tried to take you away, to alter the course of our destiny.'

'My destiny was to be with Matthew.' My words are coming out in hiccups, and as I think of Matthew, I cry even harder, my whole body shaking.

'Oh, Charlotte, Matthew wasn't right for you. Let's face it, he was a little overweight and very ordinary looking. And he was a pilot. What sort of life would he have given you? He would have been away so much, he couldn't have supported you and a family. So you see, my Charlotte, I've only done what is good for us and most of all for you. I am always looking out for you. I am sorry that Matthew needed to die. As you know, I'm not a violent man, but there really was no other alternative.'

I scream, a loud, animal-like howl. Is he admitting that he killed Matthew, the love of my life? If Rupert was the person who beat up Matthew, stole his watch and wallet, and left him for dead, then there is no hope for me. If he is telling me this, admitting premeditated murder, then it means that I too am going to die. And once again, something withers inside me.

'Did you kill Matthew?' I sob.

'Oh my darling, I only ever do what is best for you. What is best for you.'

42

RUPERT

My poor Charlotte. She is hurting. How I wish it didn't have to be like this.

I slide off the bed and step over towards the dress bag. It is heavy and smells slightly of mothballs. I pick it up and lay it on the bed, carefully unzipping it. And then I extract the dress, holding the coat hanger with one hand and ensuring the train doesn't get sullied on the floor with the other.

'My darling, this is for you. Please put it on.'

Charlotte's eyes widen, and I don't understand why her features are frozen with terror.

'You don't have to be scared, my love. Put on this dress and we will be together forever.'

'It's a wedding dress,' she says in a whisper.

'Yes. It was my mother's. She was as slender and delicate as you, so I'm hopeful that it will fit you. I would have preferred for you to choose your own dress, which is why I brought you the bridal magazines to look through, but alas, there is no time. Anyway, this dress is sentimental, and such designs never go out of fashion. Please try it on.'

'But why?'

'There is so much pain in the world. You, my love, have suffered so terribly, as indeed have I. Broken hearts, shattered dreams, a world filled with fear and no hope.'

She doesn't move.

'Darling, you don't want me to force you to put on the dress, do you?'

She shakes her head.

'I will turn around to give you privacy. Let me know when you are fully clothed.' I walk to the far side of the room and turn my back to Charlotte. I listen to her shuffling off the bed; I hear the swish of the lace fabric as she lifts up the dress and then silence. I glance over my shoulder. She has her back to me, but she is still wearing her own clothes.

'Hurry up now, love. Put the dress on, please.'

Slowly, she takes off her clothes and then there is the rustling of fabric, and when there is silence once more, I turn around. She hasn't closed the back of the dress.

'Let me do up the buttons. They are so tiny, you won't be able to reach them.'

My fingers feel thick and clumsy as I try to fasten the little buttons, not helped by Charlotte's trembling. They slip every so often onto the cool bare skin of her back. When I have finished, I tell her to turn around.

I gasp. 'It fits you perfectly.' I study her, my mouth ajar in utter admiration. My Charlotte looks stunning.

'I have more for you,' I say excitedly, reaching into the bottom of the dress bag.

'Silk stockings, a blue garter for luck and some beautiful shoes.' I hand them to her. The shoes are very high white satin stilettos, which also belonged to Mother. I'm not sure if she wore them with her wedding dress, but they go perfectly. 'Put them on. I'm going to find a mirror so you can see how stunning you look.'

'It's not necessary,' she says.

'It most certainly is.' I smile and then turn to unlock the door.

I hurry upstairs and get my cheval mirror. It's heavy and I don't want to sully my clothes, so I carry it carefully back down to the punishment room. I pick up the bag that I left outside her door and carry it in with me. Charlotte is sitting on the mattress, her slender feet in the shoes, which look a little too big for her.

'Stand up, my dear,' I say as I place the mirror in the middle of the room and the plastic bag at my feet. I hold out my hand for her, but she ignores it. I try not to mind. She walks over so she is next to me, but her eyes stay firmly fixed on the ground. I wish she would look at us in the mirror. We are such a handsome couple.

I put my hand in my jacket pocket and take out Mother's engagement ring and wedding band.

'Please hold out your left hand.'

'I don't want this,' she whispers.

'Darling, I'm not going to hurt you. I am here to protect you. Please don't be scared.'

She holds out her hand, but it is shaking so much, I have to grasp it with my left hand to keep it stable enough to slide the rings onto her finger. She is so beautiful, so natural looking, in the dress that skims her curves and cascades to the ground.

I look deep into her eyes, which is hard because she is not looking at me, but I know that is due to a mixture of coyness and ill-placed fear, so I forgive her. Still holding her left hand, I inhale deeply and speak.

'I, Rupert St John Baskerville, take thee, Charlotte Aldridge, to be my wedded wife, to have and to hold from this day forward, for better, for worse, for richer, for poorer, in sickness and in health, to love and to cherish, till death do us part, according to God's holy ordinance; and with this ring, I thee wed.' I pause to let the magnitude of the words sink in. Still holding her hand, I ask her, 'Darling, would you like to say your vow too?'

She shakes her head. I feel a splinter in my heart but try to reason that she is still too upset about the death of Jodi. Holding her hand quite firmly now, I reach down into the bag and bring out the manacles. I clasp one side on to her right wrist and the other side onto my left wrist.

'What are you doing?' She seems startled and tries to pull away, but that of course is futile.

'Come with me, my love. Don't struggle. You mustn't hurt yourself. You may need to pick up the train of the dress so you don't slip on it.'

We walk forwards towards the door, and she seems a little unbalanced in the high heels. I love her wearing those sexy shoes. The additional height means that the top of her head is almost level with my nose. I guide her carefully up the stairs, along the corridor and out of the front door. I am relieved it isn't raining. She shivers as we walk slowly around to the side of the house. It is chilly and I wish I had a fur coat to place over her shoulders. I open the door to the window-less garage.

Inside is our pale blue 1933 Rolls-Royce Phantom II Continental. I have parked it so it is facing outwards, and I've attached a white ribbon in a V shape across the front bonnet, winding around the silver Spirit of Ecstasy statue. The car is gleaming and beautiful, exactly as it was when my grandfather purchased it over eighty years ago. I have only taken it out a handful of times, not because I struggle to drive it, but because it is a priceless heirloom and I wonder if I am worthy of it. A car such as this is for special occasions only, and I can't think of a more appropriate occasion than the one I have planned for today.

The Rolls is big and there is barely sufficient space either side to open the doors and just a foot in front of and behind the vehicle. Charlotte is crying again.

'Let me go!' she cries, and then she screams, 'Help! Help!'

'No one can hear you, so you're wasting your breath,' I say, tugging at her wrist. She yelps. 'Don't make me hurt you, Charlotte.'

'This makes no sense. You can't be with a sibling. You've got to let me go!'

'Great love has always transcended society's petty rules, Charlotte. Yes, Simone was my first love, but she betrayed me with Father. It was Father who made me hurt her, and I've had to live with that forever. I don't want to hurt you today when we are celebrating our love.'

Her eyes are wide with fear. 'What do you mean, you hurt her? Did you kill Simone?'

'Simone was a slut, my dear. She was nothing like you. I am nothing like my father, and you are nothing like your mother. Although Father got everything he deserved. Now don't trouble your mind about that. Let's think about our plans.'

'No! What plans?' She is trying to wriggle away from me, but I am so much stronger than her, and all she is doing is chafing her wrist. I open the driver's door.

'Get in.'

'No, I don't want to. Where are we going?'

'To heaven, my love. Now do as I say; otherwise I will get angry.'

Tears drip down her cheeks. Fortunately she isn't wearing any make-up, so the tears shouldn't ruin the ivory lace of Mother's wedding dress. I give her a gentle shove and she slides into the car. The train of her dress catches on the heel of her stiletto, but fortunately the fabric doesn't appear damaged. After shifting around, she is seated in the driver's seat. Quickly, I undo the manacle from my wrist and attach it to the large black leather steering wheel. Then I secure Charlotte's wrists with a plastic tie, so that her wrists are secured together and attached to the wheel.

'Are you going to kill me?' Her face is etched with sadness and fear, and I wonder if now is the time to kiss all her worries away.

'No, my darling. You just need to wait for me. How much better it is to have the eternal rest of nothingness and to be at peace together forevermore. We are going to die together so that we can be together for all eternity. Killing is such a horrible word. This is an action done from love, the purest place. And we will go together, holding hands. You and me forever. Now sit back, and I'm going to prepare everything.'

She wails, but I shut the door too quickly and lock her in. I have all of the windows opened so that the fumes will take effect quickly. Charlotte is still trying to tug her wrists off the steering wheel, but it will be to no avail. Rolls Royces are the kings of cars and built to withstand rather more force that a fine-boned woman.

I stand in the narrow space between the car and the wall as I watch her. I wish she would smile, but although she is sad now, in just a few minutes she will be released from all misery, and we will be happy together for eternity. I feel an extraordinary peacefulness settle on my body, a tingling and a heaviness in my limbs, as if my whole body is being filled with my gently beating heart. Perhaps it's knowing that what we're about to do is the perfect outcome for us both. I sigh.

43

CHARLOTTE

This is the kind of nightmare scenario you read about in books. It should not be happening to ordinary me. I am about to die. I am chained to a vintage car with no possibility of getting out or being rescued.

I need to live, for Mum and for me. Not for my dead birth mother, but for the woman who has loved me ever since I was a tiny baby. This is the first time I have stared death in the eyes, and I don't want to be swallowed up by it. I want a second chance. A second chance at love. The possibility of growing old and wrinkled. Of experiencing success with my art.

And most of all, I want him to suffer for everything he has done. I want justice.

But how am I going to achieve that?

How long will it be until we are found here, gassed to death? And Mum, how will she cope? It will break her.

I watch in horror as Rupert strolls casually to the rear of the car. He bends down, so I can't see what he's doing, but perhaps he's rigging up a hose pipe. The garage is small. There are large wooden stable doors in front of the car, but no windows. The walls on the three sides are constructed from brick. How long will it be until we are fumed to death? I try to jab my foot on the pedals, twist my wrists around on the steering wheel, but without a key to start the car, all my movements are futile. I can't even see where one would insert a key. The gear stick, or at least I assume that the black stick is the stick shift, is adjacent to my right knee rather than in the normal left-hand position as in modern British cars. And now Rupert is back. He slides into the passenger seat. I move as close to the driver's door as I can. And then Rupert leans across me and presses a button. The car roars to life.

It is instinctive. I lean forwards and bite his ear, clamping down on it as hard as I can. It is disgusting and I taste the metallic tang of blood, but I keep my teeth tightly compressed. Revolting. He screams, and just as his fist comes towards my head, I let go of his ear. His fist misses my cheek by a whisker. He throws himself back to the other side of the car, and as he loses his balance, I have space to lift up my legs, ripping the fabric of the dress as I kick my feet out towards him, the sharp heel of my shoe jabbing his upper lip, causing blood to spurt out. He screams again. And then a manic force arises within me and I spear the stiletto heel on my right foot, kicking his face over and over, catching his bleeding ear, kicking out with both my feet. I think I get an eye, and he tumbles backwards, screaming, out of the car, his legs in the air, his head crashing against the wall.

The engine is still turning over noisily, and fumes are belching into the small garage. I twizzle my legs around so I'm sitting squarely in the driver's seat, and I knock the gear stick with my right knee, no idea which or even if I'm putting it into any gear. I then shove my left foot down on the clutch pedal and my right foot hard on the accelerator. Rupert has got up now, screaming, swearing. With his feet on the garage floor, he reaches across into the car and tries to grab the steering wheel, but I press down harder on the accelerator. The car jerks forwards just six inches or so, the passenger door frame slamming into him, his upper body still in the car, his legs dangling outside.

I need the car to drive forwards, straight through the wooden garage doors just a couple of inches from the front of the huge Rolls Royce. It's hard gripping the steering wheel with my wrists tied together, but I have just enough movement to control it.

I push my right foot down to the floor, as far as it will go.

'Please help me!' I yell as I shut my eyes. The engine roars like a jet plane, and the heavy car slams through the wooden garage doors, with an almighty crash. There's the shattering of glass, the splintering of wood, a massive shudder. Screams. I don't know if they are mine or his. I am thrown forwards, my chest is rammed against the steering wheel, and then I'm forced backwards into the soft leather, and still I keep my foot on the accelerator.

I open my eyes as I feel cold fresh air. I glance backwards. The passenger door has been sheared off the car chassis, and there is no sign of Rupert. He must have fallen or been crushed as the massive vehicle smashed through the garage doors.

The car is hurtling forwards along the side of the house towards the drive. I didn't even know these old cars could drive this quickly. But the steering wheel is jerking from side to side, and the car wobbles violently. I need to control it better. I lean forwards, my upper arms trying to keep the wheel straight, and then I glance up into the rear-view mirror. And to my horror I can see Rupert running behind the car, his arms waving, blood pouring from his face.

Now I reach the junction in front of the house. In a split second I think of Jodi and Matthew and what horrors Rupert has perpetrated. I am revolted by this man, horrified that such a pervert is my half-brother. I lean into the steering wheel, and somehow I manage to turn the car to the left, and I am spin-

ning around the circular drive and heading straight towards
Rupert. I press my foot further down onto the accelerator, and
the car revs up and I'm going so fast. Too fast for Rupert to get
out of the way. As he realises what I'm doing, there is a flash of
absolute terror on his face, but I don't care. I have to do this.
Faster. Faster. And when the enormous car slams straight into
him, it barely judders.

44

CHARLOTTE

I am sitting at a circular table in the ballroom at The Grosvenor Hotel in London. Mum is on my left and Rohan is on my right. Bernadette Titus is sitting opposite me, wearing an outrageous leopard-print evening dress, all loud laughter and over-the-top gestures. It seems as if she knows every one of the three hundred or so people gathered here this evening. The compere strides up to the podium, and a hush settles on the room. He is a B-list celebrity, a television news reader who claims to have a penchant for fine art.

'Ladies and gentlemen, the time has come for us to reveal the winners of this year's Portrait Artist of the Year award.' He fumbles opening the envelope. Rohan leans over and squeezes my hand. Mum looks as if she's going to pass out.

'And the winner is...Charlotte Aldridge!'

The whole room erupts into applause. Bernadette is all over me, bright pink lips puckered over my face, a cloud of sickly-sweet perfume almost gagging me. I turn towards Mum. She has tears running down her cheeks. 'You so deserve this, darling,' she says. I stand up slowly, wondering if I can do this. I didn't prepare a speech. It seemed too presumptuous. Although

I was the media's favourite, I was the professionals' outsider, and I assumed that my name was on the list simply because I was infamous for all the wrong reasons.

I can feel all eyes on me as I walk quickly, weaving my way through the tables, and up three steps to the small podium, glad that I'm wearing a trusted old black dress that skims my ankles and covers my arms. My heart is thudding, and I don't know if I'll be able to get my words out.

They have projected my painting onto a massive screen behind the presenter, and I have to bite the side of my mouth to stop myself from sobbing out loud. My winning portrait is of Jodi. I painted it for Mum and for me. I'll never sell it.

When the applause and cheers fade away, the presenter hands me the microphone, and I take a deep breath.

'Thank you,' I say. 'I feel a bit of a fraud standing up here. As many of you will know, I have only turned to portrait painting recently, ever since... Well, there have been enough column inches written about me during the past year or so, so I don't need to spell it out. Needless to say, it's been a rough time, and this portrait here is of my gorgeous sister, Jodi, whom I will miss every single moment of my life. That man stole my two greatest loves, but I am determined he will not ruin my life too. Thank you for believing in my work.'

The presenter gives me a glass plaque engraved with my name. It's surprisingly heavy. People pat me as I walk back past them; there are murmurs of congratulations and well dones, and then I sink back into my chair. I want to put all of this behind me and get on with my new life. Thanks to Bernadette's support, I have several portrait commissions and enough money in the bank to buy myself a small cottage. The people I'm painting either come to me or I paint from photographs. I'll never stay in a stranger's house ever again.

I see a psychologist once a week, a lovely lady who has helped me make sense of the horrors. The word *limerence* is commonplace now, thanks to the copious analysis of Rupert's behaviour. The official definition is romantic obsession and an overwhelming desire to have reciprocation of one's feelings.

He didn't die straight away. It took forty-eight hours before Rupert succumbed to his injuries. For a couple of days, there was talk of prosecuting me for manslaughter, but that quickly faded away when the police investigated the full extent of Rupert's crimes. They even reopened the investigation into Simone Durand's death. It came to light that the girl had given birth to Sir Oswald's child, who was put up for adoption. I suppose that baby was me, not that I wish to confirm it. Around that time, Sir Oswald Baskerville was diagnosed with cancer. It is believed that sixteen-year-old Rupert committed the murder, but his father – knowing that he was dying and wishing for the family name, hereditary baronetcy and estate to be inherited and carried on by his only son – took the rap. Mum's solicitor wants me to fight for the Baskervilles' inheritance, but I don't want their money, and I certainly don't want Sesame Hall.

'I'm so proud of you,' Rohan says, leaning over to give me a kiss on the cheek. I met him at Jodi's funeral. It may seem weird that we have become so close, but we both loved Jodi, and I don't have to explain anything to Rohan. He knows my story, he understands me, and he makes me smile. Last week, I moved out of the flat I shared with Matthew. I thought it would be hard, but actually it wasn't. The past is the past, and now I'm ready to embrace the future. Home is a little two-bedroom stone cottage on the edge of Buxton, just twenty minutes away from Mum's house and close enough for me to see Rohan in Manchester on a regular basis. I've earned enough money to buy it outright.

I feel his warm hand on my arm.

'I've got a present for you,' Rohan says.

I look at him in surprise. I am still trying to digest the fact I've won such an important art prize. He hands me an envelope.

'I would have brought him here, but I didn't think he'd like London,' Rohan says with a cheeky grin on his face.

I open the envelope and slip out a photograph.

'What?' I look at Rohan, who is winking at Mum. They must both be in on this.

'He's yours. We're picking him up at the weekend.'

I stare at the photograph that I've laid on the table in front of me. It's of the cutest, furriest, black and white puppy, with a button pink nose and large, shining black eyes.

———————————————

If you enjoyed *You Are Mine*, then you'll love Miranda's bestselling psychological thriller *Deserve To Die*, about a happily-married woman whose perfect life is abruptly shattered.

GET IT HERE!

A LETTER FROM MIRANDA

Dear Reader,

Huge thanks for reading *You Are Mine*.

Some books almost write themselves; others are harder, and this book fell into the latter category! In some of my previous books, I developed a fondness for the villain. For instance, I couldn't help but admire Tamara, in *Deserve To Die*. I never warmed to Rupert in *You Are Mine*. Yes, I intended for him to be deluded and the book was meant to give the reader the chills. He certainly creeped me out and I had to 'live' with him for the three months it took to write this novel!

Before researching for this book, I had never heard of the term limerence, but having obsessive romantic fantasies about someone is a real syndrome. One of the things I enjoy most about writing psychological thrillers is learning about states of mind.

My publishers, Brian Lynch and Garret Ryan of Inkubator Books, worked as hard on *You Are Mine* as I did. Their support is incalculable, and it is a joy to work with them.

As always, I thank my family for their unwavering support. But most importantly – thank you! Reaching so many readers through my thrillers is a dream come true. I am grateful to every one of you.

Reviews are an author's lifeblood. If you could spend a moment writing an honest review, no matter how short it is, I would be hugely grateful.

With thanks and warmest wishes,

Miranda

Leave a Review

www.mirandarijks.com

ALSO BY MIRANDA RIJKS

I WANT YOU GONE

(A Psychological Thriller)

DESERVE TO DIE

(A Psychological Thriller)

FATAL FORTUNE

(Book 1 in the Dr Pippa Durrant Mystery Series)

FATAL FLOWERS

(Book 2 in the Dr Pippa Durrant Mystery Series)

FATAL FINALE

(Book 3 in the Dr Pippa Durrant Mystery Series)

Published by Inkubator Books
www.inkubatorbooks.com

Printed in Great Britain
by Amazon